Methodical Conclusion

Methodical Conclusion

Rebekah Roth

KTYS media

Methodical Conclusion is a work of fiction based on historical facts. Some
names, characters, places, events, and incidents may be either the product
of the author's imagination or a compilation of persons the author has met.
Any resemblance to actual events, locales, organizations or persons, living or
dead, may be pure coincidence and beyond the intent of either the author or
the publisher.

ISBN 978-0-9827571-9-2

Library of Congress Cataloging-in-Publication Data
Roth, Rebekah
Methodical Conclusion
Fiction
2016944535
ISBN 978-0-9827571-9-2(soft cover)
Library of Congress Number: 2016944535

To contact Rebekah Roth:
 www.rebekahroth.com

KTYS media
www.ktysmedia.com

Printed in the United States of America

Dedicated To:

To my husband for all his patience and understanding over the last nineteen months while I researched and wrote day and night

And

To Ramjet, my show co-host for his continued encouragement to speak the truth and continue my research in the face of opposition

"The Sept 11th commission was so frustrated with repeated misstatements by the Pentagon and FAA about their response to the 2001 terror attacks that it considered an investigation into possible deception."

Thomas Kean
Chairman of the 9/11 Commission

FROM THE AUTHOR

Methodical Conclusion marks the final book in the Methodical series. The first book, Methodical Illusion, drew from my experience as a thirty plus year flight attendant with a major US airline. That experience coupled with my research allowed me to discover where the four airplanes associated with 9/11 were actually taken and landed so that the phone calls could be made. Following my interview with George Noory on Coast to Coast A.M. that book soared to #9 overall on Amazon and has continued to sell well as people replay the more than one hundred interviews I did on alternative radio.

Methodical Deception followed, which was based on nearly a terabyte of Freedom of Information Act data that was given to me. That data proved difficult to fully comprehend. From what I was able to understand, accompanied by other government documents it became apparent that the FAA was not always telling the truth when it presented data to the public about 9/11. For example, the flight paths of the four airplanes in question were loaded into the FAA computers early in the morning of 9/11 hours before any of those planes actually took off. That information along with documentation about art students traveling the country and residing in the Twin Towers found its way into the book which helped explain many of the anomalies surrounding 9/11.

Now with the third book, Methodical Conclusion, a team of commercial and military flight controllers, radar specialists, intelligence officers and eye witnesses have come together to help me fully read and understand the data found in the FOIA documents. Those new revelations are brought out in this third book and shed a bright light on aspects of 9/11 that has never before been revealed. The personal experiences of this team, along with the government documents confirm the suspicions of many that the government story of 9/11 is a lie.

These books are written as novels and use fictitious characters to bring forth the data that my research discovered. Though some of the events in the book surrounding the protagonists are fiction, you can be assured that the events explaining, detailing and exposing 9/11 information are true and can be backed up by documents found in the FOIA requests, affidavits from eye-witnesses, firsthand accounts from air traffic controllers, and through my determination to get to the bottom of what really happened. Throughout Methodical Conclusion in particular, the timelines and places are real. You can go on Google Earth and see what the characters were seeing. You can visit the places described in the book and get a better understanding of what my research exposed. I invite you to do so.

Remember that the purpose of these books is to open the eyes of the public who have been brainwashed into thinking the government was honest in reporting the events of 9/11. Do not hesitate to share these works with anyone who needs to wake up and learn the truth.

one

"Floyd, turn that damn thing off. I'm not about to listen to that lunatic dotter on about 9/11, even if he is the President of the United States," shouted Dante Wilcox, over the noise at his favorite watering hole. "It's bad enough he was never elected, but he doesn't seem to want to stop the nonsense claim that someone other than a bunch of Arabs attacked our country and caused the deaths of thousands. I'm sick of it and I'm sick of him."

The bartender tried switching the channels on the large television that was mounted on the back wall between several shelves of liquor. It seemed that President Sherman, sitting behind his desk in the Oval Office, was on every single channel—even the Shopping Network—which was unheard-of for a presidential speech. Dante nudged his buddy Jamal, seated on the stool next to him, as if to gloat about the influence he carried at the tavern. His friend was looking down at his iPhone, watching the same speech that Floyd was having trouble removing from the television screens.

"What the hell, is that boob on every electronic device with a screen?" Dante asked.

"Apparently so," replied Jamal. "The only way I can get rid of him is to turn the thing off, and I can't do that because I'm waiting for a call from Shantril telling me she got tickets to the concert next weekend. If she did then I got to get that night off, and I got to tell my boss about it when I report to work tonight."

"Well, he better be done and gone before the Nationals game tonight with the Mets. I've been waiting all day for that matchup so I could settle back here with a brew and watch Harper take apart those sorry New Yorkers."

"I just don't get you, Dante. That's the commander-in-chief. I have a beef because he replaced the first black president and all. None of us black folk liked how that went down, but you served during 9/11. In fact, I think you told me you were in Afghanistan a few days later. You fought two or three tours in that conflict and you managed to retire after twenty years with a pretty good pension. So why is it you hate this man and his desire to expose the truth about something you nearly gave your life to put right?"

"He's a Republican. I ain't got any use for those damn Republicans."

"Your mama's a Republican."

"Yeah, don't remind me. For some crazy-ass reason, she went for Nixon in college and embarrassed the whole family. They were all so proud of her at first—being the first college student and all, and with a scholarship no less. Then she basically spits in Humphrey's face and campaigned for Tricky Dick in '68. Her sister Maxine still ain't talking to her and it's been nearly fifty years. I've always thought that was why my dad left her after Nixon resigned. It was kind of an 'I told you so' she'd never acknowledge, but we've never really talked about any of that. I've just had to suffer along with her all these years. I mean I love her, but she's got the elephant disease something awful."

"That's a nice personal history anecdote, but you weren't even born in '68 and there has to be more to the story about you hating Republicans than a fifty-year family grudge."

Dante sat silently, staring into his beer and hoping to avoid where he knew this conversation was headed.

Jamal continued, "I remember hanging out with you between your tours and you were totally down with what you were doing. Bush—remember President Bush, a Republican—he started that war and you were gung-ho, Johnny on board, a last-man-standing kind of guy. Now, even the slightest mention of Iraq or Afghanistan and you crawl into your quiet place and act like you've never heard of either country. Worse yet, the mention of 9/11 in any context makes you crazy. So I'm thinking that your contempt for President Sherman has more to do with something that happened over there and not so much that he's a Republican and wasn't elected. Am I right?"

Dante took a sip of his beer and gazed up at the television, watching the president finishing his speech. He shook his head slowly, then turned to look at Jamal. "You just keep thinking, pal, that's what you're good at. Yup, you just keep thinking."

"Look, I didn't mean anything by that," responded Jamal. "I just know there's more to your story than you let on, or maybe have ever verbalized. Those of us who care about you sense your feelings through your silence."

"Hey, Floyd, he's done, switch that over to ESPN and get the game," Dante said, pointing to the television with one hand and trying to catch Floyd's attention by waving the other.

Floyd got the message and was delighted to get President Sherman off his television screens. The Nats/Mets game had already begun, but was still in the first inning. A boisterous cheer rang out when Floyd's search was successful. Dante glanced over at Jamal and gave him a thumbs-up. Jamal said nothing. He was thinking about Dante's comments about Republicans, and the inconsistencies demonstrated through Dante's actions over the years. It wasn't making sense to him. They had never discussed politics before. To Jamal it had never mattered, but he was certain that patriotism had always trumped politics in Dante's book. But now, for some reason, patriotism was on life support and Dante seemed to have no interest in resuscitating it back to health. He tried to watch the game, but his mind simply wouldn't allow him to focus on the action. He kept looking at his phone, hoping to hear from Shantril. After a while, he excused himself and moved to a far corner of the bar into a booth, where the noise level of the room was muted by the tall dividers that ran from floor to ceiling between each booth.

Dante's attention was distracted momentarily from the game, as his eyes followed Jamal across the room. He assumed he just needed to talk or text his girl in private, and thought nothing more of Jamal's departure. But later, when the game was interrupted by commercials, he glanced over to see if his friend was still there. Jamal didn't seem to be involved with his phone, and was just sitting alone sipping his beer. That didn't seem right to Dante. Such behavior was out of character for his fun-loving, baseball-crazy friend, and he made a mental note to check in on him at the end of the next inning.

It looked like the Nationals had the game pretty well under control, with a big lead of six runs before the end of the fifth inning. Dante grabbed his beer, walked over to Jamal's booth and sat down across from him. "You don't seem to be too into this game tonight. You haven't gone all New York on me, have you?"

Jamal smiled. "That would be the day. And something you never have to worry about—once a Met hater, always a Met hater."

"So what's up with you?" Dante asked.

"I guess my mind is just somewhere else tonight, that's all. I can see the game is not all that interesting anyway, probably going to be a blowout."

"Are you getting static from Shantril?"

"No, she texted and got the tickets, so we're all good there."

"So what gives, man?" Dante persisted.

Jamal sat silently, staring into his beer. He glanced up briefly, just enough to catch Dante's eyes, and then looked back down into his glass. He shifted in his seat as if he was about to say something, but the words never formed.

"I've known you long enough to know when something's not right with you, so cough it up," responded Dante to Jamal's silence.

"All right," he said, looking up. "It's you."

"Me?" repeated Dante, with a very perplexed look on his face. "What the hell did I do?"

Jamal laughed. "It's not anything you did, man, it's who you've become. Yeah, you still like to have a good time, hang out with your buddies. I mean, if you need something you call Dante. That's who you've always been and why everyone likes you, but dude, you're different. You have contempt for the government, an ambivalent attitude towards this country, and I know damn well you followed your mama and were a good Republican once. What happened to you? Tonight when President Sherman was talking, you acted like Hitler had come back to life. All the man wanted was to look more deeply into 9/11—something you gave most of your life to make right—and you acted like he was the enemy. I don't get that."

"You don't want to go there—trust me, you don't. Let's just leave that in the shadows where it doesn't bother anybody," replied Dante.

"It bothers me. And I want to know what happened to you. We've been friends since high school. You were there for me when I went through my divorce; you talked me off the ledge when I'd pretty much had it with life. You were my go-to guy. Now I can see you could use a friend like me, at least someone you can trust to talk to, and you blow me off like my ex-wife does."

"Just give me some time. It's really nothing. Just a few things I gotta work through, that's all."

"It's more than that. If it were just a few things you would have managed to overcome them by now, but you seem to be getting more defiant in your contempt for what has always been important to you and that's what worries me," Jamal replied.

Dante took a deep breath and seemed to hold it in for a long time before exhaling through his nose. He looked away from Jamal and back at a distant television screen, where it was apparent the game had resumed. "So are you going to just leave this conversation and go back to the game?" Jamal asked.

"If I were smart I would," Dante quickly replied.

"Go," responded Jamal, motioning with his hands.

Dante didn't move. He just slowly shook his head and looked down. Suddenly he slammed his open palm down on the table, which startled Jamal, and said, "You win, you win. I'll tell you what you want to know, if I can. What you're about to hear has never before left my lips. I do everything I can to hold it inside, but obviously some of it's leaked out, and to be honest, you're not the first one to notice."

Jamal tried to look as if he wasn't surprised. He didn't want to say or do anything that might change Dante's mind. He moved more toward the corner of the booth and put his left leg up on the seat, his foot dangling off the edge. He knew if Dante did decide to share anything with him, it was going to take a while, and he wanted to be comfortable. He left his beer where it had been—sitting on the table, now out of reach. He focused his eyes directly on Dante and said nothing.

Dante shifted in his seat, looking uncomfortable. Each time he caught Jamal's eyes, he would look down at the table. A barmaid came by, but before she could stop and say anything, Jamal waved her away so she wouldn't distract his friend any more than he already was. After a long pause, Dante placed his elbows on the table, put his right fist into the palm of his left hand and rested his chin on his exposed fingers. Jamal knew that would make it quite difficult to talk and feared the opportunity was fleeting. He wanted to say something, but again resisted, hoping his silence would put pressure on his friend to follow through with his promise to speak.

"I probably shouldn't be telling you any of this," Dante finally said.

"Yeah, you should, because it's eating you up and unless you tell me or someone, it'll kill you."

Dante laughed. "Yeah, kill me. The Taliban couldn't, every terror group in the world couldn't, hell even the military couldn't kill me, but you're right, this just might."

He took his arms off the table and placed his hands behind his head, leaning back as best he could. "I joined the service right out of high school. It was 1988. Reagan was still president; the world was basically at peace. There were signs that the Soviet Union was about to collapse, or at least work and play nicely with the rest of the world. The military seemed like a good idea. I could stay in for twenty years. I could be trained on sophisticated equipment, get a little schooling and basically be set up for the rest of my life. Some of that began to change as early as basic training. I had never shot a gun in my life, but my training officers could immediately see I had a deadeye and could hit almost any target right in the sweet spot from any distance. I just naturally knew how to adjust for distance, wind and caliber of the ammunition. Well, I guess that kind of talent doesn't come along every day and after basic they swept me off and put me into sniper training, and for some reason started talking about enrolling me in officer training school."

"Yeah, that did all seem kind of strange to us back home. You went into the military as a nobody private and in no time you were a second lieutenant," added Jamal.

Dante smiled. "Things just seemed to escalate from there. After a year or so I was in ranger training and being groomed as a covert sniper. Before I knew it, I was assigned to a super-secret squadron that interfaced with the CIA, MI6, the Mossad, and we took orders directly from a colonel in the Pentagon whose identity was disavowed by every agency, service branch and organization in the world. In short, he didn't exist. Which means in reality, neither did I. I worked off individual assignments anywhere in the world. I could be teamed with counterparts from the Air Force, Navy, Marines, and intelligence personnel. I never knew where I would be next or with who I'd be working. As time passed and the assignments built up, I would run across some of the same people assigned to my team in other operations. We wanted plausible deniability, but it was just an illusion. We were all directly involved and even the military couldn't hide that fact."

Jamal listened intently and then spoke. "You seemed to love that. I remember back in the day when you would come home on leave, you were happy. I could never get you to tell me what you'd been doing, but from your sheer enthusiasm, I knew you were doing what you were born to do."

Dante nodded. "For the most part that was true. I enjoyed the travel, the association with professionals and the secrecy of what I did. But mostly I felt I was helping, helping my country keep and preserve its reputation and influence in the world. I mean, there were things we did I wasn't proud of and wish I could take back, but I let the organization take the blame. I felt I was just part of the machine, well-oiled and a perfect fit."

"So when did things begin to change?" Jamal asked.

"It wasn't any one big event or some kind of blowup I had with a superior. It was a slow downward spiral that really began late in the day on 9/11."

"Where were you on 9/11?" Jamal inquired.

"The day prior, I arrived in Madrid, Spain with a small special ops force made up of a weatherman, spotter and of course me, the sniper. The spotter I had worked with before, the weatherman was new, and we were being led by a CIA agent whom I only knew by reputation. We were positioned to take out a Basque Nationalist leader when he arrived at the airport. We had intelligence he would arrive late at night on September 11th, or maybe in the wee hours of September 12th. His plane was to taxi to a remote section of the airport, and our job was to take him out before he climbed into his transport vehicle and disappeared into the city. It was to be quick and efficient. We had all the markings in place to have it blamed on a longtime rival within his organization, thereby causing chaos which we hoped would lead to self-destructive infighting. It was pretty much like stuff we had done before in other parts of the world. So Monday we scoped out our positions, made some last-minute preparations and enjoyed the nightlife in the city. It was routine stuff. Tuesday we set up late afternoon in case his plane came in earlier than planned. We had radio access to all planes contacting the tower, and we watched every plane land and every one take off. Was it boring? Yes. Was it avoidable? No. We hadn't been there too long when the airport stopped behaving normally. International flights to the States stopped taking off; others began to return. Immediately we knew something wasn't right. I deferred to the man in charge, and that's when we were told about the events that had occurred that morning in New York and D.C. That alone was upsetting, but we had a job to do and we needed to be focused. We got bits and pieces of what was going on as it related to air traffic and how it might affect our target's arrival. We knew there was a ground stop out of the US and we knew no flights were leaving Europe bound for the United States, which explained why several of the earlier take-offs had returned. We had no choice but to wait. The waiting caused me to think. That CIA agent must have known more about the 9/11 events than he shared with us. I found that disturbing. I just thought when this job was over I'd dig into it a little more with contacts I trusted. Then something weird happened."

"What?" asked Jamal, completely riveted by what he was hearing.

"Around midnight, a US Air flight radioed in for clearance to land."

"What was so unusual about that?"

"US Air had only one flight to the states out of Madrid and it left just before noon, it couldn't have been that same flight returning twelve hours later. It immediately caused me to question where this flight had originated. It also wasn't the correct flight number for the Madrid to Philly flight. We watched it land and taxi to the approximate area where we expected our target to land. That alone was weird, and caused us enough concern that it had the potential to shut down our operation. The plane, a Boeing 757, waited for a long time until the appropriate air stairs could be driven to where it was parked to allow the passengers to deplane. We scoped each individual coming out of that back door just to make certain our target wasn't on board. Then it became even stranger. Not more than thirty people deplaned. A couple of them looked to be wearing flight attendant uniforms. The others were pretty nondescript, a mixture of men and women. All of them seemed pretty tired and glad to be on the ground."

Jamal screwed up his face and tugged at his right ear. "I'm having a hard time following you on this one. Other than the fact the plane was in your target area, what seemed to be the problem?"

"One of the pieces of information that the CIA agent divulged early on was that US Air had been the first to issue a ground stop of all their planes in the United States. In addition, Brussels had issued an order for all planes bound for the US to return or divert. With those two facts in play, where could this flight have come from? It was too late at night for it to be a returning US flight, and why wasn't it parked at a gate? I would have thought it was a plane coming from the US, but a 757 doesn't have that kind of range, so it had to have originated from the continent. Nothing about it made sense."

"That's interesting, but it doesn't really explain your change in attitude," Jamal said softly.

"That didn't change my attitude, but it was the beginning.

That damn CIA agent knew more about that US Airways jet than he was sharing. I could tell it from his voice, and I could sense he didn't seem at all surprised when it landed. It didn't even seem to bother him that it parked where it compromised our mission. I've always wondered about that plane. It was the first disconnect for me about 9/11, but I had a job to do and was committed to fulfilling my assignment."

"So did the terrorist land?" asked Jamal, sensing the story was losing some steam.

"Well, he never landed that night. The mission was aborted towards dawn. Perhaps 9/11 turned out to be his lucky day, and all the air traffic confusion ultimately saved his life. I don't know—maybe another unit picked up his trail and was assigned to take him out. We slept through most of the next morning and when I awoke, I had orders to go to Afghanistan."

"You mean just like that, you left Spain and were headed for someplace new?"

Dante smiled and then began to chuckle. "Snipers like me never adjust to the water in any one place. If I were someplace long enough to down more than a canteen or two, I had permission to call it home. The following day I hopped a British C-130 transport to Ramstein, and later that night I was in Kabul meeting up with another secret Special Forces group and reporting to a CIA officer whom I knew quite well."

"Are you saying that two days after 9/11 you were in Afghanistan? Why?" Jamal asked.

"The elusive Osama bin Laden, of course. Don't you know that within hours of the 9/11 attacks he was identified as the culprit and had to be taken out?" Dante said with a touch of sarcasm in his voice.

Jamal was in the middle of downing the last swallow or two of his beer when Dante's comment caught him off guard and he spit what was in his mouth back into the glass. "You say that as if you don't think he was responsible for what happened that day."

Dante laughed. "How about I share with you what happened in the next ten days, and you tell me how responsible you think he was."

Jamal motioned with his two index fingers to bring it on.

"I've never really shared this with anyone. Maybe enough time has passed and the official story is so entrenched that I won't get in trouble for divulging what occurred. But promise me you'll keep this to yourself and just refer to it as another layer of crap that has caused me to see the world like I do now," Dante pleaded.

"Sure, buddy. I'm just trying to figure out who you are and what caused you to change. I won't breathe a word to a soul."

Dante took a deep breath and held it in for several moments before audibly exhaling through his teeth, making a hissing sound. "We had excellent intelligence and knew exactly where Osama was. He obviously knew from the television reports that we were blaming him for what had occurred, and I'm sure he knew we were going to be hunting him down. What's interesting is he didn't really do anything to protect himself. I mean, he was an easy target—almost too easy."

"What are you saying?" Jamal questioned.

"It took us several more hours for our entire team to arrive and get prepped for our mission. My CIA friend laid it out for me, and we had our spotters and informants keeping watch for bin Laden while we waited for the arrival of our weatherman from the States. Our plan was fluid, since we anticipated bin Laden moving to avoid what he knew was coming. Odd thing was, he didn't move. He was like a sitting duck. We watched him move about his apartment for hours. Never did he try to avoid the windows or even the open courtyard in the middle of the complex. Once it got dark we moved to a permanent location, but completely out of view from the street or from anyone inside the building. It couldn't have been more perfect. I set up from a hundred fifty yards with an AR-15, which we don't normally use, but it was such an easy kill and with the silencer it was pure stealth. Our orders were simple—one shot through the forehead and into oblivion we would vanish. Next day we expected to read that the 9/11 mastermind had been taken out by Special Forces and we were well on our way to a victory in the war on terror."

"I don't think I ever read that story." Jamal smiled. "So what happened?"

"I had the bastard dead to rights, crosshairs right above the nose. We couldn't get permission to fire. All our actions were being reported up the chain. When I gave the green clearance I got back in my earpiece, 'no go.' We stayed for another hour, running through the same exercise, with the same response from upstairs. As we were about to shut it down, an F-16 flew overhead and dropped an ordinance which blew half the building to rubble. They used our reports to position bin Laden. There was no question in my mind that bomb was laser-guided to the outer edge of the building, completely away from where we told them he was. It was like a calling card, 'Hi Osama, we know where you are and can take you out any time.'"

"And he fled that location to Tora Bora, correct? But why wouldn't they let you shoot?"

"We tracked him the whole way. In fact, had we wanted to, we could have had a welcome wagon at the entrance to his cave when he arrived. But no, we slogged our way up those rugged mountains with the same orders to take him out. Three days later, I was set up with my team positioned for the kill shot. Bin Laden didn't seem too concerned. He was outside his fortress most of the time. A twelve-year-old could have taken him out."

"And?" Jamal prompted, hoping for a better end to this part of the story.

"Same damn response. Had him in my sights and again got

the 'no go.'"

"So you're telling me that we could have captured or killed Osama bin Laden at the outset of this whole fiasco and somebody at the top wouldn't allow it to happen?"

Dante looked Jamal directly in the eye and replied, "That's exactly what I'm telling you. And it got worse from there."

"How so?" he inquired.

"As you know, I was deployed to either Iraq or Afghanistan three different times after that initial deployment. I worked undercover most of the time as a sniper assigned to protect our troops. But I wasn't hidden under camouflage twenty-four hours a day with my rifle pointed at potential terrorists. There were extended periods of time when I was out and about mixing in with the people we were trying to liberate from oppression. I got to know many of them on an individual basis. You know me well enough to know I like people, always have. Given the opportunity I'm going to mingle and mix in with anyone, no matter who they are or what they believe. I got that from my Republican mother." Dante laughed, and nudged Jamal's elbow with the back of his hand. Jamal nodded, indicating he understood the connection Dante was trying to exploit.

"But you never voted for any of them, right?" Jamal chided.

Dante looked closely at both of his index fingers and responded, "If I did, the purple has worn off and no one's the wiser."

Jamal excused himself to get another beer, and took Dante's empty glass along with him. When he returned he said, "So explain what you meant by things getting worse. I can't imagine anything worse than not having the support of your superiors when you're lined up to accomplish the job you were sent to do. That's crazy, man."

"I really don't know how to explain this. I'll give it a shot, but if it doesn't make any sense that's too bad. Because I spent time with the people and got to know them, I began to understand who they were and what they were all about. I know here at home we think they're all terrorists plotting day and night to blow something up. That's just not the case. They, for the most part, are mothers and fathers trying to make a life for their kids under impossible circumstances. I'd break bread with these people once they learned to trust me. I learned a little Farsi in Afghanistan and some Arabic in Iraq. Between that and the little English they knew, we were able to communicate. The point is, we didn't really need all the words. If I saw they needed something I would break a few rules and do my best to get it for them. It wasn't much, maybe a bar of soap, a roll of duct tape or a pot to cook in that didn't have any holes. You know the kind of stuff that happens when people care about each other. And they did the same for me. During the dust storm season they would make—not give, but actually make me scarves to wrap around my nose and mouth to protect me from the elements. I didn't ask them for that; they saw a need and cared enough to do something to help me. They lived in makeshift shelters and struggled to keep themselves fed, but they were happy in spite of the death, chaos and war that went on all around them. Jamal, they are like you and me with a different set of challenges, but with the same end in mind. Can you understand that?"

"I don't think I've ever met an Arab, but I think I get what you're saying," Jamal replied. "What I don't get is why this caused a problem for you."

"I was the son of a bitch that in the dark of night blew their fathers and sons, neighbors and friends into oblivion."

"But you were protecting the lives of United States soldiers," responded Jamal.

"Was I? What was I was protecting them from in the first place, a country that had been invaded for no particularly good reason other than the fact that our president wanted to look tough in the aftermath of 9/11?"

"Okay, now I'm beginning to see where the bitterness stems from, if you really think that 9/11 was something other than Islamic terrorists taking out their aggression on the United States. You don't really believe that, do you?" Jamal asked.

"I certainly didn't think that when I first arrived in the Middle East, but the more time I spent in those countries and the more tours I did, the more I began to question what occurred that day and who was ultimately responsible," Dante shot back. "Worse yet, look at where we are today. Thousands of lives lost, tens of thousands of soldiers crippled and maimed for life, and for what? We left those countries in far worse shape than we found them in, and have primed the pump for them to be taken over by autocratic regimes far worse than the ones from which we supposedly liberated them. Go ahead, tell me I was just doing my duty night after night, and kill after kill."

Jamal was silent and could not look directly at Dante. He wanted to say something, but the words seemed jumbled and the thoughts in his head all seemed to be missing their salient points. So he said nothing. He sipped from his beer and tried to figure out where their conversation would lead. He was beginning to wish he had never pushed the issue.

Dante, however, was not through. His thoughts had taken on an aura of clarity for the first time and needed to find their voice. "So, go ahead, ask me why I hate Republicans. Of course my mama was a GOPer and you knew I'd been a Republican all my life. So what changed? Ask me. Here's your big chance. Don't blow it."

Jamal placed his elbow on the table and leaned his forehead into his open hand. He looked over at Dante with the one eye that wasn't blocked and softly said, "So what happened?"

"Nothing happened. They primp, they preen and they promise, but in the end, nothing happens. They don't do a damn thing. And if you look at it carefully, over all these years since 9/11, they've done nothing but promote the war effort and pander to their special interests. They're lazy liars who line their pockets with the lucre they lust after and expect their constituents to support their lunacy. I hate them. And the damn Democrats are worse. In the house I grew up in I was nearly eighteen before I knew damn Democrat was two words. They all make me sick. That's why when President Sherman comes on the television I want him off. He's a liar and he can't be trusted. They're all losing liars."

That was not exactly what Jamal expected to hear come out of Dante's mouth, and it made this next question more difficult to ask. "But you still love your country, don't you?"

Dante stared at him in disbelief. "Of course I love my country. That's why I kept going back to those hellholes and fighting the demons that haunted my soul. I kept hoping and praying that things would change. I wanted my country to be what I had grown up thinking it was, and I was willing to do my part to make that happen. I guess I failed it, and I know it's failed me."

"But if you listen to President Sherman, he's talking about trying to open a new 9/11 investigation and having citizens come forward with information they may have from that day. I think he's crazy, but doesn't that appeal to you?"

"Is he a politician?" Dante cynically blurted out.

Jamal nodded.

"Well then, it really doesn't matter what he says or what he wants to do, now does it?"

"Look, I don't know. My concern is you and what you're becoming. I can't imagine you enjoying what's happening to you. Unless you're into a good baseball or football game, it's almost like I hardly know you anymore. And look at us now; we blew off this game tonight. So there's not even that," Jamal said, shaking his head slowly.

"I put in my time in the service. I have a good pension that allows me to do pretty much whatever I want to do. For that I'm grateful, but let's face it, Jamal, it was time wasted. And I have to agree with you, I'm not sure who I am anymore, and I struggle daily to cope with all the horrific things I've done in the name of my country. I feel like an orphan without a future."

Jamal waited until Dante's eyes were focused on him and he knew he had his attention. "I had no idea what you've been going through. You hear about PTSD and all the problems that so many of the veterans have when they come back, but I thought you were immune to all that. I mean, you had ribbons and medals on your uniform that would rival most generals. I just thought you could handle anything thrown at you. Now I can see you need help and I have no idea what to do."

Dante snorted slightly at Jamal's comment about the ribbons and medals. "I doubt there's anything you can do. It's felt good to get this off my chest. I never talk about it, except to myself, and I'm not sure that is mentally healthy. Like most things in my life, I guess I'll just have to gut it out and hope for the best. Thanks for listening."

The phone Jamal had placed on the table began to light up with an incoming call. It was Shantril. "I'd better take this. Why don't you go get us another round of beer? I'll only be a minute."

Dante nodded and stood up, stretching his legs as his friend placed the phone to his ear and did his best to try to hear what his girlfriend had to say amidst the noise of the bar. Jamal watched him walking up to the bar to find Floyd. Shantril did all the talking, which required all of Jamal's attention. As he had assumed, the call only lasted a minute or two, but when he finished there was no sign of Dante. He scanned the crowd all around the bar, but Dante was nowhere to be found. He waited for ten or fifteen minutes, hoping he would return. Nothing. Dante had left the bar and headed into the night, alone once more with his thoughts and all his memories.

.

two

President Sherman called the meeting in the cabinet room to order with a strike of the gavel. It wasn't necessary; he just liked how the wooden mallet sounded when it was struck against the metal base. The gavel had been a gift from some of his former football teammates at Stanford when he took the oath of office as president. The inscription at the base read, 'Never be afraid to call an audible.' The purpose of the meeting was to coordinate the follow-up effort from the president's address to the nation the night before. Since the president had kept the tone and message of his remarks secret, a great deal of work needed to be done to facilitate the influx of information they hoped would follow. Around the table were Jerry Reitz, head of the NSA, Jim Bowman, Special Assistant to the President, and Max Hager, Director of Research, along with the members of his team, Gil and Ruth Ann. In addition, the president had asked Vera to accompany him to this meeting, as well as his Chief of Staff, the US Attorney General and the Chairman of the Joint Chiefs of Staff.

"Jim, share with us where we're at in the planning and implementation process," said the president.

Jim took from his briefcase a file marked '9/11 Leads,' and opened it across the table. He spread a few documents out so that he could easily refer to them in case questions arose. "I've been working with Gil to create a website that invites the public to share information with us, including their contact information. Naturally, we'll capture their IP addresses and if there develops a compelling need to make contact with an individual, we'll have that option as well."

Vera glanced at Jim, and he could tell from her raised eyebrows and the angle of her head that she didn't approve of capturing their IP addresses. Jim knew her well enough to nod slightly in a way that invited her to speak her mind. "With all due respect, gentlemen, if you're going to allow people to think they're divulging secrets to the government anonymously, you can't violate that trust at some later date."

Max piped up and asked, "If we receive as much data as we hope, we're going to have to hire a staff to filter through the details that are salient to our research."

Jim thought for a moment and responded, "You're right about needing a staff to sort through the information. My hope would be that not everyone who divulges details will want to remain anonymous, but more particularly I would hope that a lot of the data that is shared overlaps and has more than one source. Does that make more sense to you, Vera?"

"Well, it's a start, and I do like it better than what you just proposed," she replied.

"I think it would make sense to have Ruth Ann coordinate and organize the incoming data," Max said, looking in Ruth Ann's direction.

Ruth Ann smiled as the group turned to look at her. "I'm sure I'd love doing that, but I have to tell you, after what happened to me, I need to take a little time off and visit my favorite getaway in Las Vegas. I've been putting it off, but both my body and my mind are telling me to book some time at the M Resort. My enthusiasm for this work needs to be recharged. My commitment hasn't changed, but I do need some rest and a good massage at a spa where I can refocus my thoughts and rebuild my drive and determination to get to the bottom of 9/11."

"I'm surprised it's taken you this long to come to that conclusion," said the president. "I told Max the day after you were rescued to make sure you had the latitude to come to grips with what happened and to not overburden you with more assignments. For the most part he's done that, I know, but we all fully expected you to take some serious down time. So by all means do what you need to do."

Max stuck his index finger in the air as a gesture to be recognized. When he was acknowledged he proceeded, "As long as you're going to Las Vegas, would it be too much trouble for you to stop by the coroner's office and pick up the last of Bob's personal effects that were found when he was brought to the morgue? The coroner placed them in his safe until we could send someone with the proper credentials to pick them up."

"I'm sure that wouldn't be too much trouble at all. I'd be happy to do that," replied Ruth Ann.

"Great," said Max. "I'll tell the coroner to expect you."

"That doesn't solve the problem of the data collection and how to organize and disseminate it to your team," inserted Jerry. "I could assign NSA personnel to assist you, if you think that would help solve the problem."

The president stroked his chin and looked at Jim. "This little group has been working under my authority for a while now. Our circle has been tight and the information has been confined to those with a need to know. That's worked well. If we incorporate NSA staff into our team, do you see any problem with that?"

"That might be a better question for the attorney general," Jim responded, deflecting the president's question in the direction of Rudy Rathburn.

Rudy, who was always focused on what the president needed from a legal perspective, was quick to respond, "Jerry and Jim can assign their people to do whatever needs to be done, even if it overlaps with work in some other branch of government. I would advise, however, that NSA personnel don't work inside the White House. Have them fulfill their assignments from other locations here in the D.C. area. I assume that's possible?"

Max asked Gil to respond to that inquiry.

"It'll be easy to assign work through the website to any of Jerry's people without giving them access to anyone's personal information. I can have that file sharing feature ready in a day."

The president turned to the chairman of the joint chiefs and asked, "I suppose you're wondering why you were invited to this somewhat informal meeting?"

"No, sir," came the reply. "I know enough about what you're looking into to know that there will be a military component to the information you process through your analysis, and you'll need my input to help make sense out of some of that data and most of the procedures."

"Exactly," replied Jim. "You'll no doubt be asked a lot of why questions, which I hope you'll have the answers to."

The chairman of the joint chiefs chuckled. "When the military isn't executing a how proposition, it's up to its ears in whys. So I'll be in my element."

The president smiled and nodded his approval.

The president's chief of staff had been taking notes, and motioned with his pen to be heard.

"Allen, I hope you're going to share with the group what we talked about earlier this morning. I think it's time," said the president.

"Yes sir, Mr. President, that's exactly what I had in mind. As you all know, in the president's address to the nation, he laid out a plea for the citizens to bring forward any information or anomalies they might have witnessed on 9/11 that could be helpful in getting Congress to open a new investigation. To assist them in that effort, we will be airing a number of public service announcements explaining how they can access the website. These messages will begin airing in a few days and will continue to air on television and radio until we feel they are no longer effective. Hopefully, they'll generate more leads than you can follow up on, and you'll demand more resources. Should that occur, I assure you that the funds and assistance will be provided. You can coordinate anything you need through me. I'm sure I don't need to remind you that our findings need to be kept under the radar until we're ready to release the information to the public so they can put pressure on Congress. If they get wind of what we're doing I can assure you that Congress and their lobbyists will do everything in their power to discount and discredit our efforts. This is ultimately a grassroots effort on the part of the public, with just enough catalyst from us to prime the pump. Furthermore, we already have some idea of the guilty parties in this crime, and we know they weave their tentacles in and out of almost every organization and government agency. They'll be poised to protect themselves from any kind of intensified scrutiny, especially after so many years of complacency and acceptance of the official government story. So be circumspect in all your communications, and to whom you extend your trust. This effort is our last chance to get to the truth."

"Once again, Allen, you've summarized my thoughts and feelings precisely, and directed them to their exact target. Keep it up and you'll cause me to be obsolete," said the president, chuckling.

"Not a chance, sir. Without you and your dogged determination to penetrate this holocaust, we'd all be sipping the Kool-Aid that's been flowing for nearly two decades."

"If there are no further questions or comments, let's adjourn this meeting for now and get to work on making it all happen. And Ruth Ann, enjoy your stay at the M Resort. I've stayed there while traveling to Nevada as a member of Congress, and I have to agree with you, it is like going home. There's no other hotel like it in all of Las Vegas—maybe anywhere," added the president.

three

"Ladies and gentlemen, we are now in our final descent into McCarran International Airport. We ask that you please place your seatbacks and tray tables in their original upright and locked position, and make certain that the aisle way at your feet is clear of all carry-on items. We will be on the ground in just a few moments."

Ruth Ann had fallen asleep after the meal service. She had heard the flight attendant announce their arrival, but was not awake enough to follow her commands. Just as she realized the flight was on final approach, she felt her seatback lift into its upright position as the lead flight attendant's soft voice informed her, "Ms. Lowy, we're about to land in Las Vegas."

"Thank you. I was so sound asleep," Ruth Ann apologized.

As soon as the aircraft door opened, Ruth Ann stepped into the aisle and quickly pulled her small suitcase from the overhead bin. She nodded to the lead flight attendant and thanked her for the pleasant flight. She hadn't been to Las Vegas for quite some time; the crime problems and the ailing economy over the past decade had put Vegas near the bottom of her list of favorite destinations. She preferred to vacation instead in quiet out-of-the-way resorts that provided her a more secure feeling.

The airport seemed bigger and busier than she remembered. Perhaps there were more slot machines scattered about the terminal, or just more people traveling. Her new bright purple luggage was already at the baggage claim area, circling around on the stainless steel carousel, when she descended the escalator and found her flight's claim area. As she stepped out of the terminal and into the dry desert heat, she felt her skin begin to tingle. She stopped to remove her lightweight jacket and noticed several yellow taxicabs parked nearby, waiting for fares. It reminded her of her yellow Lexus, and the horror she'd experienced when she was kidnapped. She reached in her purse for her cell phone, and quickly stepped back into the air-conditioned comfort of the terminal. The phone number to the hotel was already in her phone memory, so she pushed the call button and waited.

"The M Resort, this is Julia, how may I be of assistance?" a cheery voice answered.

"This is Ruth Ann Lowy. I'm at McCarran airport; would it be possible for you to send your limo to pick me up? I'm at the American Airlines baggage claim area."

"By all means, Ms. Lowy, our limo driver is just on his way to drop off a guest now. I'll let him know to pick you up. He should be there in a few moments. May I give him your cell phone number?"

"Of course. I'm sure you captured it on your system when I called," Ruth Ann replied, not wanting to repeat her phone number in a crowded area full of strangers.

"Yes, Ms. Lowy, I have your number. It's also noted here on your reservation," Julia replied.

Ruth Ann rolled her suitcase closer to the wall of windows to keep an eye out for the limo. She began to feel a sense of nervousness as the terminal continued to fill and became more crowded with arriving passengers. She was more than ready for her vacation to begin. She had discovered the M Resort by accident the first year it opened. She had been driving from Los Angeles to Chicago, and was just approaching the outskirts of Las Vegas when the stunning design of the hotel drew her attention to the neon 'M' logo. Without thinking, she took the St. Rose Parkway exit off the freeway, drove around the hotel and pulled her car in under the massive wooden and glass portico at the main entrance to the hotel. She politely asked the valet if he would keep her car close by because she was only stopping to see if the hotel was as magnificent inside as it was from the freeway.

The lobby was more spectacular and elegant than she'd imagined. The walls surrounding the reception area were massive sand-colored stone, over which a thin layer of water cascaded down from ceiling to floor. The view through the lobby opened up to a panoramic display of the Las Vegas strip miles to the north. She passed the beautifully appointed office of the concierge, who was standing just outside with his hands clasped in front of him. He smiled and nodded in Ruth Ann's direction. "Good evening," he said. "May I help you?"

"Well, you might be able to. I was driving past and your gorgeous building drew me in like a magnet. When was this resort built?" Ruth Ann asked. "I've never seen it before."

"Oh, it's brand new, and I would be honored to show you around if you have the time." He held out his hand and said, "My name is Vik. I'm the lead concierge at the M Resort Spa and Casino, Las Vegas' newest and finest resort."

She shook his hand and introduced herself. "I'm Ruth Ann Lowy, currently residing in Chicago. I'd love a tour, thank you."

The concierge closed the doors to his office and walked to the front desk to gather several room keys and to make certain there were no guests booked into the rooms he was planning to show her. "Come right this way." Vik motioned toward a wide corridor which led to the elevators. It was accented by raw silk curtains that matched those in the main lobby. The interior design and accent furnishings created a calming effect that Ruth Ann could feel beginning to envelop her entire being. It had begun with the stone walls of cascading water, and flowed from the placement of stylish leather furniture, unique floor lamps and tall glass vases that were positioned in the most appropriate locations.

Vik showed her all the various room options, from a glorious mountain view that extended into the desert for miles, to rooms with a magnificent view of the Strip glimmering off in the distance as the setting sun radiated against the colored glass walls of Vegas' prestigious resorts. Without question, the most breathtaking offering Vik showed her was one of the two-story lofted suites situated in the triangular corners of the hotel, which displayed a view of both the desert and mountains on one side, and the incomparable lights of the city on the other. In addition, the soaking tub with its amenities and the impeccable attention to detail throughout the suite created a space in Ruth Ann's senses that would constantly invite her to indulge.

"I was planning on making it into Mesquite or maybe as far as St. George tonight, but your tour has pushed that idea from my mind. I'd like to stay here a couple of days and enjoy this resort to its fullest. The Spa Mio and that wine cellar are just too fabulous to not experience. Call this an unexpected vacation on the way home." Ruth Ann smiled and assumed that Vik would provide the accommodation.

"Ms. Lowy, it would be my pleasure to secure you a room for the next two evenings. Having seen them all, which type of room would you prefer?" Vik asked.

"Since it's just me and I doubt I'll be in my room much, one of those sweet resort rooms with a view of the Strip would be perfect. I can enjoy the view and be reminded how fortunate I am to be here and not there."

Vik smiled. "I'll take care of that for you. Step into my office while I make the arrangements. Do you have a car parked with the valet?" he asked.

"Oh, my, I almost forgot, I did valet my car, but I thought I'd just be here a few minutes. I'll take care of that and ask the bellman to bring my things to the room." Ruth Ann laughed. "I wonder how many other people have stopped in to take a look at this place and ended up staying?"

Vik looked up from his computer screen. "Oh, you'd be surprised how many people have done the same thing, including many locals who avoid the Strip altogether."

The enjoyment of that first experience at the M was consuming Ruth Ann's memories. As she was about to revisit her relaxing day at the spa, her cell phone rang. It was the driver informing her that the limo was waiting for her nearby.

The ten-minute ride to the resort allowed Ruth Ann to center herself and relax, just knowing that she was about to spend quality time at her favorite place away from home. She was not looking forward to the trip to the Clark County Coroner's office to collect Bob's personal possessions, but she felt that Bob most likely had a flash drive or two in his pockets that might hold some vital information about some of the 9/11 details. Bob's style of research and organization was always a mystery to Ruth Ann and everyone else. He had his own way of filing, and it often was much more complicated than her own logical, straightforward method. She remembered her last visit with the research team in Minnesota, looking over Bob's shoulder at his computer screen in amazement as he recited to her the many avenues of data he was pursuing. That fond memory of their last meeting was quickly pushed aside by the realization that she would be collecting all his personal items and death certificate the following morning.

four

The next morning, Ruth Ann opened her eyes to a panoramic view of Las Vegas. Airplanes were landing at McCarran every few minutes, and the sunrise cast beautiful gold and pink hues upon the Luxor and the Mandalay Bay. At that hour of the morning, the Strip was a kaleidoscope of colors that accentuated its uniqueness. For this particular stay Ruth Ann had chosen to nestle into a spacious two-story loft suite. The massive windows on the opposite side of her suite looked out upon the Sloan Canyon Conservation area, the McCullough Range, and the Spring Mountains, all bathed in a mixture of pink and lavender hues from the rising sun. She settled into one of the swivel chairs, which provided her the choice to view the vistas from either direction. It was a relaxing beginning to what she knew would be a busy day.

The daunting task of visiting the coroner would soon be upon her, and she wanted to get it out of the way as soon as possible so she could enjoy the day at the spa and continue relaxing at the pool. She showered and took her time getting ready. She chose a casual business suit for the ordeal, then headed downstairs to the Baby Cakes coffee shop for a cup of coffee and an almond croissant. She stopped by Vik's office to reconfirm that the limo driver would be available to take her to her appointment and bring her back. "I'll only be there long enough to show my identification and collect some items," she assured him. "Tell the driver to meet me in the coffee shop, and to please wait for me at the coroner's office. It shouldn't take more than five minutes, since they're expecting me."

"Ms. Lowy?" asked the limo driver as he approached her small table in the bakery.

"Yes," Ruth Ann answered, standing as she spoke. "I'm ready to go if you are."

They walked together through the elegant lobby to the waiting limo, parked directly in front of the hotel entrance. Once seated comfortably inside, Ruth Ann reached into her purse for the address. "One seven zero four Pinto Lane," she informed the driver as the limo began to roll through the expansive driveway onto Las Vegas Boulevard.

"Sure thing, ma'am," the driver replied, as if he were already aware of her destination.

The drive into town had a few traffic slowdowns, but twenty minutes later they pulled up to the front of an orange sandstone stucco building. "I can wait for you right here, Ms. Lowy," the driver informed her as he parked along the street.

"That would be perfect," Ruth Ann agreed, and waited for the limo door to be opened.

Once inside the coroner's office she approached the receptionist and waited to be recognized. "I'm Ruth Ann Lowy and I believe you have a packet for me to pick up."

"Yes, a Mr. Max Hager called and said you'd be coming this morning. I just need to see a photo ID," she said, smiling for the first time.

Ruth Ann showed her Illinois driver's license and waited for the receptionist's nod of approval.

"I have all his things right here for you," the young woman said as she placed a large sealed envelope on the counter. "Now if you'll just initial here." She turned a plastic clipboard around and pointed to the area that corresponded with Bob's name. Ruth Ann quickly jotted her initials, thanked the young woman and was pleased she had not even taken the five minutes she had told her driver.

"Traffic's very light going south this time of the morning. I'll have you back at the M in no time," the driver said to Ruth Ann as he opened the door for her.

The maids had already straightened her suite by the time she returned. She changed into something more comfortable and summoned the courage to open Bob's envelope. She spread the contents out across the dining room table and sat down to investigate his last unexamined possessions. It wasn't long before she looked skyward and proclaimed out loud, "Sure enough, Bob, only you." There amidst his things were two more flash drives. She picked them up and could see they were thirty-two gigabyte drives. She laughed to herself, knowing that Bob always had more data hidden somewhere, and she wondered if they would ever find it all.

She started to go upstairs to retrieve her laptop, so she could examine Bob's data, but before she made it to the first step, the doorbell rang. "Now who in the world could that be?" she wondered aloud.

"Delivery," came a woman's voice from the hallway.

Ruth Ann opened the door to see a small Hispanic woman peering from behind a very large basket wrapped in cellophane. She could clearly see two bottles of wine, and what looked like apples and some chocolates neatly tucked inside the large basket.

"Oh my, please come in and you can set that basket on the bar," Ruth Ann directed. She pulled a five-dollar bill from her pocket and handed it to the woman.

"Thank you, ma'am, what a beautiful basket," the young woman remarked as she backed out the door and into the hallway.

"Yes, it is. And what a nice unexpected surprise it is too, thank you again," Ruth Ann said, closing the door to her suite and hurrying over to the gift basket. She pulled away the cellophane wrapping and reached for the card. She noticed fruit, chocolates, a pair of crystal wine goblets, two bottles of wine, several packets of nuts, and some cheese and crackers. Her fingers quickly flipped the small envelope open. The card read, Wishing you a relaxing and refreshing stay. Enjoy! Love, Vera and Joel. She grabbed her phone and texted a 'thank you' to Vera, knowing that she would share her appreciation with the president.

She retrieved her laptop, returned to the dining room table and inserted one of Bob's flash drives into the USB port. She clicked on the icon and waited for it to open. Several files appeared, all of them carrying a designation that only meant something to Bob. The first file Ruth Ann opened was appropriately titled FOIA, but inside that file were many other files, each with an unrecognizable title. She clicked on the first file. It was huge and took several minutes to load. It looked like a radar file for one of the flights on 9/11. Her eyes scanned down the left column of numbers, looking for an aircraft identification or a transponder number that would correlate to one of the flights. There were X and Y coordinates, and something that looked like altitude and distance from the radar station; she wasn't certain what all the numbers meant.

"Ok, I'm going to need some help here," she thought. She began to feel overwhelmed at the massive amount of incomprehensible data. She clicked open another file and again the screen filled with numbers. She saw Flight 93 in the right column, then noticed that the numbers were recorded every twelve seconds. "No wonder these files are so huge," she thought. She took note of the starting and ending times. As large as this file was, it only covered a ten-minute period of time. "Oh, man, I sure hope Bob has these files sorted somewhere in a manner that will make some sense." This time she spoke out loud.

She continued to click on several files randomly, even though their names meant nothing to her. Freedom of Information Act data was confusing enough without Bob's special touch added to the offerings. She hoped he had left an index somewhere that might be found. Each file she opened seemed larger and more confusing than the last. Her head began to pound with each keystroke. She looked heavenward again and sighed. "Bob, come on, Bob, nobody will ever figure out your crazy codes. Leave me an index, and give me a clue."

After more than an hour of opening files and trying to comprehend what it was Bob had found, she realized she wasn't going to be able to put it all together. Worst of all, she wasn't sure she knew anyone that could help. Perhaps someone in the Federal Aviation Agency that Jim Bowman or Vera trusted might be able to read these radar files and make sense out of them, but even that seemed to be a stretch. One particular file was clearly marked 'Daily Log,' and she could see what she hoped were airport codes with the familiar JFK and BOS marked near the top. They appeared to be daily log sheets from Air Traffic Control Centers. She closed the file and made a copy of it onto her desktop to examine later. Some of the codes were unfamiliar to her; she assumed they might be radar sites or perhaps a control center that was not located at an airport. Then again, they could be almost anything.

Ruth Ann's cell phone beeped, indicating a text message had come in. Glad your basket found you safe and sound. Enjoy your time, you've earned it. Keep in touch and most importantly, stay safe. It was from Vera. They had not known each other long, but the time they had spent together as hostages had created a special bond between them. Vera had been her hero before the ordeal, and they shared only an enhanced admiration afterward. Ruth Ann understood how important finding and exposing the entire truth about 9/11 was to Vera and the president. Vera had shared with her how connected the airline family was, all around the world. She also knew that President Sherman had learned enough from Vera, Jim and the entire research team to not settle for anything but the entire truth, no matter where it led or who it included.

She ejected the flash drive, picked up the other drive and tucked them both neatly into a zippered side pocket in her purse. She carefully slid Bob's wallet and other personal items back into the envelope, sealed it, and placed it under her jogging suit, which was still folded in the bottom of her suitcase.

Feeling frustrated, she lowered herself into a comfortable leather chair and turned toward the view of the Strip. She felt her shoulder muscles begin to tighten, reminding her that her spa appointment was rapidly approaching. She planned to indulge herself in the luxury of the Spa Mio, relax by the pool for a while, and then enjoy a nice dinner at the Pasta Bar. She had the rest of her day and evening well mapped out.

The visit to the spa lasted over three hours. Ruth Ann felt totally renewed by the time she put on her swimsuit, grabbed a robe and headed for the pool until it was time to return to her suite to dress for dinner. She assured the professional attendants at the spa that she would be back in a couple of days.

When she arrived back at her suite, she quickly checked her email for any updates from Max or Gil—nothing. Good, she thought, and then quickly checked a few news sites for any headlines of importance. "Not much going on worldwide, it seems," she said to herself. "Good, good, good, just what I needed to see."

She grabbed a small bag of chocolate-covered almonds from the gift basket and nibbled a few as she applied a touch of makeup and fastened her hair loosely with a beaded hair clip she had bought in Morocco years earlier. She chose a cobalt-blue linen dress to wear for the evening and headed out the door to one of her favorite restaurants in the hotel.

The hostess welcomed her and seated her at a table for two near the small chrome and glass elevator that separated two of the casual dining establishments on the lobby level. Her waiter approached her table and immediately recognized her. "Ruth Ann, isn't it?" he asked.

She had not been to the M Resort in well over a year, and was surprised that he recognized her—even more astonished that he remembered her name. She glanced up at his nametag. "Chris, yes, it is Ruth Ann, thank you so much for remembering."

Chris smiled and replied, "I never forget anyone as impressive as you."

"Do you say that to all of your customers?" she asked.

"Only the ones whose name I remember," Chris replied, laughing. "Now, what wine may I offer you this evening?"

"Oh, I'd love a nice glass of Pinot Grigio," she answered, "and a small caprese salad. For my entrée I'll have the salmon, which I remember was fabulous."

"My pleasure," Chris replied, just as another waiter delivered some Italian bread to her table.

It never bothered Ruth Ann to dine alone. She was comfortable being in control of the situation, even though she was aware of a lingering paranoia brought on by her recent kidnapping. It caused her to become keenly aware of strangers, particularly those in close proximity. Here at the M, she felt safe; only a handful of people knew where she was, and they were the ones who had rescued her. Her mind began to flow into the soft music playing in the background while she waited for her food and drink to arrive.

The hostess seated a gentleman at the table next to hers, and as he set his menu down, his eyes met Ruth Ann's stare. He readjusted himself in his chair and said, "Good evening," with a warm smile to back it up.

His words startled her and brought her back into the moment. "Oh, my apologies, I wasn't staring, I hope. I was just lost in thought," she explained.

"Not a problem at all! You were looking right through me and I didn't want to startle you when you came back to the real world and found me sitting nearby," the man clarified. "My name is Mark Stillman, Colonel Mark Stillman."

Ruth Ann smiled and extended her hand across to his table. "Nice to meet you, Colonel Stillman. My name is Ruth Ann, Ruth Ann Lowy."

"The pleasure is mine. Are you dining alone this evening?"

"Yes, as a matter of fact, I am." Ruth Ann smiled, feeling strangely comfortable, yet not sure why.

"I would be honored if you'd join me." Colonel Stillman pointed toward the empty chair across the table. At that moment Chris, the waiter, pulled the chair out for Ruth Ann and transferred her place setting to her new location. Ruth Ann found herself suddenly seated across from a stranger and felt perfectly safe.

"Actually, I should have introduced myself as Colonel Mark Stillman, retired, US Air Force," he continued. "I'm recently retired and I'm not used to adding that to my name. I'm sure before long I'll just be Mark, with no mention of the military."

Ruth Ann was not very familiar with the military and its rankings. "Colonel—that's pretty high up there, isn't it?" she asked.

Mark smiled. "A colonel is a pretty high rank, I guess. There are several ranks that are higher, but then I'd have had to be a general and nobody likes generals, even if they're retired. What brings you to Las Vegas?" he asked, clearly wanting to change the subject.

"Oh, I came here for a little vacation. I've had a rather hectic few months and I love this place. Years ago I used to enjoy the excitement of the Strip, but now I rarely venture in that direction. This is one of my favorite places to come to relax and renew myself. How about you—what brings you to the M?"

"Oh, I had a little reunion of Air Force guys, a group I'd not seen for quite a while, and several of us had retired in the past few years. It was great fun to see everyone, but I'm not much of a gambler and quite frankly the Strip has never been my cup of tea."

Ruth Ann listened carefully for clues, but she still had questions about Mark's career. "What does a colonel do in the Air Force? Did you have a specific job or duty?"

"Yes, I was a pilot," Mark answered, but not wanting to be more specific.

"Oh, I suppose that's what the Air Force does, silly me," Ruth Ann replied, but her thoughts shifted to the idea that this was someone who might understand radar, and maybe Bob's files.

"Well, not everyone in the Air Force is a pilot, but that branch of service certainly has more pilots than any of the others, because we have most of the airplanes," Mark said with a smile.

Chris brought Ruth Ann's wine and salad, and Mark ordered an entrée and a glass of wine. They enjoyed the ambiance of the Pasta Bar and their casual questions as they began to learn more about each other. Even though they both felt comfortable sharing aspects of their lives, they were careful not to divulge too much. Caution and a sense of privacy were traits both of them shared, which made dining together pleasant, without expectations. When they were finished the waiter came by with their checks in separate leatherette cases. Mark quickly picked them both up and insisted, "Let me get this."

"Why, thank you, Mark—or should I call you Colonel? Which would you prefer?" She giggled to herself, knowing no matter what his answer was, she wasn't going to call him Colonel.

"Please call me Mark," he responded. "Now, how would you like to head downstairs to the Wine Cellar and do a little tasting? Have you been down to the Hostile Grape yet?"

"Funny you should ask, I was already planning to go there

after dinner," Ruth Ann admitted.

The Hostile Grape wine cellar was the most unique wine bar Ruth Ann had ever experienced. Not only did it have hundreds of wines from around the world, but it had a wine tasting area that dispensed wines in one, three or five-ounce samples. Using a wine card, one could choose from wines in every price range, and taste as many as desired.

Together they enjoyed the experience of tasting several unique wines and relaxing on the comfortable leather sofas, while chatting about places in the world where they had sampled the fruit of good grapes. They laughed at each other's tales and were beginning to truly enjoy one another's company. Finally, Mark rested his glass on the table in front of them and said, "Ruth Ann, my dear, I'm going to have to call it a night. May I escort you to the elevator? It's been a long few days for me, and after that excellent dinner and the discovery of a few new wines, I'm ready for a little shut-eye."

"I would appreciate that," Ruth Ann said. She stood, smoothed out her dress, and reached for her purse.

As they walked toward the elevators, Mark inquired, "Will you be staying here long?"

"I have no definite plans. I'll probably be here a week or two," Ruth Ann responded, purposefully being vague.

"Well, do you have plans for tomorrow?" Mark asked.

"Yes, I do, I plan to be in a cabana at the pool with my laptop," Ruth Ann answered, smiling.

"A perfect place to be, I'm certain," Mark agreed.

"If you're looking for someplace to hang out, you're more than welcome to come to the pool and find me," Ruth Ann offered.

"I just might do that in the afternoon, if you're still there. I have an old friend from the academy I want to try to connect with and I'll probably spend my morning either talking with him, or hopefully having breakfast or lunch."

Just then the elevator opened and they stepped inside. Mark pushed ten, and Ruth Ann pushed fifteen.

"Good night, and thank you for sharing your evening with me," Mark said as he stepped off the elevator.

"Good night, Mark, and thank you for dinner and the wine. I do hope you come and find me tomorrow at my cabana," Ruth Ann said, surprised that she had offered a second invitation for him to join her.

five

Ruth Ann, having fallen asleep in the shade and warmth of the cabana, heard a voice echoing as if in the distance. "Are you awake?"

She sat straight up at the sound, turned around and was pleasantly surprised to see Mark stepping into the cabana holding two large glasses.

"How does an iced coffee sound?" he asked. "I had them add a touch of cream and a shot of vanilla in one, and caramel in the other. Which one do you prefer?"

"Oh, caramel is my favorite. Did I mention that to you last night?" she asked.

"No, it was just a wild guess on my part," Mark admitted, as he took a seat beside her in the shade.

"This is just what I needed. I buried myself in some research last night and this morning. I even tried digging into it again out here. Quite frankly, it wasn't in my vein of expertise. I guess I found it difficult to stay awake in the heat and whenever I have to force myself to research beyond my capabilities, it makes me really tired," Ruth Ann tried to explain as she sipped her iced beverage.

"Sorry to hear that. Researching is tough enough when you know what you're doing," Mark consoled her.

Ruth Ann closed her laptop and slid it into her tote bag. "Enough work for today." She lifted her drink toward Mark's, touched hers to his and proclaimed, "Cheers! Now, do you have a swimsuit on under those pants?"

"I most certainly do," Mark said, setting his drink down on the table and reaching for his belt.

"Meet you in the pool." She laughed and quickly darted out of the cabana, and dove into the water.

She swam underwater for as far as she could in the enormous pool. When she finally lifted her head out of the water, secured her footing and turned around, she could see Mark underwater just a few yards from her. Before he reached her his head popped up to the surface. "Now that really clears your head. I have a whole new perspective on life," he said, laughing and shaking off the water.

"Back to those iced coffees. I'll race you," Ruth Ann said, leaping forward and trying to get as much of a head start as possible. When they were back in the cabana she toweled her hair and asked, "Did you find your buddy today?"

"Yes, I did finally get ahold of him; unfortunately, he's not doing too well health-wise. We did manage to have a late breakfast/early lunch at a little hole-in-the-wall joint he frequents in Henderson. It was a nice reunion; he missed the get-together the other night due to a family commitment," Mark explained.

"Glad you two got reconnected," she said, recalling her recent reunion with Gil and Max.

"Hey, are you interested in joining me again for dinner tonight?" Mark asked, hoping that she was available.

"I have no plans other than a little research, and the information I've uncovered might as well be written in Greek. It's got me pretty frustrated. I have to admit, dinner tonight would be a welcome distraction." Ruth Ann could feel her sense of caution begin to gradually dissipate with each conversation they shared.

Mark seemed to pick up on her hesitation to divulge her research subject. "Hey, you don't have anything to worry about; I once held one of the highest security clearances in the United States government."

"You did?" Ruth Ann asked, curious to know more and hoping he would offer some details.

"Yes, I did." He smiled, but said nothing more.

"Well, I might have to pick your brain a little to see if you can help me," she said, hoping to spark his curiosity enough that he might offer up more about his mysterious background.

Mark reached for his cell phone. "What do you say we meet at that M Bar in the casino about six?"

Ruth Ann agreed, stood and saluted him. "Yes, sir," she said, laughing.

Mark chuckled as he turned back toward the hotel. "Six it is," he said, holding up six fingers above his head.

Ruth Ann was hoping she could solicit Mark's help in reading some of the FOIA files. There were so many acronyms that she was not familiar with, she needed to find someone with an aviation background. A pilot, an air traffic controller—somebody that could read the data and explain it to her.

Her cell phoned chimed a text message. It was Vera: Just checking in, hope you are relaxing and enjoying your time.

She typed back: Thanks Vera, I'm at the pool and I've taken care of the business at the coroner's office. Digging through his flash drives trying to dissect any information I can.

Ruth Ann's text message to Vera reminded her that she had a little time before dinner to slog through more of the files. In spite of her desire to stop, they kept calling her back. She grabbed her towel and tote bag and headed up to the suite. She indulged in a long shower before diving back into what had become a grind. Six o'clock could not come soon enough.

six

Dora Wilcox was now in her seventies and lived alone in Richmond, Virginia. Her two daughters lived nearby and would come and visit often with their children and families, but not Dante. For the most part he kept his distance since retiring from the military. He would occasionally drop in to check on her when he was in the area if it was around lunchtime; otherwise Dora never knew where he was or what he was up to. She wasn't even sure where he lived. The last cell phone number she had for him always went to voicemail when she called. It didn't matter how many messages she left with him inquiring as to his well-being, there was never a reply. In fact, the last time she called the number, someone she didn't know answered who had never heard of her son. This was a wound she kept concealed. She and Dante had been close all through his growing-up years. He was her last child and only boy. That alone reserved a special place in her heart for him, especially after her husband left. The responsibility of being a man came early to Dante, and his mother cherished the way he'd accepted the challenge. She liked how he always put her first, no matter what endeavor he was pursuing. If his friends came over to play ball, he would often make them wait in the living room until he finished his homework. That was a habit she had instilled in him from the time he started school, and it warmed her heart to see it take root and flourish in him in his later years. When he entered the military she received a letter from him almost every week. Even when he was on special assignment in remote corners of the world, letters would come. They always began with an inquiry as to her health and well-being before he ever shared with her how he was or what the military would allow him to tell her of his missions. As opportunities presented themselves, he would call her. He never missed her birthday or holidays. One week out of every month of leave Dante always spent with her. She would plan short trips for those days, often to Washington D.C. where she delighted in showing him the historical and political sites in the area, and he would share with her the inner workings of the military and get her into places most civilians never went. It was a time they enjoyed together, full of laughter, insight and memories. But those days seemed to be over now and Dora could not understand why, or even receive a plausible explanation.

As midmorning approached, Dora found herself in the garden. She had tended to her vegetables on the side of the house where they received the most sunlight, and now was tending to her flowers, which lined her walkways in the front. It was the flowers that set her house apart from the neighbors, whose yards were neat, but did not have the radiant beauty that had been a hallmark of hers for years. As she was leaning over to clip the dead leaves from her peonies, she heard a car engine rumble as it pulled up to her curb and quickly shut off. She wanted to look, but she was more comfortable just hoping that car was Dante's. She remained bent over, only now her eyes were closed, transforming her hope into a silent prayer.

"Hello, mama. Your flowers are as beautiful as ever."

"Oh, Dante," she cried, rising up and turning around to get him in full view. "To what do I owe the pleasure this time?"

"Oh, the other night I was drinking with Jamal and you came into the conversation, so I thought I'd swing by and see how you were doing. Did I catch you at a bad time?"

"There's never a bad time for a son to come see his mama. And how is Jamal? I haven't seen him in years."

Dante took the clippers from his mother's hand and gave her a big hug. "Jamal is fine, still stuck on that Shantril. I doubt they'll ever get married. And as usual he asks a lot of questions, but I can never tell if he's listening for the answers. Anyway, let's go inside and see what's for lunch."

Dora laughed. "One of these days you ought to come and take your mama out to lunch, but I won't let the fridge go empty waiting."

"Probably wise," commented Dante. He found his favorite overstuffed chair in the living room and settled into its comfort. Dora washed her hands and began making his favorite corned beef sandwich on rye bread. She never had to ask. If she had the fixings for it, that was the ticket, and probably the real reason he ever came to see her anymore. He always told her that her corned beef sandwiches were the finest in the land, and he'd enjoyed them in all corners of the world.

"Did you hear the president's speech the other night?" she called out from the kitchen. She knew she shouldn't ask that question. It had all the ingredients to ruin a good visit. She asked anyway. That's what mothers do.

Dante was silent until he thought to change the subject by telling her Jamal was thinking of moving to Baltimore, which was a total fabrication, but the consequences for lying seemed, at the moment, benign compared to the pain that would be inflicted upon him if he allowed his mother to commence a political discussion.

She brought his lunch to him and sat on the sofa nearby. It made her happy to just watch him eat, but inside she wished he would open up and talk to her. "It's nice that Jamal is moving, but you never answered my question about listening to the president's speech the other night." She waited, feeling the tension begin to build in between bites of the sandwich.

"I saw that he was on, yes, but I didn't pay any attention

to what he had to say. I was busy talking to Jamal, and not too interested in his message," Dante replied.

"Well, it wasn't very long. The point of his message was to solicit the help of the public in providing evidence and anomalies surrounding 9/11 that could help him persuade Congress to open a new investigation. I liked what he had to say, and I hope it makes a difference in how the public feels about looking into the past and for once finding the truth."

Again Dante was silent. Dora knew that if she persisted he would rethink his reason for coming to visit, and before long he would be finding his corned beef sandwiches elsewhere. In spite of that she continued. It had been too long, and it was too confusing for her not to release what was inside her soul, even if it meant alienating her only son.

"Surely you must know things about that day that have never been revealed. You used to tell me about some of the missions you were involved in while fighting the 'war on terror' and I just have to think that as smart as you are, you figured out things that this president needs to know." She stopped talking and just looked at him as only a mother could, pleading with her eyes and yearning with her heart for answers.

He couldn't face her. He finished his sandwich and placed the plate on the coffee table, then just stared out the window. His recent conversation and confession to Jamal was fresh in his mind, and he still questioned if he should have unloaded that burden. He didn't feel any better having shared what he harbored inside, and now his own mother was getting close to dredging that same conversation to the surface. Dante didn't know if he could stand to relive the emotions he'd felt the other night.

"Can we just drop it, mama?" Dante barely whispered.

"We can, but you know it's not going away. It's the wedge that now resides between us. A wedge I don't understand, and maybe in reality you don't understand it either."

"Oh, I understand all right. I hate Republicans and this Joel Sherman is a Republican, therefore he's as good as dead to me," Dante shot back.

"I guess you don't remember how in 1984 you sat in that same chair on election night and cried your eyes out because you weren't old enough to cast a vote for Reagan, and you knew that was his very last election. And then just four years later, after graduating from high school and enlisting in the military, you called me from boot camp to tell me you had voted for George H.W. Bush and it was the happiest day of your life. Now how do you go from that to hating Joel Sherman, who wasn't even elected, and is only trying to do what's best for this country? You of all people should be able to see that doesn't make a lick of sense."

Dante shrugged his shoulders and turned his head to face her. "Yeah, well, maybe it doesn't make any sense. I'm not sure I make any sense, and you pointing it out doesn't help. I spilled my guts about my experiences overseas for the first time the other night, talking to Jamal. I'm wishing now that I had just kept my damn mouth shut. It brought too many things to the surface I don't think I can deal with, and now you want to make me rehash them again."

"Look, honey, I'm not trying to harm you in any way. If you can't talk about some things, I can understand. What I just want to know is why the change in you. How could you go from a patriot wanting to serve your country and to support your leaders, to a shell of a man who hates his government and loathes his homeland? As your mentor for most of your young life, that's difficult for me to understand. As your mother, the pain I feel inside you is unbearable for me to ignore."

"For now, let's just say having been there and having done that has about done me in, and I'm unable to deal with the confusion in my head, heart and soul. I've stopped coming around because you don't seem to want to let me deal with this on my own terms. You know I love you, but when you question me constantly about what I'm going through I kind of don't like you, if that makes any sense."

Dora rose from the couch, picked up Dante's plate and carried it into the kitchen. She knew him well enough to let him stew over the words he had just spoken to her. They hurt, and she didn't have an adequate response to them, so she slipped away to attend to her motherly duties in hopes her son would somehow come to grips with the fact that his anguish was not only affecting him, but that it also had a detrimental effect on others. She had tried this approach before without positive results, but it was all she had and so she employed it again.

Dante eventually followed her into the kitchen and stood behind her as she was washing the dishes. "Mama, I'd like to find my way back to peace, but I don't see how that's possible with everything I have seen and done. I'm in this hellhole and I'm afraid there is no escape for me. Just forgive me if you can. I don't want to hurt anymore, and I especially don't want to hurt you."

Dora turned around and reached out her arms to embrace her son. He was much taller than she, and so it became her best bear hug around his chest. He rested his chin on the top of her head and let her hold him for as long as she wanted. He knew it wasn't what she wanted, but it was the best he had to offer. He could hear her softly sobbing as her grip on him slowly tightened. When she finally let go she said, "I've lived in that hellhole. I don't know how you managed to get into yours, but the only escape from mine was to be of some service to others. When I could force myself to stop thinking about me and to do something for someone else, then—and only then—could I see the faint glimmer of a doorway out. That's the only advice I can offer you—that and the fact that I love you no matter what you've done or what you will ever do. I'm your mother, and mothers love their sons no matter what."

"Oh mama, you frustrate me, but you can always make me feel better. Thank you for that. I don't know if I can follow your advice—that kind of thing has always come back to bite me in the ass—but I won't forget what you've said." He hugged her around her shoulders, then wiped the tears from her eyes with his thumbs.

"Okay, I just have one question to ask you, and I promise I won't ever bother you again about all the things that cause you so much stress."

"Go ahead, ask," said Dante.

"Do you think you have information that could possibly help President Sherman in his effort to find out more about 9/11?"

"Probably," he answered.

seven

At exactly six o'clock, Mark arrived at the M bar in the middle of the casino and found Ruth Ann already waiting for him. Based on his wine preferences from the night before, she'd known exactly what to order, and a full-bodied Merlot had been placed in front of his empty seat.

"What a pleasant surprise," he said, smiling his approval, and sat down to relax for a few minutes before dinner. "Where would you like to eat tonight?" he asked.

"Oh, I think it's a perfect evening for the Jayde Fuzion, right over there," she replied, pointing through the bar in the direction of the restaurant.

"I've eaten there before when it was located where the pasta bar is now. Good call," he answered.

After they finished their wine, Mark took Ruth Ann by the hand and helped her to stand, then escorted her through the bar and casino towards the maître d' station, where reservations were not necessary.

"Please follow me," a young hostess said, smiling as she led the way to a solitary booth near the back of the restaurant.

The dimly lit Asian-style restaurant offered a perfect atmosphere for the two of them to engage in a quiet conversation without being overheard. Ruth Ann broke the silence. "Mark—" She paused. "The other day you told me you were a pilot."

He nodded, but could sense she was having a difficult time phrasing the follow-up question, so he began to explain. "My father was a pilot, my mother was a flight attendant, and one of my grandfathers was an aeronautical engineer. I grew up with planes on my bedspread, propellers on the curtains and airplane talk almost every night at dinner. Flight played a big part in my life. I traveled around the world before I started third grade. I guess I didn't have much choice; growing up around planes, pilots, flight attendants and engineers, it was only natural to seek appointment at the academy in Colorado and become an Air Force pilot. Oh, and my uncle, Mom's brother, was an air traffic controller before their big strike in 1981."

"Have you flown only military planes?" Ruth Ann asked.

"Well, I've flown several types of military jets, if that's what you mean," Mark replied, but he wasn't sure he wanted to go into detail about his flying career.

"So, you must be familiar with radar stations, flight plans, and that sort of thing?" Ruth Ann asked.

"Yes, ma'am, very familiar," Mark responded without hesitation.

She was pleased at his response, but remained silent. She recalled his comment the other day about having a top security clearance, but she still felt apprehensive about sharing her research subject. She knew she needed help, but she didn't want to scare him away by saying anything about 9/11. Before his untimely death, Bob had texted her phone that he had found proof that long range radar all around the New England area had been out of service on the morning of September 11th. That subject wasn't something you could throw out to an unsuspecting acquaintance, even if he was taking you to dinner again.

"Do you think I might be able to help you with your research?" Mark offered. "If I can't figure it out, I probably have colleagues who can. My circle of friends goes from Washington D.C. to California, and from air traffic controllers to astronauts."

"Where were you when the terror attacks of 9/11 hit?" she asked.

"I was in Peru, on an assignment," Mark revealed.

"An assignment in Peru?" she questioned, screwing up her nose.

Mark leaned forward to be closer to Ruth Ann and whispered, "Long story, but I had flown the Secretary of State to Lima, Peru."

"You what?" she asked.

"I was a pilot not just for the US Air Force, but for the White House and the Pentagon," he said, his voice still a whisper.

"I probably can trust you, then," Ruth Ann replied, feeling her apprehension begin to dissolve.

"Oh, I'm trustworthy," he said, speaking in a slightly louder voice and leaning back in the booth.

They both paused their conversation each time the wait staff came close to their table. A bond of trust was beginning to form between them, which was able to pierce through the barriers that each had erected to prevent the details of their lives from being brought into the open.

They talked all through dinner, paying little attention to what they were eating. As good as the food was, the excitement they shared learning more about each other's careers and experiences seemed more important. Ruth Ann offered to pay the check, but on one condition—Mark had to follow her to her suite and look at the data with which she had been struggling.

"Sure, I'd be happy to do that for you. It sounds like a fair trade," he said.

Ruth Ann pushed the key into the slot in the door of her suite and walked inside. She turned on the lights, which caused the magnificence of the suite to come alive. Mark followed her inside and looked around, in complete awe of what he was seeing.

"This is spectacular," he exclaimed. "I had no idea there were rooms in this hotel as breathtaking as this one."

Ruth Ann said, blushing, "Another reason I love this hotel. You can't duplicate this anywhere in the world. Once I saw this room on my first visit, I knew I would have to come back and stay in it. You can see why I think of this place as my home."

She directed Mark to the dining room table, where her laptop was casting screen saver images across the room, making it look almost like a disco parlor from the eighties. Ruth Ann instructed Mark to take a seat at the table while she ran upstairs to retrieve the flash drives she had stored in the safe.

"What kind of project are you working on, exactly?" Mark asked when Ruth Ann returned and sat down in the chair beside him.

"Well, to be perfectly honest with you, I'm digging into the supposed terror attack of September 11th. But don't go thinking I'm one of those internet conspiracy nuts with a tinfoil hat and a Facebook page. I'm working with a team of highly respected researchers directly under the president," she replied.

"The president, you mean as in President Joel Sherman?" Mark asked.

"Yes, that president," Ruth Ann answered as she pushed the flash drive into the USB slot and waited for the file information to fill the screen.

"Great guy, Sherman. I liked him from the day he took office," Mark said.

This was the moment where Ruth Ann felt it was time to explain what she was doing. If Mark could be of any help to her, he needed to know the full scope of her project, including a lot of the background research that had yet to be made fully public. She turned her chair slightly so she could face him and said, "This is kind of a long story, but if you heard the president's last address to the nation, you'll have a good idea what my research team is working to uncover. You see, after several FOIA requests and thousands of hours of research, our team has found some very disturbing anomalies, or perhaps something much worse."

"What do you mean?" Mark asked.

Ruth's apprehension was beginning to bubble up again. She wanted Mark to know everything, but she wasn't positive how he would accept information that was contrary to the Bush administration's story. She realized he had essentially worked in the Bush administration as one of its pilots. She took a deep breath, weighing the risk, and said, "Most of the information our team uncovered, Jim Bowman and Vera, the president's wife, discovered together."

"I'm listening," Mark assured her.

"You see, they discovered the four commercial planes we were led to believe hit targets or crashed that day, were hijacked electronically using the flight termination system, or possibly another remote-control system."

"DARPA's Operation Homerun?" Mark asked. "You know about that?"

"Yes, I'm aware of that program, and I'm aware that there was more than one remote control system that could have been used. We know that the two airlines involved both had SPC's Flight Termination Systems onboard, which certainly could have been used. Of course, we have uncovered Operation Homerun and have a pretty good idea how SPC got ahold of that technology as well. Not many stones have been left unturned by this team; they've dug deeper than anyone ever has into the entire 9/11 operation."

"Where are you at now with your research, and how can I be of help?" Mark asked.

"We know that the pilots, even if they knew the Flight Termination System was installed, would never have dreamed it had taken control of their plane. Since there were no hijackers or intruders inside the cockpits, it appears the pilots suddenly lost the ability to control the aircraft and were most likely busy trying to regain that control. This is the only possible reason eight highly trained pilots, all of them with military backgrounds, did not squawk the universal hijack code. It also explains why there was no communication with the flight attendants in the cabin. Once the remote system takes over, it makes all communication impossible, including the onboard interphone system between the pilots and the flight attendants. We're pretty certain that some of the passengers onboard were there for the reason of facilitating this electronic hijack by taking control of the flight attendants or other devious actions. One member of our research team is a retired senior flight attendant; she has been instrumental in determining that this was not a typical hijacking. She has scrutinized the FBI's transcripts of all the phone calls made by both passengers and crew members, and has come to the conclusion that the government story is a lie. Once this realization was made, the team was able to set the official story aside, and look with a new set of eyes. We've done that, and we've discovered that all four planes were remotely commandeered by someone in the air or on the ground, and landed at a reserve base in western Massachusetts."

Mark interrupted her. "Westover."

"Yes, Westover. It's just outside of Chicopee. Are you familiar with that base?" she asked.

"Oh yes, very much so." Mark's words were slower now, as his mind was engaged in the details of the remote control device landing the planes, and what the pilots must have been thinking as the planes stopped responding to their commands.

"Most of us, the researchers and those that began to question the official story, had trusted that the FAA and the National Transportation Safety Board were telling us the truth. We followed the supposed flight paths all around the country, and collectively tried to make their storyline fit. Unfortunately, the one detail someone forgot was the cell phones, and the fact that they did not work at cruise altitude. The airline professionals that have contributed to our research have guaranteed us that it was impossible for a cell phone to make a connection above fifteen hundred feet. Several American Airlines employees have contacted us to reconfirm the impossibility of CNN commentator Barbara Olson using an onboard air-phone. American had deactivated all the phones on their 757's by the end of January 2001, some eight months prior to 9/11," Ruth Ann said, nearly out of breath by the time she finished.

"I'm aware that cell phones don't work at altitudes above fifteen hundred feet or so, on a commercial jet. I never had much luck with those air-phones either, to be quite honest. The first time I saw one installed, I had to use it just because of the novelty of being able to place a call from altitude. The call dropped twice, which explains why those air-phones were short-lived," Mark added.

Ruth Ann got up and poured a glass of water for both of them. It was clear to her that Mark comprehended everything she was telling him and that he believed her, which meant it was going to be a long night of conversation.

She took a sip from her glass and continued, "The retired airline pilot and flight attendant on the team added inside information none of us had access to, and quite frankly, they brought the missing piece of the puzzle to us. Once we understood the remote control system and the failure of all those crew members to follow the FAA hijack protocols, we began to look at the government documents and their claims with a new perspective. These two airline professionals discovered Westover Air Force base by the timing of the phone calls from the planes. Since cell phone calls were impossible to make from altitude, they wondered where all four planes were when the calls began. They then realized that the calls, whether made from cell phones or onboard air-phones, were most likely made from the ground. They also knew those planes, full of fuel, would need at least a ten-thousand-foot runway to land, and since the first phone calls from two flight attendants on Flight 11 came within twenty minutes of Boston, they knew when they saw Westover that they had found the location. The flight times from Newark and Washington's Dulles to Westover also coincided with the start of the phone calls from flights 93 and 77. Their discovery has been reconfirmed by reservists who were activated that morning, who arrived at the base gate and were told the base had been evacuated of all personnel. They had been locked out and were housed for the next few days at hotels in the area. Several eyewitnesses in western Massachusetts have now come forward who saw the commercial planes dangerously close to the ground that morning, but once they saw the television broadcasts from New York and D. C., those sightings went out of their minds."

"Westover certainly has a long runway—that's a C-5 transport logistics base. They received millions of dollars for renovations shortly after the terror attacks," Mark added.

"The flight attendant dug up several versions of the FBI's initial interviews and recordings from that day. When those documents were entered into hearings and trials, she noticed that some accounts had been changed or removed entirely. This caught her attention, and when she discovered a quote from one of the flight attendants onboard Flight 11 that said he stood upstairs, it dawned on her that the plane was more than likely in a hangar."

Mark sat quietly, nodding his head. "Yes, there are five or six very large hangars on that base. With no ground traffic, a plane could be taxied into one of those hangars very quickly. Some of those hangars can fit a C-5 Galaxy, and that bird makes the 747-400 look small."

"One of our research team members was here in Las Vegas. He was killed by a couple of petty thieves—street thugs that wanted the few bucks he had in his pockets. What they didn't know, fortunately for us, was that he was one hell of a researcher.

He could dig into documents like nobody else. He was relentless in his determination to get to the truth. Like so many others that day, watching building seven at the World Trade Center collapse exactly like a controlled demolition was the commencement of his pursuit."

Ruth Ann paused to make certain Mark was still taking all of her information in and that he had no questions concerning what she was telling him. Then she continued, "This researcher had a rather large file from the Freedom of Information Act that he and others had accumulated over the years. That's part of what I picked up here from the Clark County Coroner's office. His personal effects included these flash drives filled with information that we need to fully comprehend. Obviously, I don't understand it. I could take it back to Washington and let the rest of the team dive into it, but I have a gut feeling that what's contained on these drives has something to do with this Mojave Desert area; otherwise, he would not have been in this area when he was killed."

"So, what you really need is help reading the information and making sense out of it?" Mark asked.

"I'm going to say yes," Ruth Ann acknowledged. "If I can show you what type of files these are, perhaps you can make more sense out of them than I can." She clicked open a large file titled AAL Flight 11. "Some of these are huge files and can take a while to open. May I pour you some wine from my gift basket?" she asked, pointing toward the large basket on the other table. "You won't believe this, but this gift was given to me by the First Lady, Vera Sherman, upon my arrival."

"Seriously, you're friends with the First Lady?" Mark questioned.

"I am. We actually met not very long ago. It's a long story and someday I might have to share it with you," Ruth Ann said, smiling and taking careful note of the expression on Mark's face.

"That would be great. I'd love a glass of presidential wine, and I wouldn't mind hearing your story when you have time. Right now it sounds like this research project, and what might be in these files, may cause me to need something a little stronger than water," he said, as he watched the file open and fill the computer screen.

Ruth Ann pulled the wine goblets and a bottle of merlot from the basket, noticing that Vera had even included a wine opener among the assorted snacks. She smiled. Only a flight attendant would think of that, she thought to herself as she pulled the cork.

The text file had finally opened when she returned to the table with the wine. Mark began scanning the document in silence. Occasionally an audible noise could be heard coming from his mouth, but it was as if he were talking to himself in some foreign tribal language. Ruth Ann could not tell if they were good sounds or bad ones. After several minutes and nearly a half a glass of wine, Ruth Ann asked, "Are you familiar with this? Does it make any sense to you?"

"This is a radar strip; it looks like it scans every four seconds. These X and Y coordinates are the distance from some point. I'm not exactly sure at the moment where that point is. This here is the transponder code of the aircraft, as long as it's transmitting. These numbers in this column represent the plane's altitude. I would have to spend some serious time looking in order to find any significant anomalies. I'm not as familiar with this type of data as an air traffic controller might be," he admitted, taking a sip of his wine. "However, I know plenty of tower jockeys that can easily read and understand all of this information."

Ruth Ann reached over and closed the radar file, then clicked on another icon. As it opened, several pages lined up on the desktop. She clicked on the first file at the top of the list. It was something she had looked at earlier, but it had not made any sense to her. She turned to Mark and said, "There's some notation here marked ACARS, whatever that means."

"ACARS is a type of text message system on the aircraft," Mark explained he scanned the document. "This 'FP' here indicates a flight plan. These codes are way points along the route from point A to point B. This particular FP is the flight plan for American Flight 11, and it shows the way points from Boston into Los Angeles. The flight definitely took off from Boston. That's a fact. That information has been typed into the onboard computer and acknowledged by the airline's operations dispatcher, here," he said, pointing to something on the screen.

"So tell me again what exactly these way points are," Ruth Ann said.

"Any pilot would easily recognize this as a flight plan, and these points are like a highway in the sky. There are several different highways, so to speak; often an airline will usually fly on one given highway for a specific route, say Boston to Los Angeles. You see this particular flight path takes the 767 along slightly north of Westover," he remarked. He looked closer at the codes as if he were memorizing the details.

"That's starting to make some sense." She sighed.

"Let me stop for a minute and check a map," he said, pausing to type a web address into the computer. Mark pointed to the screen. "This is called a vector map, and it shows those way points you saw on the flight plan. And this is the northeast end of that eleven-thousand-foot runway at Westover. The flights could have landed here in a matter of minutes from Boston."

"Well, there are also lots of reports on this drive that look like daily logs from all over—air traffic controllers, radar centers, interviews from the FBI and lots more. They aren't quite so complicated; at least they're in Word documents or PDFs and use written language. Unfortunately, much of what I've looked at so far contains some type of acronyms, like airport codes, but not any airport codes I recognize," she explained. "It's getting late, but I'd be happy to show you some of them tomorrow."

"I might be able to help you with some of those, but if it is air traffic controller lingo, I may have to call on a friend that doesn't live too far from here. We can get him to help," Mark suggested.

Ruth Ann stared out the window, gazing towards the Strip, but thinking about the flash drives. "There are literally hundreds of files on these drives. How long were you planning to stay in Las Vegas? Not to mention Bob's filing system, which is so complicated it might take me a few days and nights to gather everything together," she said, laughing, but wanting to cry.

Mark could sense her frustration and remembered how long she said she was planning to stay. He replied, "I'd planned a couple of weeks here, and just got checked in the day we met at the Pasta Bar. I've got some time and I can extend my visit if necessary. I'm retired now, remember?"

She was relieved to hear Mark was planning to be around for a while. "The biggest question is: are any of these radar files real? We discovered that several of them were somehow uploaded to the FAA computer system in their headquarters before the first flight departed from Boston. Actually, several radar and voice files were uploaded around six that morning. The first flight pushed back from the gate one minute before eight. That discovery really shook us up, and sent us down the road of questioning everything the FAA said or did."

The expression on Mark's face was priceless. It was a combination of surprise and incredulity. "Uploaded two hours before departure?" Mark repeated, hoping to reconfirm what she had said in case he had not heard her correctly.

Ruth Ann just nodded, and Mark understood.

"How in the world did that happen?" he asked.

"That's what we're looking for. Pretty mind-blowing information, isn't it? Many of those radar files we have are obviously faked, and whoever was involved forgot one tiny little detail. Each time a file is uploaded and saved, the computer stamps it with a time and date," Ruth Ann answered.

"The meta tags? You're talking about the computer meta data?" he reconfirmed.

"Amazing, isn't it? A very small but rather important detail somehow was just overlooked."

Mark finished his wine and moved to the more comfortable leather chair which looked out over the city. He wanted to digest what he had heard and learned in the past few hours. When he finally spoke he said, "So let me see if I have this all straight. Your team knows that the four planes were commandeered remotely using a flight termination system, and landed at Westover Air Force base. The base had been evacuated and the reserves were locked out for a few days. The phone calls from the planes were not made while the aircraft were in the air at all, even though several of the phone callers accentuated that they were, quote: 'up in the air.'" Those words coming out of his mouth made both him and Ruth Ann laugh. He continued, "Actually, if you were reporting a hijacking, there's no reason to say you are 'up in the air'; of course you would be in the air, or it wouldn't be a hijacking. What an interesting choice of words."

Ruth Ann moved over and sat in an adjoining chair. "Oh, the flight attendant that joined our team pointed that out too. To include those words, she likened it to being in a carjacking and telling the 911 operator: I have been carjacked while I was in my car."

Again they laughed at the absurdity of it all.

Ruth Ann continued, "All the anomalies of the phone calls are in a file I created. In fact, I printed it out and it's in my briefcase. If you'd like some bedtime reading material, there's probably enough to read and think about to keep you up until dawn. I'm sure you'd find a flight attendant's take on all the anomalies in the phone calls compared to where the FAA said the planes were at the time, fascinating. The last page in this report is a notarized affidavit of an eyewitness that saw the second plane, United 175, landing in western Massachusetts. The poor woman was in a panic; she said the plane was so low to the ground, she was certain it was about to crash just up the road. It's really interesting, because she knew within five minutes the exact time of day when the plane flew over her house."

"I think you mentioned eyewitnesses. I would love to read her account," Mark said.

"Yes, both military and civilians have come forward to share information about the base evacuation and closure, along with sightings of the commercial planes."

She handed him the folder and said, "Let's meet for coffee in the morning, and I'll have all the information we have gathered so far laid out for you. We can chart a course for going through Bob's information and see what we can uncover, but it might mean we'll have to pay a visit to your air traffic controller friend."

"He's just across the desert, a short drive from here. I'll give him a call in the morning and see what his schedule is like for the next couple days, and let him know we might be calling on him to pick his brain. He'll prove to be invaluable; there's no doubt in my mind. He questions most of the things the government does anyway. Even better still, all that radar text you have, he wrote some of the software that the military and then the FAA used to create those files. The guy knows code, he knows radar, and there is nothing in the world of aviation he can't talk about."

"Sounds like he's exactly what we need to get this air traffic control information unscrambled and fit for human consumption," Ruth Ann said with a laugh, refilling their wine goblets. "Let's toast to a successful methodical conclusion to this research. The other team members are in the Washington area, following up with several other leads. One is a retired commercial pilot, really great guy—I think he flew for the military too, not sure though. The goal is to uncover all the details of what really happened that day and who was behind the planning and execution of the event that I like to refer to as a psy-op. One of my fellow researchers calls it a card trick, 'an illusion.' That event changed our country and the entire world, everyone everywhere lost a great deal of freedom, and many in the Middle East lost much more than their freedom. President Sherman would like to set the record straight and take the nation in a new direction, one of peace for a change, not these unending wars."

They lifted their goblets and clinked them together. "A new direction, one of peace," they said in unison.

eight

Ruth Ann's phone chimed a text message alert. It was Mark: I am at the Baby Cakes Bakery—up all night reading. Text me when you're on your way down I'll order up a coffee or latte. Ruth Ann showered and dressed as quickly as she could. She was excited to see and hear Mark's reaction to the information she had given him the night before.

"Over here." Mark waved as Ruth Ann stepped into the bakery.

"Top of the morning to you," Ruth Ann greeted him.

Mark shook his head and rolled his eyes as she approached. "You know, these printouts kept me awake reading all night. Luckily for me this bakery is open twenty-four hours a day. I wandered down here about two o'clock for a double shot espresso. This information is incredible. I find myself without words. You were right, it's mind-blowing. Your team has uncovered details about this supposed terror attack that most people would find impossible to believe. I've experienced first-hand how difficult it is to accept government corruption and black ops dealings. None of this comes as a total shock to me, but I'm amazed that anyone could've figured out how this was pulled off and by whom."

"Well, as you saw last night, we're still working on exactly how and by whom," Ruth Ann said, reaching for her latte. "President Sherman's serious about getting the perpetrators brought to justice. I have to tell you, the First Lady is even more determined to find answers and to execute justice. You do realize she was a flight attendant for more than thirty years, and it was she who, with the help of Jim Bowman, discovered the planes were taken to Westover."

"I kind of assumed that. I did know she flew for a major carrier. But I want to talk about what I read last night. The document from 84 Rades out of Hill Air Force base, stating that Flight 93 was a 747, is rather concerning. It's hard to believe they could make a mistake like that, considering the date on their report was two full days after the attack," Mark said.

Ruth Ann nodded in agreement. "It's almost like that report was written for a drill of some kind." She laughed. "It was that report alone that caused me to look into all the military drills going on that day. When the elite radar specialists of our military can't get the type of aircraft correct in their report, you have to ask yourself, what else do they have wrong? Obviously, they thought most Americans would buy into their story and never question what really happened."

"Well, they never dreamed that someone would gather up all of this Freedom of Information Act data," Mark added.

"The team and the president want to gather up the rest of the details, which won't be an easy task. There's something missing. I can feel it, but I can't quite put my finger on exactly what it is."

"Well, I'm curious as to the 'who' part. If this was an illusion, who planned it, who carried it out, and where are they now? I got the feeling, reading through the details of the phone calls last night, that some of the callers were not innocent or random victims. When I looked at some of their backgrounds, their work histories, and their connections to the military-industrial complex, my Spidey senses began to tingle. If some of these phone callers and passengers were not victims, but perpetrators, what happened to the real passengers and crew members? And where did the perpetrators go, or are they still floating around under new names?" Mark wondered.

"That, sir, is one of the important details we're searching for in Bob's drives and the information we're trying to glean from the documents you read last night. We know the people behind the Project for a New American Century, you remember, those neo-cons that actually wrote how a 'New Pearl Harbor' type event was needed to rally the American people behind all the wars they planned in the Middle East. That's the tip of the iceberg," she explained.

"Those guys might have been behind the initial planning, but some intelligence agency does the dirty work, not the elite. The elites buy stocks, drink martinis and plan wars," Mark replied, knowing this from his own experiences with both the military and black operations carried out by the CIA. "The most concerning document in your folder was the sixty-six-page Drug Enforcement Agency report. How or why would the head of the DEA not be concerned with foreign military intelligence agents traveling around snooping into federal employees' homes and offices? They were even caught on military bases. Even more disturbing was the fact that some of them were ordinance specialists for the Israeli Defense Forces. Then, when I saw the New York Times article from just a few weeks before the supposed attack, about the foreign art students and how their team, Gelitin, was actually living in the World Trade Center towers, that blew me away. The facsimile of the temporary construction pass the artists were given while they lived in the towers was very telling. They had the run of the buildings day and night. Why would security not think that was suspicious, at least in hindsight? After they watched the towers explode, why didn't anyone think that maybe those artists were possibly up to something other than art? Now their book, The B Thing, that was really surreal. I have to think that building a balcony, and taking a window out of the 91st floor of the tower, was not an art project as much as it seemed to be a test run to see what kind of security was monitoring the towers. It's very disturbing to learn about this so many years later," Mark admitted.

Ruth Ann agreed and then added, "I have to guess that someone in New York City must have connected those dots, but with the media showing it was a plane and telling them that jet fuel could melt steel, nobody gave the story about the artists living in the towers a second thought. If anyone did find a concern with the artists, who would they have reported it to?" She paused a moment to drink her coffee, then looked at Mark and continued, "Are you aware of the eighty-five security cameras that surrounded the Pentagon that the FBI confiscated within minutes of the explosion? Some of those cameras were from hotels, gas stations, and businesses surrounding the Pentagon. What those cameras filmed hitting the Pentagon should have been released to the public to show a large commercial airplane; instead they were sealed away from scrutiny for over a decade. That act alone supports the discovery that the official story of a 757 hitting the Pentagon was a false narrative, at best."

"Let's hope that if the president can get a new investigation going, those eighty-some cameras can be unsealed and the video shown in court. Now let's finish up here and head out to visit my air traffic controller friend across the desert. When I called him, he said he'd be around most of the day. If we text him when we leave Las Vegas, he will be home when we arrive," Mark informed her.

"That sounds great. Give me about twenty minutes to get my computer and a few things thrown in a bag. I'll meet you in the lobby," Ruth Ann said, checking her watch.

They met the concierge in the lobby and mentioned to him that they would be out most of the day. He wished them safe travel and waited with them under the portico for the valet to bring them their vehicle.

The two headed out in Mark's rental car toward the I-15 freeway. Ruth Ann activated a wireless connection and opened her laptop as they sped along. "Let me take a look at the traffic westbound; I know this route is famous for being nearly gridlocked on Sundays. I should be able to pull up some information on Cal-Trans' website."

Mark didn't seem to be bothered or worried by traffic. He thought it would be a good idea to tell Ruth Ann a little more about his friend they were going to meet. "My buddy is a great storyteller, and you'll really have fun listening to him. He's the kind of guy who has racked up so many unique experiences in his lifetime that he can spin yarns for hours. I hope he has time to tell you about the day he learned there was a Flat Earth Society and its president lived not far from the entrance to Edwards Air Force base. He heard about this guy from two astronauts, but he wasn't sure he believed them. I won't do his account justice telling it, but if we hit a quiet moment in our meeting, remind him to tell you that story."

Ruth Ann laughed and added, "I can only imagine. The first time I saw a video about the Flat Earth Society, I honestly thought it was a joke; someone was deadpan seriously putting on one heck of a spoof. I figured they were a government psy-op of some type, out to make anyone looking into the 9/11 event look as insane as they were. I recall someone—it might have been President Bush or even Obama—comparing 9/11 'truthers' to 'flat earthers' at the time. I wasn't aware anyone really thought the earth was flat. How do they explain the International Space Station and the photos we get from space?"

"I'm sure Tom will be able to tell you word for word that old guy's explanations. I seem to recall one of their theories has to do with the government faking everything."

"But for what gain?" she asked. "What benefit would there be for the cabal or the elite to lie about the shape of the planet? I can see them lying about a cooked-up event or false flag like 9/11, but I may never understand what lying about the shape or size of our planet could do to benefit the government or anyone else."

"I hear you," Mark agreed. "But Tom's story of driving out to meet this old guy in his beaten-down single-wide trailer in the middle of the desert is a classic."

Ruth Ann refreshed the Cal-Trans webpage. "Oh dear, trouble ahead. It says there's an accident between Barstow and Victorville. The delay right now is about ninety minutes."

"I'd planned on passing through there, but I can turn off before Barstow and take old Highway 58. It's the scenic route," Mark said, laughing.

"Looks like you know your way around here pretty well," Ruth Ann replied.

Mark nodded.

"We'll have to swing in through the town of Mojave. Have you ever been there?" he asked.

"I can't say that I've ever had the pleasure," Ruth Ann admitted.

They drove for nearly a half an hour through the desert, commenting at the many dilapidated buildings and abandoned businesses. As they entered the town, she looked up from her computer and saw a sign that read, 'Mojave Air and Space Port.' Across the street she noticed vintage stucco homes, yards full of junk, and plywood coverings on many of the windows. "This town is the spaceport? You mean the spacecraft and rocketry factories of Paul Allen and Richard Branson, SpaceShipOne and Virgin Galactic? This place looks more like a scene from The Twilight Zone."

Mark chuckled. "It's quite the dichotomy, isn't it? These old boarded-up houses everywhere, and the most high-tech spacecraft and experimental aircraft anywhere in the world right across the street. You can bet that anyone living in this town is not directly involved in the production of these top-secret high-tech spaceships. The guys that own these companies are serious about civilian space travel. I'm not sure if it'll happen in our lifetime, but it will happen someday. I believe the people that work at the spaceport live down by Tom, either in Lancaster or Palmdale, or maybe even as far away as Los Angeles."

"I can see why," Ruth Ann commented.

"Hey, it's well past lunchtime. I'm getting hungry, how about you?" Mark asked.

"I could do with a bite to eat, and I sure could use a stretch of the legs too," she admitted.

"I haven't been through this town in years. Let's take a quick spin around and see if we can find anything open. It seems awfully quiet around here," Mark said as he turned right at the intersection and headed toward the main part of town. "Most everything seems to be closed."

"Or out of business," she added.

As they turned northwest on Highway 14, Ruth Ann spotted a number of large aircraft parked closely together. "Is the spaceport also an airport?" she asked.

"That," he said, "is more commonly known as a boneyard. I don't know much about this particular yard; it's rather new. I think they started storing aircraft here for Eastern Airlines in the early nineties, right as the airline was starting to go under. I know Tom knows a lot more about the history and what's going on than I do."

"Can you pull over into this wide spot?" Ruth Ann asked.

Mark turned off the highway and parked the car on the side of the road where they could get a better view of the parked airplanes.

Ruth Ann was awestruck. "Look at all those 747's and 747-400's parked there. That one over there looks like the doors have all been removed. Atlas Air—I remember them from Florida, a charter outfit I believe. See those Southern Air 747's? I seem to recall they were associated with the CIA."

They sat in silence until Mark asked, "Are you ready to move on and grab a bite to eat? The most inviting place I've seen so far was Denny's. Does that work for you?"

She took one last look at the parked aircraft, then flipped open her laptop as they drove back to the restaurant. "Southern Air Transport was based in Miami. It was a cargo airline best known as a front company for the Central Intelligence Agency, and for its role in the Iran-Contra affair in the mid-eighties. Southern Air carried four loads of US weapons bound for Iran from the US to Israel, and on the return flights, carried weapons for the Nicaraguan Contras from Portugal. It was Southern Air that was shot down in Nicaragua. The two pilots died, but an ex-marine parachuted to safety, only to be arrested by the government. They were carrying arms to the Contra rebels. It isn't any wonder these events caught the attention of the US government and the press. Do you remember any of this?" she asked.

Mark pulled the rental car into a parking space in front of Denny's. "Oh yeah, it's very familiar."

She sensed Mark knew more than he was letting on, but was unsure if she was reading more into his abbreviated comment than she should. The hostess seated them at a booth near the window, facing a massive wind farm covering the hills west of town.

"It'll be interesting to hear what Tom knows about this place. I'm afraid most of my time was spent on the east coast. I knew about the intelligence agencies having involvement with some of those airlines over the years. I think everyone has heard those stories." He recalled watching the news after a Southern Air Transport plane had crashed, carrying small arms and ammunition for the anti-Sandinista Contra rebels. The lone survivor had been the skydiving ex-marine Ruth Ann mentioned, named Hasenfus. The CIA had been prohibited by law from assisting the rebels with military supplies. Both the CIA and the Reagan administration denied any connection to the cargo of arms or the C-123 cargo plane. Hasenfus told of nearly twenty-five members of the Southern Air Transport team in El Salvador that oversaw all of their dealings, including their flight plans. In particular, Mark remembered how Hasenfus had been captured, convicted of terrorism and sentenced to thirty years in prison, yet was miraculously released only three months later and returned to the States.

The waitress glided to their table with two coffee mugs in one hand and a pot of coffee in the other. "Coffee?" she asked, almost as if she knew they would say yes. She lowered the mugs and filled them. "Have you two decided what you would like?"

Ruth Ann ordered the Cobb salad and Mark ordered the burger of the day. "This place is like a functioning ghost town," Ruth Ann whispered.

Mark smiled. "I'm sure there must be more to it, but from what we've experienced so far, you're correct. It sure has untangled some cobwebs in my memory banks, just thinking about the connection between the CIA and Southern Air Transport, and to find their planes in a boneyard makes it all very real. When you brought up the Iran-Contra affair and all that it entailed, those familiar names like Robert McFarlane, Caspar Weinberger, Richard Secord, Oliver North and John Poindexter came back to life."

"I wonder if anything out of the ordinary happens here. Seeing all those Southern Air 747's parked, and knowing about their CIA involvement, makes me curious," Ruth Ann said.

"That's hard to say. I never associated the CIA with this place, though I was aware they were very active in Marana down by Tucson, Arizona," Mark replied.

Seated at the counter between their table and the kitchen was an older gentleman wearing worn overalls that appeared, from a distance, to be an oversized dark gray flight suit. Just as the waitress brought their orders, he swiveled around on his stool and looked at Mark and Ruth Ann. He confessed, "I've been eavesdropping on your conversation. Are you just passing through town?"

Mark answered, "Yes, we are. We're headed to Lancaster. The lineup of 747 tails caught our attention as we pulled off the highway. This is quite the interesting town you've got here."

The old man took a sip of his coffee. "Oh, we've had some interesting happenings around here. The problem is, you never know what it might be or when it might happen."

"Please join us," Mark said. He stood up and slid into the seat next to Ruth Ann, and pointed to his former seat.

"Mighty nice of you folks," the man said. He hopped off his stool and balanced his coffee cup carefully on his way to their booth. He reached out his hand first to Ruth Ann, and then to Mark. "Name's Jack, Jack Cooper."

"Mark and Ruth Ann," Mark said with a smile.

"So, you two are curious about our spaceport and what goes on around here?" he asked.

"Well, who wouldn't be curious?" Ruth Ann replied.

Jack let out a big belly laugh that seemed to come from the bottoms of his well-worn boots. "I guess you have a point there, missy. To the outsider it must be a very strange and mysterious place indeed. To those of us who live here, we understand."

"Understand?" Mark asked.

"Ask anyone that lives here what goes on over at the airport, or you can call it the spaceport if you'd rather. We have one stock answer: Everything around here's a secret." Jack smiled and raised both eyebrows high on his forehead. "Get it?"

Ruth Ann and Mark nodded in the affirmative.

"Do you work at the airport?" Mark asked, being unsure of exactly how to word his question.

"I've been around planes and this place all my life. Off and on

I've worked here and there, and yep, sometimes I worked at the port," Jack answered.

"Do they launch rockets there now?" Ruth Ann asked.

"Like I said, everything around here's a secret." Jack let out another belly laugh, winking at Ruth Ann as he spoke the word 'secret.'

"And that's because of the rocket technology?" Mark inquired, hoping Jack would open up a little more.

"Well, we have an interesting situation around here; you see, we have mysterious planes coming and going. We have planes that come and stay, and get parted out. We have military planes and commercial planes both large and small coming and going and staying. We also have foreign planes that stop by," Jack offered.

Mark could feel Jack wanted to tell him more, but was holding back. "Foreign planes?"

Jack didn't answer; he just turned the conversation to other topics while they finished their meals. As they were getting ready to pay the check, he asked, "Hey, you two got a minute?"

Mark and Ruth Ann both nodded that they did indeed have time.

"Follow me in my van; it's that dark blue Chevy parked out front. I'll pay up here and when you see me finally get that old engine to start up, get in your rig and get on my tail," Jack said in a loud whisper, scanning the room to make certain no one was listening to him.

While Jack got into his van, Mark paid their bill. As he was handing the cashier a couple of twenties she remarked, "Don't pay no mind to old Jack. He and his brother are well-known around town for making up stories, especially about airplanes."

"I'll take that advice under consideration, thank you," Mark said.

Jack's old blue van turned northeast on Highway 14, the same route Mark and Ruth Ann had driven earlier. The van slowly pulled off the highway onto a paved auxiliary road that offered only a narrow gravel shoulder. Jack pulled off and stopped. Mark followed.

"You all got any binoculars with you?" Jack asked, holding out a small, well-worn cardboard box.

"No, we're in a rental car," Mark admitted.

"Figured as much," Jack said, placing the cardboard box on the hood of the rental car. "Grab yourselves a pair of eyes."

Ruth Ann and Mark each pulled out a pair of binoculars and waited for Jack to instruct them.

"Take a look over there in and amongst those 747's. Can you see there's a row of smaller 757's parked by them?" Jack said, as he guided them with his finger.

Ruth Ann scanned the rows of planes. "I see them," she said.

"Well, not all the planes parked in this place are permanent. Some of these planes, they come and go. Not sure where they come from or where they go. Now that means something is going on here that needs explaining. My brother Elmer, he's a photographer; he's also a serious airplane buff. Combine those two hobbies and situate him right between Mojave and Edwards Air Force base, and you got yourself some real off the wall entertainment. I wish you two could meet him, but he's up by Tonopah today, not sure when he's headed back. He just lives a few minutes from here. He's been watching the planes parked here for years; he keeps track of tail numbers and he can tell you some real interesting stories about a lot of these birds."

"I'd love to hear what he has to say," Mark replied.

"All of us that live here, not many pay any attention to what goes on at the port. But Elmer, he doesn't miss much—he rarely leaves town and has himself several hidden viewing spots around where he can sit with his dog and take pictures of airplanes. He might not know what the military is going to call them, but he probably has a black and white photo of a top secret plane as well as other things that fly around here. Before you leave town, head over to the entrance of the spaceport where you saw that big old Convair 880 parked, and grab yourselves a map. You'll have to use a computer to get the full effect, with the runways and taxi ways and all, but I suggest you do that so you'll have a better idea of what happens around here. And when you look real close at the map of this place, don't be fooled by the building calling itself the National Test Pilot School. It's really the CIA."

"The Central Intelligence Agency?" Mark queried, making certain he'd heard Jack correctly.

"Yep. Spooks, as we like to call them. I tell you, if you could talk with my brother, he could tell you a lot more than I can. I know what he's told me, but I'm afraid I might not get his stories straight if I was to tell you. Probably would be best to hear it right direct from him."

"We have to head to Lancaster, but it would be great to get together with you and your brother in the near future," Mark told Jack, certain Ruth Ann was in total agreement.

"Neither of us packs one of them cellular telephones, but you can find me every day right where you met me today, at Denny's at the counter, twelve-thirty sharp. Elmer usually joins me." Jack laughed. "We are what you'd call regulars, and we are on time, like clockwork. We never miss lunch."

"Great, we'll have to make it a point to get back here to Mojave and have lunch with you and Elmer." Mark smiled as he reached his right hand toward Jack's. "Thanks for your time. We'll be back."

"Strange old man, isn't he?" Ruth Ann commented as they got back into their car.

"The cashier warned me about him, but I have a feeling he knows things that could be very helpful to our research. I guess we'll know more when we meet up with Elmer, which should prove to be an interesting lunch if he's anything like Jack," Mark said.

There was no gate at the entrance of the airport. Next to the large sign that read 'Mojave Air and Space Port – Imagination Flies Here,' sat a parked Convair 880. Mark slowed the car to a stop. "They only built sixty-five of those planes," he said. "And here's a bit of trivia for you—Elvis Presley bought one, and refinished it inside to include amenities such as a queen-sized bed and gold bathroom fixtures. That fighter jet behind it is an F-4 Phantom, probably one of the loudest jets ever built."

Ruth Ann pulled up the website to the spaceport on her laptop and was reading the driving tour. "The F-4 Phantom II fighter jets were given a second life here in Mojave by BAE Systems. Retired F-4s were converted to fly without a pilot on board to serve as target drones for military radar and missile testing. The unmanned version was painted with an orange tail and wing tips, and was re-designated as a QF-4. Since 1997, the Air Force has flown 315 QF-4 drones as targets for training and weapons testing. This tells me that drone technology was in use long before 9/11."

"Long before," Mark added, saying no more.

As they drove up to the main building below the air traffic control tower, Ruth Ann remarked, "There's no one here. This is kind of creepy, isn't it? I mean, there's all this space technology and yet from the surroundings, you'd think we were in the early sixties."

They drove past several large metal hangars, most marked with numbers. Only a few carried signs with a company name. They drove along Sabovitch Street and along several side streets. No airplanes were taking off or landing, and very few cars were in the parking lots. It was very still and almost too quiet.

"OK, I think we've seen all there is to see here. How long will it take to get to Tom's place?" she inquired.

Mark laughed. "Pretty unimpressive as spaceports go, don't you think?"

"That, my friend, is one very large understatement," Ruth Ann replied, feeling like they had just been fooled. The sign bragged of a spaceport, but they'd found only an abandoned boneyard of aircraft in various stages of disrepair or dismantling.

"Tom's place is about thirty minutes from here and as you can see, there's not much traffic on the road, so we should be there in no time."

"Great, that gives me some time to pull up this crazy functioning ghost town on Google maps and maybe read up on what we apparently missed." Ruth Ann was still laughing at the letdown the Mojave Spaceport had been. Her browser tab was still tagged to Southern Air Transport. She clicked on a link to Evergreen International Airlines. "Hey, did you know this? Evergreen International flew the Shah of Iran out of Iran and into Egypt."

"I didn't know that, or if I did at one time, the memory has escaped me. Well, now, that's interesting. I had several Iranian friends in college; they always said the CIA flew the Ayatollah into Iran. I guess someone must have seen the airplanes. So, Evergreen International flew a plane into Tehran, loaded up the Shah Mohammad Reza Pahlavi, and flew him to safety in Egypt," Mark said, shaking his head.

"Then they also flew him into Panama and later on into the United States," Ruth Ann added.

Ruth Ann's mention of the CIA caused Mark's thoughts to return to Jack. "I'm still trying to figure out how it is old Jack knows the CIA is operating out of the spaceport hangar disguised as the National Test Pilot School. You'd think that spooks would be better than that at keeping their presence a secret."

"Yeah, good question. I wonder what else he knows," Ruth Ann replied.

Mark's cell phone rang and he quickly hit the speakerphone button. "Mark, Tom here, just checking on your ETA. You didn't get caught up in that traffic on I-15, I hope?"

"Nope, we stopped in Mojave for a bite to eat and a quick tour of the spaceport," Mark explained. "The computer in the car says we're eight minutes away."

"Great, I'll get some of my favorite wines opened and wipe down the patio furniture. This is one of those rare perfect weather days here, not too hot, not too windy. I can finally use the new patio furniture. See you in eight," Tom said, and ended the call.

nine

As tips began to flow into the website that Gil had set up in the White House for citizens to share information about 9/11, Max was overwhelmed with the amount of data and follow-up that was going to be necessary to weed out the salient information from the dross that always follows a call to action from the public. Unfortunately, President Sherman's invitation opened the door for weirdoes, wackos and winos to vent their feelings on any governmental conspiracy they might have harbored for decades, most of which had absolutely nothing to do with 9/11 or any of the events surrounding that day. In most cases, their emails began with words like: I'm really not comfortable divulging what I know through email or over the phone. I can only share this information in person and even then I would need to be assured of my safety so it would be necessary for you to fly me to the nation's capital. Then I would be willing to tell you all I know. At first these types of letters had a humorous ring to them and Max would share them with his colleagues, but as they continued to proliferate, the humor turned to frustration.

"Gil, isn't there some way you can filter these emails based on the common denominators in their offerings?" Max asked.

"Well, I can do that, now that I have a general idea of what to look for. I can build an algorithm into the software which will put all these types of tips in a folder marked 'woo woos.'" Then you can look at them at your convenience and perhaps we can fly them all here next April Fool's Day," Gil replied.

Max laughed, but was expressly grateful for any help he could find that would begin to segment the incoming information into categories that he could then assign to others to follow up. Originally he'd had the incoming email sorted into four distinct areas: Washington D.C., New York, Shanksville, and other. This allowed him to glean the information that might be germane to the Pentagon, the Trade Towers and Flight 93. To his surprise, much of the data fell into the 'other' category, most of which had a direct bearing on the scenario Vera and Jim had established about Westover.

One email in particular stood out, which caused Max to call Jim Bowman to his office. "Jim, you're going to love this tip that came in this morning. A man who lives outside Stockbridge, Massachusetts claimed at around 8:45 on the morning of 9/11, his wife was stopped at a light on Highway 7, when a huge American Airlines plane flew low over the top of her car, heading in the direction of Westover. According to the calculations you and Vera postulated, that would be exactly where Flight 77 should have been, on its way to a hangar at Westover."

"Wow, another eyewitness," Jim excitedly proclaimed.

Max smiled knowingly. "I think it would be best if you handled this one. Contact this man, who was kind enough to leave his phone number, and see if you can talk to him and his wife. I want on tape, if possible, the closest thing you can muster to a deposition, verifying what she actually saw and the time she saw it. You do realize this now is the second eyewitness to come forward that saw commercial planes in and around the Chicopee area? One was United Flight 175, and now this would be American Flight 77."

"I'll contact him tomorrow morning. I get the impression this is another example of somebody who saw something out of the ordinary that Tuesday morning, but couldn't place it into context, so it was simply never mentioned again. Obviously, however, she told her husband and he remembered. Joel was exactly right in doing what he did. If people's memories can be jogged, we'll find all we need to convince Congress to do their duty," Jim replied.

"You know, I've got another one here that isn't in any way earth-shattering, but my gut tells me there's something here and we need to do some investigation," Max added.

"Oh, what is it?" Jim asked.

"It's from a young Saudi national named Farouk. Now at first blush, the fact that he's Saudi Arabian raises flags all by itself. I mean, since most of the hijackers in the government story were Saudis, that makes this email stand out, but that's not what's driving this for me," Max explained.

"So, what did he say?"

"When I tell you, you're going to think I'm crazy, but there's something here. I can just feel it inside. What he says is that he lives in Fredericksburg and drives to work every day to Alexandria. That's about a fifty-mile drive. For years he was able to cut through Fort Belvoir on Highway 1 to save time. There was a gate, but it was unmanned and the public could drive through the base twenty-four hours a day. He goes on to say that early in the morning on September 10th he was driving to work as usual, but when he gets to Fort Belvoir, the gate is manned and closed. He asks the MP what's up and he's told that the base is now off limits to all non-military personnel, and that he'll have to find some other way to get to Alexandria. Okay, so the next day, September 11th, he again attempts to drive through the fort. He meets the same armed guard, who recognizes him and is a bit rude this time, telling him that the route is never going to be open to the public again, and especially not today."

"That's it? That's all he had to tell you?" Jim shook his head in disbelief.

"I told you it wasn't earth-shattering," Max responded.

"I'm not sure that's even noteworthy. What aren't you telling me, Max?" Jim asked.

"I agree with you that something this mundane would not be noteworthy on the surface, but you know me, I always want to know why. Why did this kid send this to us? He must have felt it had some value. And the fact he is a Saudi—he's obviously trying to be helpful, if only to put a plus in his country's column."

"Yeah, or maybe he's trying to waste our time and his letter should go into the woo-woo file," Jim suggested.

Max stared at his friend in a way that made Jim squirm just a little. "I guess you're not seeing it, are you?"

"Seeing what?" Jim shot back.

"What do you think hit the Pentagon that morning?" Max asked.

"Well, obviously not American Airlines Flight 77. You just told me we had an eyewitness who saw that plane in Massachusetts around the time it should have been headed toward the Pentagon. I've always thought that some kind of missile hit that building."

"Based on the cordite smelled at the scene, I'm sure you're right. Now, who has access to missiles, and where could one have been launched from?" Max wondered out loud for Jim's benefit.

"You don't think from Fort Belvoir, do you?" Jim asked, beginning to hone in on Max's line of thinking.

"Have you ever been on that base?" Max asked.

"No, I haven't," Jim replied.

"It's huge, diverse, and secluded enough to launch a missile without anyone noticing, if Route 1 was closed. So if somebody launched a missile from that base, they definitely would want the public removed so they could not report anything they might have seen," Max asserted.

Jim scratched his head, trying to think how any government base could possibly be used to launch a weapon that would strike at its own command and control center. Finally, he asked, "Does the CIA have access to that base?"

"You're damn skippy it does," Max said, pointing his finger

at Jim because Jim had finally merged his thought process with what he was being told. "They also have access to the kind of missiles that could have struck the Pentagon and done the type of damage we saw."

"Well then, perhaps we should have a talk with Farouk," Jim suggested.

"My thought exactly. I'm going to ask him to come and meet with me personally here in the White House. Whether or not he accepts will tell me what side of the equation he's on. And then if he's willing, I might get permission to take him on the base and have him show me the exact route he normally would have taken, had he been allowed to pass through on Monday and Tuesday of horror week," Max said.

"I hope it proves fruitful for you. You know, I sometimes question your methods, but I can't remember a time when you were wrong. You'd think after all these years I'd learn to shut up and follow you wherever you want to take me," Jim said.

"To be perfectly honest with you, it was another letter I received that caused me to think Farouk's email had some serious validity. This one came from a guy who claims his brother-in-law was called to the Pentagon prior to 9/11 and was told to shut down all the defense systems. Unfortunately, he didn't leave us any way to get in contact with him, and from the tone of his post, I doubt he could or would be able to tell us anything more specific. He didn't identify his brother-in-law, who I'm sure wouldn't be cooperative even if we found out who he was. If he really did what this letter says he did, I would suspect he would be so wracked with guilt that he's managed to justify himself into total denial. My point here is the timing of this letter. I received it about the same time Farouk's email arrived, which got me to thinking there is something out there at Belvoir we need to look into. I'll get back with you on this after I've had a chance to talk with Farouk," Max concluded.

Jim leaned back in his chair and put his hands behind his head, pondering what Max had just told him. Max, thinking the meeting was over, stacked his papers into a pile and was about to make a phone call. Jim pushed his chair forward and forcefully placed both his hands on Max's desk and blurted out, "That brother-in-law, no doubt, had to have done what the letter said he did. I mean the Pentagon is the most heavily protected building in the world for a reason. Any airplane approaching it would have been spotted, tracked and shot down before it could have hit that building. And a missile could never have penetrated its defense systems unless they had been turned off. I still have some interesting contacts over there, and I'm going to do a little investigation on my own about this if you don't mind."

"Mind?" Max laughed. "I was hoping you'd come to that conclusion and offer your special kind of research. I know the president invited the chairman of the joint chiefs to our meeting the other day, but I'd prefer to keep him out of this until we have something more solid to go on. Then we could use all his muscle to get to the bottom of the pile."

"You mentioned the CIA having access to missiles and Belvoir, but certainly they don't have the ability to shut off the Pentagon's defense systems, do they?" Jim wondered aloud.

"I wouldn't think so. That could only come from the military brass, or the Defense Secretary himself. Rumsfeld never would have made such a direct order, even if he were in on the whole thing from the beginning. Let's play this from the bottom up and see what we can find, but you're definitely on the right track here, Jimbo."

ten

Tom invited Mark and Ruth Ann into his large stucco home. A beautiful water feature with a tiny creek surrounded the entryway, and welcomed them into a tranquil environment.

"I would have liked to have made my creek larger, but this drought in California makes it hard to keep my neighbors at ease and the water police from charging me fines. It's all recycled water, and the design was my own. After retirement, I got interested in things like Feng Shui and energy alignment, along with doing some landscaping," Tom explained as he led his guests to the patio.

"Ruth Ann has some radar files in text format that we're having trouble understanding," Mark said. "We'd like to leave some of them with you and when you have time, take a look and see what you can make of them."

"I'd be happy to do that," Tom replied.

"I don't know if you've ever looked at the anomalies surrounding the terror attacks of 9/11, but these are FOIA files a friend of Ruth Ann's compiled. Your air traffic control expertise is needed here. Some of it looked a little familiar to me, airport codes and the like, but this is way over my head."

Ruth Ann slid the flash drive into her laptop and brought up a few different files to show Tom. "I suspect you'll recognize these."

Tom scanned the radar text file. "Oh, yeah, I can read this easily. Is there anything specific you're looking for?"

Ruth Ann and Mark looked at each other, each hoping the

other would answer Tom's question.

"Well, yes, we think so," Mark answered.

But before Mark could finish telling Tom what they were looking for, Tom interrupted, "It would be ideal if I could upload these files into an external hard drive. That way I'd have them all in one place and could easily search for exactly what it is you're looking for when the time comes. I happen to have a brand-new two terabyte external I just picked up. I was thinking about saving a bunch of data, and I know I don't have two terabytes' worth on all of my computers around here."

"That would be perfect. I have a few flash drives here we can upload, and anything else we need you to look at can be transferred using Skype," Ruth Ann suggested.

Tom retrieved his new external hard drive and installed the software onto his healthiest computer. "All right then, let's upload those files and while they're doing their thing, I'll grab us some snacks and refresh your wine."

Mark and Ruth Ann used the upload time to brief Tom on all the details the research team had uncovered surrounding 9/11, the intentions of President Sherman, and the leads the other researchers on Ruth Ann's team were following.

"Well now, that sure gives me something to think about," Tom said. "You know I was working the Los Angeles Center, down the road here in Palmdale, that day. My shift started at seven in the morning and by the time I showed up for work, confusion and some pretty hairy moments ruled the day. I remember a small civilian plane had taken off from a rural airport, headed for Phoenix or someplace. The pilot obviously had no idea the rest of the country was in full freak-out mode. They surely had no idea the FAA had closed the entire country's airspace. I have no doubt those two senior citizens came apart when fighter jets scrambled to their wingtips and ordered them to land. It's funny now looking back, but I remember how frightened I was for them until they were escorted to the ground. Out here in California, we were a long way away from the action. Other than a couple fake bomb threats at LAX, and a whole lot of commotion and confusion coming out of the FAA, there wasn't much action. I'll go over those facility logs you have; they should tell me a lot. It looked like you had one from just about every airport east of the Mississippi. Now that I have an idea of what I'm looking for, it should be easy. So, your research team uncovered remote landings at the reserve base?" he asked, directing his question toward Ruth Ann.

"We found that and a lot more. We need you to reconfirm what we've found, if that is possible. The chairman of the 9/11 Commission hearings, Thomas Kean, said that the commission felt that the FAA was making what he referred to as 'misstatements.' That right there told us we had better take a good look at everything coming out of the FAA, for starters. So, we requested all this data through the Freedom of Information Act. And now it's all yours. We discovered a couple corporations situated in the basement of the FAA headquarters that had access and ability to upload bogus radar and voice recordings. If you're willing to help, I'll be able to connect you to the rest of the team. There are a few missing pieces still, but we're confident that we'll be able to find them. There's no money involved; we just want to expose the truth for honor and country, and to credit those that lost their lives that day, as well as the lives lost in the Middle East," Ruth Ann explained.

"It looks like your team has uncovered more details than I've ever heard about, or even suspected. Because of my career and with my military background, nothing would shock me. I read the Project for a New American Century, I'm familiar with the Council on Foreign Relations, the Bilderbergs and those elitists that plan to move this country and the rest of the world toward a global economy, a global currency, and a global government. This event is starting to look to me like Operation Northwoods out of the sixties, the Gulf of Tonkin, and a few other well-planned and executed false flag operations to stir the pot, get us into a war, or keep us involved in one," Tom said. His voice faded into silence.

"Here's my Skype number," Ruth Ann said as she handed Tom a business card with her cell and Skype contact information. "You can text me anytime you find something you want to share. If I'm not near my computer when you text, it will only be a few minutes before I am."

"That's for sure. This girl is surgically attached to her computer," Mark added.

For the next several hours the three of them discussed the events of 9/11, and Tom shared many of his stories, including his experience with the president of the Flat Earth Society. Mark was correct; the story was hilarious, and Ruth Ann asked Tom's permission to retell it to members of her team.

"Tom, I'm afraid Mark and I had better start back to Las Vegas. It's getting late and it's a long drive," Ruth Ann said.

"You two stay in touch. I'll dig through these files and see what I can find. I also have a few colleagues from around here that might recall unusual events surrounding that day, they were in positions at either the Air Force base or the air traffic control center. I'll gingerly see what their feelings are, and if they happen to mention things that were out of the normal procedures, I'll ask more pointed questions."

Ruth Ann and Mark thanked Tom for his hospitality and help as they headed toward their car.

"I really love your water feature," Ruth Ann complimented him.

Mark glanced down at his watch as he started the car. "What do you say we spend the night in your favorite ghost town?"

"Mojave?" Ruth Ann asked. "Seriously?"

"I was thinking that if we spend the night there, tomorrow we can check out the spaceport in the morning when it is hopefully populated, and maybe have lunch with Jack and his brother, if he's back in town. After that we can head back to Vegas," Mark explained.

"Sounds like a good plan. I did see several hotels in town, but only one that looked like it might be an enjoyable place to stay. After the M, I'm a little picky." She laughed.

"Yes, that was the Mariah Hotel; I remember seeing it right by those planes at the entrance to the spaceport. See if you can get adjoining rooms, non-smoking—and if possible, a view of the airport," he said, handing her his credit card.

eleven

Ruth Ann sat straight up, having heard a sound in her sleep. Shaking her head awake, she became aware of how fast her heart was pounding. In her confusion at being suddenly wakened by the strange sound, she had forgotten that she and Mark had decided to stay in Mojave. She heard the sound again. It was Mark tapping on their adjoining doors.

"Ruth Ann?" he whispered.

"Hey, sorry, hold on a minute," Ruth Ann answered. She quickly pulled her clothes on and walked across the room. "I hope you have coffee," she said, laughing.

"I thought we might head over to the spaceport and grab a little breakfast at that restaurant under the control tower, the Voyager," Mark suggested.

"Is it that late? I have no idea what time it is. I was so sound asleep. But I like your idea. Give me a few minutes and I'll meet you in the lobby," she said.

Driving into the spaceport, Ruth Ann noticed the place had come alive with activity. The parking lot in front of the Voyager was full, but Mark found a place to park on the other side of the main offices. It looked like all of the parking lots had plenty of cars in them, quite a different sight than on the weekend.

Once inside the Voyager, they noticed the restaurant was situated right along the runway, which gave them an even better view of the 747's parked in the boneyard. They were fortunate to grab a freshly cleaned booth by the window. Behind them sat two men wearing florescent construction vests. Ruth Ann turned around and boldly asked, "You guys work here?"

The older gentleman answered, "No, we work for the county. We come here once a month for breakfast. It's our little treat."

"Interesting place you have here," she remarked, at a loss for a better comeback. "Do you guys know anything about the planes parked here?"

"Well, this isn't a boneyard where planes go to be parted out and die. Though there are exceptions. For the most part, this is a storage yard; almost every plane out there can be made airworthy in thirty days or less."

"Really? I wouldn't have thought that. Who owns the planes?" she asked.

"That I'm not sure about," the man admitted.

The second county worker chimed in, "Some are owned by the company whose logo you see on their paint job, others are owned by leasing companies, and some have private individuals as owners. The important thing is that these facilities here can get most any plane airworthy, whether they need doors, like that 747-400 you see there, or new paint or some other type of maintenance. Everything can be done right here," he finished, sounding as if he had more knowledge than most about what went on at the airport.

Just as Ruth Ann turned back to Mark and her breakfast, two F-14 jets taxied in their direction. "Look there," Ruth Ann said, pointing her index finger at the planes.

"Fourteens," Mark commented as they watched the duo taxi toward them, then turn to the east end of the taxiway.

When they finished eating and returned to the rental car, Mark suggested that they drive around the spaceport again. They drove due east, past hangars marked discreetly with red numbers. At the east end sat the National Test Pilot School building. Mark slowed the car as they noticed two pilots dressed in flight suits walking out of the building.

"Those guys look like they might be the pilots of those two F-14's we just saw taxi in," Mark said in a low voice. He turned down White Street, then back onto Sabovitch Street, heading toward the exit. While they were stopped next to the Convair 880 at the entrance, waiting to turn left onto the highway, a car pulled up on their right. The driver's window was rolled down and they could see that both pilots they had just seen were in the car. The driver was wearing a flight suit with an Italian flag emblem on his left arm. He quickly pulled out and drove into town toward the Sierra Highway.

"What do you suppose Italian F-14 pilots were doing at the CIA front company?" Ruth Ann quietly asked. "And since when does an F-14 pilot from Italy learn how to be a test pilot crawling out of a US F-14? What do you make of that, Mark?"

Just then the roar of the two F-14's filled the air, taking off one right after the other. "Well, you have to wonder who's flying those planes now, don't you? This is somewhat puzzling, and quite frankly, I don't know what to make of it," Mark said, shaking his head.

"Let's head back to the hotel. I want to shower and get cleaned up a little better. Then we can check out and head over to Denny's, and wait for Jack and his brother to show up," Ruth Ann suggested.

They had no sooner ordered coffee at Denny's when Jack Cooper walked through the door. "Hey! Fancy meeting you two again. My brother came home last night and will be five minutes behind me."

"Join us, please," Mark called out. "We grabbed the biggest booth we could find so we would all fit."

Jack had just gotten himself situated and a cup of coffee poured when his brother walked through the door. "Elmer, over here," he shouted, waving his arm in the air. Jack then turned to Ruth Ann and said, "This ought to mess up his gyroscope; we always sit at the counter."

Jack quickly introduced Ruth Ann and Mark to his brother, and explained their interest in the spaceport and the goings-on around the airport.

"We heard this morning from a couple of county workers that these airplanes parked here can be made airworthy with a thirty-day notice from their owners. Some of them are missing their doors and engines. Can they really get these old birds operational again?" Ruth Ann asked, leaving an opening for Elmer to fill in the details.

Elmer grinned, exposing a couple of missing teeth. "If a person keeps their eyes open, and a lot of this town's folk don't, you can see some real crazy things. Several years back, might be fifteen or more now, we had a huge Russian plane come in every Saturday night. It parked over near the east end of the taxiway. After noticing that huge bird come in several weeks in a row, I got my cameras and tripods set up so I could follow it and take some photos of that gigantic bird. Biggest plane I ever saw—made those 747's seem small, like the 757's do parked next to them. So, I noticed that this plane was on some type of schedule but hey, nothing here really runs on a schedule. Mojave is a hit or miss operation. Most planes fly in, park, and stay put for months or longer. But this big Russian plane, it came in from an unusual approach over Edwards, and came in every Saturday like clockwork. One night I was ready for her. I set up my gear and just as it got dark, I saw it on final approach. That bird took up most of the runway, it did. It pulled over between two hangars and when that cargo door opened and the lights came on, all you could see was gold. It was so bright inside that I couldn't get the right exposure on my camera. Those guys worked like fools unloading pallet after pallet of gold bullion, and stacked them damn high too. Whoever was loading that plane on the other end must have had billions of dollars' worth of gold in a mighty big vault somewhere."

Mark and Ruth Ann were fascinated by Elmer's story. "Wow!" Ruth Ann exclaimed, not wanting to say more and interrupt Elmer's storytelling.

"That's not the only strange thing that was happening around here about that time. A few months, maybe six or so, after that Russian plane stopped coming here, another strange thing happened. It was again on Saturday nights and if I recall, it was four or maybe five months before the terrorists blew up those towers in New York. We had, oh, I'd say maybe a dozen US Airways planes parked here. Most of them were being parted out. But one bird that was parked right smack in the middle of the row was pulled out of the line—the coverings over the jets and windshield were temporary. Those were removed and that plane would be loaded with what at first I thought were stewardesses—flight attendants I guess they're called these days—but both men and women. Yep, they each carried the same black suitcase on wheels rolling behind them, and they boarded that plane and it took off out of here, just about sunset. Very strange—those passengers would all show up on a bus. I never paid much attention until I noticed it was doing the same thing every weekend. I have a bad habit of watching all these planes," Elmer said, as he smiled his toothless grin again.

Mark kept sipping his coffee and listening at full attention. "You really do keep an eye on things around here."

"Oh, listen, I have a friend that works on the inside. The crazy thing about that US Air 757, was he said they installed a fuel bladder on that baby. That meant she could carry enough fuel to fly nonstop all the way to any city in Europe, maybe farther. Yep, when she flew out of here last, she could go a heck of a long ways without stopping if that fuel bladder was full. If you had more time, I could show you all my photographs of those planes the military thought were top secret. They ain't all that smart; they think none of us around this town pay any attention to what goes on around here. From down by Edwards up to China Lake, I've seen things that would make your hair curl and tie your tongue in knots trying to explain what it was. Yep, they must think we're all deaf and blind—that we ain't aware of some of the goings-on around here," Elmer repeated, as he slapped his brother Jack across the back.

"Wow, Mark, you've flown the 757. Have you ever heard of adding a fuel bladder to one so that it could fly longer distances?" Ruth Ann asked.

"You put a fuel bladder on one of those airplanes and it could easily fly halfway around the world," Mark said, collecting more questions in his head to ask. He looked at Elmer and asked, "Did they change the paint job, or did it last fly out of here under the US Airways logo and colors?"

"It was still flying the US Air paint and logo. I asked the guy that installed the bladder, because I couldn't imagine a commercial carrier doing that. Why not just use a plane that could fly farther? Made no sense to me, guess that's why I never forgot about it. But he also wasn't sure US Air even owned that plane, which made it all the crazier," Elmer reconfirmed, confident in the details he was sharing.

"That does sound suspicious," Ruth Ann added.

Elmer scratched his head and continued, "I tell you, we had lots of stuff going on here years back, seems like it was right around the time when everyone was thinking their computers were going to go crazy when we hit the year 2000."

The four of them chatted about all kinds of things while they enjoyed lunch. The conversations always seemed to keep coming back to the boneyard and the planes that flew in and out. Jack was right; Elmer was a wealth of information that provided Mark and Ruth Ann with thoughts that were beginning to dovetail with some of the other data they were investigating.

"We'd better get ourselves headed back in the direction of Vegas, you two. I'll pay the lunch tab as a thank-you for all your stories and information. It's been very enjoyable and extremely enlightening, to say the least," Ruth Ann offered.

Mark joined her at the cash register. It was attended to by the same woman cashier from the other day. She looked at Mark and rolled her eyes. She apparently wanted to warn him again about those two brothers, but he smiled and she seemed to get the message.

Ruth Ann paid the check and Mark peeled off several one-dollar bills and handed them to the cashier. "Would you give this to our waitress? I think her name was Candy," he said.

twelve

Mark's cell phone rang as he was resting in his room back at the M. "Tom, my friend, what's up? Find anything interesting in those files?"

"More than interesting. These files are all over the map. I was looking for facility logs, because they would note any irregularities with the air traffic controllers in either the tower or the approach. What's a little disturbing is that I'm finding files that are similar, but the time is off and entries have been both added and removed. That's not right. Those facility logs should note specific details, and they would never be changed."

Mark was taking notes on the small tablet on his desk. "So, does it look like someone has come in say, after the fact, and made changes? I'm not sure I understand what you are saying."

"Oh yeah, this is a problem. Someone has come in and typed up these reports. I'm still looking for the originals, which should be handwritten. It's not so much a problem that the reports are typewritten, but the information contained in them looks to be entered by someone who really didn't understand what an air traffic controller would log. Some of these logs read like news reports and contain information that had nothing to do with the facility. To tell you the truth, so far, my mind is boggled with what I'm seeing. Where did Ruth Ann get these files? Does the government know she has them? Mark, from what I'm initially looking at, something isn't right here. I would not be shocked to find some very damning information in these files and I've just started looking," Tom said, barely taking a breath in between sentences and never waiting for a response from Mark.

"I can sense you're pretty wound up by them. I'll probably have to take notes in order to answer all your questions," Mark responded with a chuckle.

"Take notes, record it, do what you have to do. I'm diving in headfirst and don't plan to come up for air any time soon," Tom replied.

"Well, to start answering your questions, I think her team of researchers has done thousands of FOIA requests over the years. I don't know how many of those, if any, Ruth Ann did personally, but my gut tells me, knowing her, she was very involved. She's very dedicated to this cause and her team has already uncovered details about 9/11 that have never been uncovered before. I think what they need now is confirmation that the FAA and possibly the higher-ups at the Pentagon were involved."

"Well, I know Westover air base; I had family that lived not far from that base. I used to spend summers up there, and a few Christmases, too. The base is huge as far as area is concerned; it's one of the largest bases, and the runways were certainly plenty long enough to land those planes full of fuel on 9/11. The flight attendant was correct about cell phones not working above about 1,500 feet in 2001, and those flights were all above that altitude when the calls were made, according to the official story. Knowing about the remote takeover and landing of the aircraft sheds a totally new light on the event. Listen, Mark, I don't know what your assignment was at the time, but I had buddies that were inside the Pentagon that day. They all told me the smell of cordite was overpowering, and every one of them was certain that they smelled only cordite and not jet fuel. They also heard multiple explosions going off in that wing."

Mark found himself doodling on the tablet as Tom spoke. He had always known there was more to the supposed terror attacks than advertised, mainly because of the way the Bush administration and the president's Secret Service detail acted that morning. Their job was to keep the president safe at all costs; they were trained to take a bullet for him, to lay their own lives on the line to protect him. That morning, President Bush sat among elementary students in a classroom in Florida. When the second plane hit the south tower, under normal circumstances, his Secret Service detail would have scooped him up and removed him immediately, even if he protested. Nothing like that happened. He remained seated while he was informed of the second strike on the World Trade Center Towers, and didn't move until moments before the Pentagon was struck. Only then did he calmly, and of his own accord, move toward his limousine and on to Air Force One. That was telling to those who understood what the Secret Service should have been doing. The rest of the country thought we were at war, the media had banners across the television screens reading: America Under Attack, yet the Secret Service did not seem concerned, nor did the president. That always bothered Mark, but he'd managed to set his doubts aside until he met Ruth Ann.

Tom interrupted Mark's thoughts. "Well, I wanted to touch base with you. I got up bright and early and started looking at the files. I might have to print them out to keep them all straight. I'm seeing multiple accounts and varying times for the same event. There should only be one time noted for a specific event at a facility. Just let Ruth Ann know she's definitely roused my curiosity, and I'll call you the minute I find anything else noteworthy. I have to admit, at this point, I feel as though I'm looking at faked documents. If what you and Ruth Ann told me can be verified in these files, well, I guess the official story and the 9/11 Commission hearings were the real conspiracies, not the people out there saying jet fuel can't melt steel. Mark, this could be serious, and this is the type of information people get taken out over. I hope your friend Ruth Ann is careful. Her life is probably in grave danger, especially if her name is on the FOIA requests," Tom said, his voice becoming calmer, but more serious. "Mark, I can't imagine the government would really release documents that could blow their cover. I know some of these files are looking complicated and they sure aren't organized, but I have a hunch that buried in there is something that could change our lives forever. You two watch your six. I'm damn serious, Mark. I have a real deep-seated feeling that something is in these files that nobody was ever supposed to find, and when we do find it, we'll all be in danger."

"Well, Tom, I have to admit, in the last few days I've learned more about that point in our history than I ever thought possible. I know that President Sherman is involved and dedicated to not only finding the truth, but getting that truth delivered to the public. On the other hand, I'm not naïve. I understand the entities that were most likely involved in the planning and execution of this event, and they do mean business. They'll do anything to stop this information from being exposed to the public," Mark acknowledged.

"I'll continue looking through these files, but Mark, I think we should be as discreet as possible when talking. I'm not afraid for myself as much as I am for you and Ruth Ann. The walls have ears these days, and you never know who's snooping around. Hell, who knows, they could be snooping to see who's found condemning information about the government and we could be on their radar right now. I'll text you in a few days, and maybe you two can meet me in person again where we'll all feel safer."

Mark relayed the information to Ruth Ann over lunch, after her morning visit to the spa. "I'm sharing his warning with you because I feel the same way. We could be on the verge of uncovering some very monumental and dangerous information. I know Tom, and he is thorough in everything he tackles. If there's something amiss in this official story and it's in those files, he'll find it."

"I'm no stranger to the dangers that investigating 9/11 can bring," Ruth Ann admitted, without sharing the details of her recent kidnapping. "I think it's time for me to check in with Washington. We would be wise to take some precautions, at least when it comes to our communications with Tom. Let me make a couple phone calls, and while we wait for responses why don't we do something relaxing. I have a cabana reserved at the pool for the day, and the massage I just enjoyed has me feeling like a day of rest is just what my body is crying out for. How about I meet you at the pool in an hour," Ruth Ann suggested.

"Perfect. I could use a day to rest, and the pool here is probably one of the best places in the entire world to do just that," Mark agreed.

Ruth Ann picked up her cell phone and dialed. "Max, Ruth Ann here," she said in a precise, businesslike tone.

"What are you doing calling me? Were you able to pick up Bob's personal effects?" Max asked. "Hey, I hope you're about to tell me you are having massages every day and getting plenty of sleep." He laughed, waiting for Ruth Ann's response.

"Well, not exactly. I did manage to pick up Bob's personal things at the coroner's office. I've spent some time looking through the files; he had lots of files, Max. And his crazy method of organizing said files, well, what can I say? I can only look at them for a period of time before I'm forced to either have a massage or head to the pool," Ruth Ann said, laughing.

She informed Max about meeting Mark, and giving him as much personal information as she felt comfortable with. She knew Max would be doing some background checking. Then she told him about Mark's friend, the retired air traffic controller, who was looking through the FOIA data. "He's already found what he calls serious irregularities in the facility logs. I don't have all the details, but he's certain something is suspicious," she said.

Max listened intently as Ruth Ann filled him in on the developments on her end. "Text me the address of your hotel and tell the concierge that you will be expecting a package. I'll get a couple secure encrypted laptops for you to use to communicate with this guy."

"I'll let the concierge know as soon as this phone call is over," Ruth Ann assured Max.

"Just an update on the situation here—we have some news coming in and the websites have been proving to be a great way to allow the American people to feel safe with the information they're sharing. Don't want to take up your time, Ruth Ann—remember you went to Vegas to rest, relax and recover. I'm not surprised that you've stumbled on to people that can help you, because I know the research never really leaves you," Max said with a laugh. "I never have to say, 'You go girl' to you, Ruth Ann. I know there's no keeping you down. I'll get those laptops out tonight. Enjoy your day, stay safe, and Ruth Ann, be aware of your surroundings. Don't let your guard down. We don't want to lose you, or any of Bob's information. You hear me?"

"Yes sir, I'm on my way to the pool via the concierge as we speak," Ruth Ann acknowledged. She was already out the door and waiting for the elevator when she told Max goodbye.

thirteen

Farouk was a devout Sunni Muslim who had come to the United States to attend the University of Virginia. Though he was not part of the royal family, he was able to attend the university on a royal scholarship as long as he majored in electrical engineering and he graduated in four years. That proved to be a significant challenge for him, since his English was rudimentary and he knew no one in Virginia from back home. He was on his own and under a ticking time clock from the moment he set foot in this foreign land. Naturally, he found the nearest mosque in Charlottesville and immediately made friends with the Imam. That association and familiarity provided enough grounding for him to succeed at his goals. The mosque offered English classes for those who were interested, and Farouk never missed a session. He knew that being able to function proficiently in English was the key to his success. The engineering studies would come easier for him if he could read and speak the language. He had been a top scholar in math and science at his high school in Riyadh, which was why he was offered the scholarship. As time passed, his ability to communicate in English grew from functional to exceptional. So fluent had he become that his Imam friend often teased him that his mother was really a British maid who spoke English to him as a small child before she fled the kingdom and went back to London. They laughed about such a scenario and its impossibility in Saudi Arabia, but whatever the reason, Farouk communicated in English almost as well as a native speaker when he graduated with honors from UV.

With permission from his government, he accepted a job in Fredricksburg with a high-tech startup company producing home surveillance systems. Unfortunately, that job only lasted a couple of years before the seed money dried up and the business had to close with no warning early one Monday morning. He thought about returning home, but the kingdom had contacts with a firm in Alexandria and arranged for him to interview the very same week he had lost his job. He seemed to be a perfect fit and was not only hired, but also encouraged and tutored in how to extend his H1B visa and to eventually obtain a green card. He chose to keep his apartment in Fredricksburg because he was dating a girl he had known from school who also lived there, and it was worth it to him to engage in the long daily commute to be able to be with her as often as possible.

A few nights back, when he and his girlfriend Karen were sitting in his apartment watching their favorite television show, President Sherman interrupted with his call for action on the part of United States citizens. Karen was upset that her show was delayed, and said to Farouk something to the effect that even if she knew something about 9/11, she wasn't going to give it to anyone who butted into her favorite program. Farouk disagreed with her. He thought that if anyone knew something, it was their duty to do as their president asked and share the information. This led to a heated discussion about politics in general, and Karen's contempt for President Sherman in particular. She had been a lifelong Democrat and President Sherman's ascension to that office had never set well with her. The two of them had never discussed politics before, primarily because Farouk wasn't a citizen and his personal experience with the monarchy had always been positive. However, this argument with Karen struck a chord in him that cut across the grain of his desire to be loyal to whatever government he was subject to. He could not understand her contempt for a leader who was only trying to do what he felt was best for the country, and wanted the public to assist. Even if he despised the politics of such a leader, it was important to him to be loyal to his country, and that meant helping when asked. Their night ended on a sour note, and Farouk went home questioning the future of the relationship with the girl he had dated for so long.

For several days, the fight with Karen played over and over in his head. One evening when he was sitting alone in his apartment, watching television, a public service announcement was broadcast, informing the public of the website available to share information about 9/11 with the White House. It was at that very moment he decided to write them about his experience commuting to work in the early morning of September 10th. He didn't think it was anything very valuable, but it was his way of doing what the president had asked, and subconsciously his way of saying 'thank you' to a country that had offered him so much. It also served to assuage some of the guilt he felt as a Saudi subject who was led to believe it was mostly Saudi hijackers who commandeered airplanes that day.

A few days later, he was more than surprised to receive a call from the White House.

"Farouk, this is Max Hager, special assistant in the White House for 9/11 investigations."

"Yes, sir, Mr. Hager, how can I be of help to you?" Farouk asked, though he was rather confused as to why anyone from the White House would be calling him.

"I have in my hand the email you sent to us, telling us how you were denied access to Fort Belvoir the day prior to 9/11, and then again on that fateful morning. I was wondering if you could arrange some time to come to the White House and meet with me. I have some questions that are related to what you shared, and frankly, I want to pick your brain on what you remember from your days traveling through the fort. If it works out, we may even go visit the route you drove every day. Would that be possible?" Max asked.

"I don't know why you would want to talk to me. What I sent you was true, but probably not very helpful," Farouk replied.

"Son, it may not seem all that helpful, but then again it might be the doorway to answering a question we've had, and talking to you might be the key to that door. So if it is possible, could you come to Washington at ten o'clock next Monday? All you need to do is drive up to the gate and give your name. I will have made all the arrangements for you to pass through security. You'll need your Saudi passport and your Virginia driver's license. They'll probably fingerprint you, and I'll have an escort waiting to direct you to my office."

"I can arrange to get off work next Monday. And I'll come, but I don't know how much help I'll be," Farouk replied.

"I'll be the judge of that. I thank you for your willingness to help, and apologize for the inconvenience that it will cause for you that day. If all goes well, I might be able to introduce you to the First Lady, but don't get your hopes up too high—she's a busy woman. However, she's very engaged in what we're doing here, and she likes to personally thank anyone who's kind enough to assist us," Max explained.

"I'm looking forward to coming, Mr. Hager. Thank you for your invitation, and I'll see you at ten Monday morning. Goodbye, sir."

Farouk smiled inside and thought, Imagine me meeting the First Lady! That's reserved for dignitaries like our king, not ordinary Saudi citizens.

The weekend seemed to drag on slowly and Monday could not arrive soon enough for Farouk. When it did, he was ready to leave at his usual time for work, but since his appointment in Washington was later, he tried to keep busy around the apartment, hoping it would calm his nerves. It usually took him an hour and a half to drive to Alexandria. Washington was a little farther, but since he wouldn't have to fight the rush hour traffic, he decided to leave at around a quarter to nine.

About an hour earlier that morning, Dante left Richmond, where he had spent the night at his mother's place. He headed out on I-95 toward Alexandria, to meet with a friend to discuss a business opportunity they had been chasing together for several months. The meeting was more about their friendship than it was about making money, and so there never seemed to be a rush to consummate the deal. This time of year was usually hot and humid, but fortunately not this morning, so Dante lowered the top on his Corvette and looked forward to a pleasant drive. As he approached Fredricksburg, traffic began to back up, and he had to slow down to allow merging traffic to enter the freeway. Ordinarily that would cause Dante to put the Vette through its paces and weave through that kind of mess until he could once again accelerate past the posted speed limit. Since the top was down and he wasn't in a real hurry, he decided to go with the traffic flow and enjoy the ride. Eventually, the traffic thinned out and he remained in the right lane with his cruise control set to the speed limit, following behind a black Toyota Camry.

Twenty minutes outside of Fredricksburg, Dante heard a rifle shot ring out. Looking to his left, he knew the shot came from a small hill on the other side of the highway. Even with the noise from the roadway, he recognized the type of rifle used to execute the shot. When he looked forward, he could see that the Camry had blown its left front tire and was starting to slow down and make its way to the shoulder. Another shot was fired, and this time Dante could tell the round tore into the back tire of the Toyota. Instinctively, he pulled alongside of the Camry, blocking the sniper's view. He ducked down, then opened the passenger door and crawled out on the ground between the two stopped cars. He opened the driver's side door of the black car. With one hand he pulled Farouk onto the ground, protecting him from any further sniper attack. He made Farouk keep his head down, and together they waited.

When sufficient time had passed that Dante felt it was safe, he stood up, but told Farouk to remain where he was. He inspected the tires to see if either of the rounds had remained in the tire itself, or if they had blown through both sidewalls. It seemed that the rear tire might have a slug lodged inside. He knelt down and tapped Farouk on the shoulder. Farouk rolled over on his back, then sat up.

"I'm Dante Wilcox," he said. "Who do you think might be shooting at you?"

Farouk looked puzzled and replied, "I have no idea. My girlfriend's mad at me, but she wouldn't go to this much trouble. You probably saved my life. Thank you."

"Whoever it was wasn't trying to kill you. He was too good of a shot. Had he wanted to kill you, I'd be wiping up brains off your seats and windshield. He was trying to warn you, or stop you from going somewhere," Dante explained. "Now the police are going to be here any minute, and before they get here, I want your permission to cut into this rear tire so I can find the bullet. I want to confirm my suspicion, if that's okay with you."

"Well, I guess that would be okay, but won't it disrupt any police investigation?" Farouk asked.

"If these bullets came from where I think they did, the police will never be able to conduct an investigation that leads to the culprits," Dante replied.

"I owe you my life, so go ahead,"

Dante took out a serrated knife from his glove box and began to cut into the back tire towards the bottom. Just as he suspected, there was the slug, resting in the well of the tire. He examined it and placed it in his front jeans pocket. "May I ask you where you were going?"

"I'm on my way to the White House to talk with a Max Hager. I'm supposed to be there at ten this morning, but now it doesn't look like I'm going to make it on time," Farouk responded.

"Who's Max Hager, and why were you going to talk with him?" Dante asked, his curiosity beginning to stir.

"I'm not really sure who he is, but I was going to talk with him about some anomalies I saw on 9/11 around Fort Belvoir. To me it didn't seem all that important, but he thought it was, and so he asked me to come see him today."

"Did you tell anyone where you were going this morning?"

Farouk, still sitting on the shoulder of the highway, thought for a moment and said, "No. I would have told my girlfriend, but like I said, she's mad at me, and thinks I'm crazy for trying to help President Sherman." He paused. "No, wait, on Friday I went to the bank to get some cash for this trip in case I had to buy somebody lunch or something, and I told the teller, whom I've known for years. That's all, no one else."

"What bank?" Dante asked.

"Sun Trust Bank, why?"

Dante shook his head. "Never mind, but that explains a lot."

"What, what does it explain?" Farouk begged.

Dante looked around to see if the police or highway patrol were on their way. Someone else must have heard the shots and reported it, but if not, two cars parked side by side on the shoulder of the highway would cause enough suspicion for any passing motorist or peace officer to report it to 911 or the highway patrol. "You know, I'm probably going to hate myself for doing this, but since your car isn't going anywhere soon, I'll take you to the White House. But you're going to need to get on your phone and call that Hager guy, and explain to him what happened. I doubt he'll be overly surprised. Tell him my name, Dante Wilcox, tell him I was Special Forces in Afghanistan, and give him my license plate number. That should be enough for him to look me up and get permission for me to accompany you. Tell him I have information he'll need about this sniper attack and I'll share it with him when we arrive. Can you do that?"

Farouk began to feel frightened. He was sure he was into something that was way over his head, and began to wonder if maybe his girlfriend had been right all along. Perhaps he should have just minded his own business—if he had, none of this would have occurred. Now he wasn't sure what was going on or who this Dante guy was, but he was stuck and had to trust him. If the White House gave the okay for Dante to bring him there, he would go along with that, but he was certainly having second thoughts. "I'll do it," he replied. He got out his phone and called Max.

Just as the call connected and Max answered, the highway patrol arrived.

"You just keep talking and keep Hager on the line. We may need him to talk to the police. Got it?"

Farouk nodded.

Dante approached the officers and began to explain to them what had happened, but kept what he suspected to himself.

Jim Bowman was in the office when Farouk's call came in. Max listened carefully to what he was being told and took a few notes. He asked Jim to look up this Dante character, and kept talking to Farouk.

Dante was having a hard time getting across to the officers what he thought had occurred. He pointed to a small wooded hill on the other side of the freeway where he thought the shots had come from. The officers were more interested in getting identification from him and Farouk and assessing the damage to Farouk's car. They didn't notice the slice in the rear tire.

After several minutes, Jim got back to Max. "This Dante guy is golden. A retired lieutenant colonel, three tours of duty in the Middle East, secret Special Forces unit, three bronze stars, a silver star, two purple hearts. He's been awarded everything but the Medal of Honor, and reading his service record, I would guess you could make a case for that on his experience alone."

"Let me talk to Dante, Farouk," Max said.

Farouk took the phone over to Dante and said, "Max Hager wants to talk to you."

Dante took the phone from Farouk's hand and the police officers descended upon Farouk.

"Mr. Wilcox, Max Hager and Jim Bowman here, we're special assistants to the president. Farouk gave me an idea of what happened out there this morning. I've read your service record and know this kind of thing is not foreign to you. Farouk was fortunate you were in the area. Can you shed any light on what you think might have happened?"

Dante stepped away from the area just far enough so that the officers would not hear what he had to say. "It was a CIA hit. Not a hit, more of a warning. For whatever reason, they didn't want Farouk to meet with you."

"How did they know he was even coming?" Max asked.

"On Friday, Farouk mentioned the whole thing to a teller at Sun Trust Bank, and we both know who runs that bank now, don't we?" Dante said.

Max chuckled in a way that suggested he knew exactly who controlled that bank, and wasn't surprised at the outcome. "Do you have anything else, or is that just your hunch?"

"I extracted a bullet from one of his tires. It's not a round you can buy at Kmart. I've shot that same caliber many times, and I know their sole source all too well. Trust me, this was CIA all the way," Dante assured them.

"I'm glad you offered to bring Farouk to D.C.; now we're going to want to talk with you too," Max said.

"I felt sorry for the kid. I'll bring him to the White House, but I'm not so sure I want to get involved in what you people are doing. It's just not my thing anymore. Oh, and in order to get Farouk out of here I'm going to need you to talk to the police who are here investigating. I doubt they're going to want to let us go anytime soon. At this point, we can't be much more help to them. They should just impound Farouk's car and do whatever they are going to do. I'm sure they'll never get to the bottom of what really happened, but if it's not too much trouble, I'd like to give the phone to the lead patrolman and have you explain to him that we have to go now," Dante suggested.

"By all means, let me talk to that flat-footed note-taker. I'll set him straight," Max said, laughing.

Dante handed Farouk's phone to the officer in charge and said, "The White House wants a word with you, officer."

"Yes, sir," he replied, placing the phone to his ear.

"This is Maxwell Hager, special assistant to the President of the United States, and I need to ask you to allow Mr. Wilcox and Farouk to leave immediately. They're to be in my office in less than an hour, and time's a-wasting. I'm sure you have their contact information. Impound the car and if you need anything from me, have Farouk give you my number. I'll help you any way I can, but it's a matter of national security and I need these gentlemen in my office sooner rather than later. Can you do that for me?" Max asked.

"Yes, sir, Mr. Hager, I understand what you're saying and I'll see to it that they're free to go immediately. And say hello to President Sherman for me; he's the best and has this officer's full support."

"Will do, officer, and thank you for your help and understanding," Max replied.

The officer handed the phone back to Farouk along with his business card, and then motioned with both hands for the two of them to get in the Corvette and be on their way to Washington.

Farouk climbed into Dante's car and fastened the seatbelt,

while Dante pushed the button to raise the roof back into place. Farouk took one last look at his Camry as Dante signaled left and rapidly accelerated onto I-95 headed north once again, only this time through Alexandria and into the nation's capital.

fourteen

"Ms. Lowy, your package has arrived. Would you like me to deliver it to your room?" the concierge asked.

"That would be wonderful, thank you, Vik. You're the best; you always make my stay here so pleasant," Ruth Ann replied.

After the package was delivered, Ruth Ann opened one of the laptops and found a note from Max: Here is your secure laptop. I set it up with your sign-in and password, you will find a post-it note on your keyboard. The other one is set up exactly the same, but only you will know that. Be safe, Max.

That Max, she thought. He thinks of everything. Understanding that the second laptop to be shared with Tom was set up the same exact way as hers meant she could access it should anything happen to Tom. She reached for her cell phone to call Mark. "Have you heard back from Tom yet?" she asked.

"No, I was just going to give him a call. What's up?"

"The secure laptops arrived; it would be great to get this machine to him as quickly as possible. Why don't you call him and see if we can arrange a time and place to get it into his hands? I'm fine with driving back to Palmdale if you are," she informed Mark.

"I'll do that right now. I'm certain he'll want this laptop; he was a bit apprehensive the last time we spoke. Let me see if, when, and where we can meet up with him, and give you a call back," Mark said.

"I can be ready about as fast as the gals at the bakery can whip up a few pastries to go," Ruth Ann said, laughing, and thinking about how fast things were beginning to move.

"I'll meet you downstairs. Order me a large coffee and get me one of those Italian donuts," Mark instructed, feeling certain that the arrival of the secure laptop would be important enough for Tom to change any plans he might have. It was also a four-hour drive to Tom's place, so even if he couldn't reach him by phone, there was plenty of time on the way to make contact and arrange a rendezvous point.

"Well?" Ruth Ann asked when Mark entered the bakery.

"He suggested we meet him at a location he'll text to me in a few minutes. He asked if we'd be okay with him inviting another retired air traffic controller to join us. His friend was a controller at Edwards for a number of years, so he had top security clearance. Tom said his buddy has a wealth of knowledge, and never forgets a detail involving anything with wings attached to it."

Ruth Ann was excited. "Let me run up and get the computers, and I'll be ready to head out."

The valet pulled the rental car up to the curb. Ruth Ann loaded the boxed computer for Tom into the backseat and made herself comfortable in the front, while Mark tipped the valet and shared a short conversation with him.

"I told Tom we'd head out in his direction and wait for his instructions," Mark informed her. "Looks like another nice day with no traffic, perfect for a long drive."

"Exactly. It's my kind of day, full of the unexpected," Ruth Ann gleefully replied.

About twenty minutes into the drive, as they were passing through the town of Jean and almost to California, Mark's cell phone beeped the sound of an incoming text message. He handed his phone to Ruth Ann.

"This looks like a latitude/longitude coordinate. It says, thirty-five degrees twenty-two minutes and zero seven seconds, if I remember how to read these. The longitude is one hundred seventeen degrees thirty-nine minutes and twenty-nine seconds. You don't happen to know where that might be, do you?" Ruth facetiously asked. Knowing that an answer wouldn't be forthcoming, she quickly typed the coordinates into her laptop. "The map says it's a town named Randsburg, in California." She zoomed out on the map so she could see the surrounding towns. "It looks like we'll be taking that Highway 58 out of Barstow until we connect up with Highway 395, and then we'll take a right up to Randsburg. So it's not all that far away from Mojave," she said.

The cell phone indicated another incoming message. "It says 'The Joint,'" Ruth Ann read aloud.

"I'm not sure what that means. I know Tom doesn't smoke joints, so maybe he has a problem with his knee he's trying to tell us about," Mark said with a laugh.

Ruth Ann was already typing on her computer. "Oh my, it's the local bar in town, and does this place have a colorful history. Randsburg is an old gold mining town; looks like the town got started in 1896—at least that's when their post office opened. It's considered to be a living ghost town, with a population of about seventy people. During the California Gold Rush days, gold was discovered in the Rand Mine in 1895. A mining camp was quickly formed, being named after the Rand gold mining region in South Africa. Now, The Joint is along the main street and from the photographs online, I'm sure it's not a bar we would have ever visited—maybe never even noticed. I'm sure this will prove to be a very colorful afternoon."

They passed a huge solar farm on the way up Highway 395, and as they climbed higher toward the mining area, old wooden shacks and abandoned trailers dotted the barren landscape. As they crested the top of the hill, they noticed a small green sign that pointed toward Randsburg. Mark looked at his watch. "Well, we're right on time. Let's see what Tom's found, if anything. Once we get this laptop into his hands, I know he'll feel a lot more comfortable sharing information with you and your team. After all those years in air traffic control, Tom has an uncanny way of seeing details and keeping more than one iron in the fire."

"Great, those are necessary attributes when digging through government files. After the 9/11 Commission hearings, they brought an eighteen-wheel trailer full of data to the National Archives. Very little information was saved electronically. I assume that whoever was in charge at the Department of Justice didn't want anyone to find anything like what we've found. The people, the survivors from the towers, and even some airline employees and FBI agents that we suspect knew something, started mysteriously dying not long after the attacks. Some of those deaths were labeled as suicides, but a right-handed man has a difficult time shooting himself in his left temple, if you get my drift. The mysterious deaths also included family members of some of the airline crews. Nothing we can accuse anyone of doing, but the timing of their deaths is difficult to explain. The people that were behind 9/11 are very wealthy and very connected to a large pool of psychopaths. We're collecting data on some of the people that spun off from the Central Intelligence Agency and started their own army of rogue mercenaries. We don't know if it will lead to something substantial, but I know we're on the right track."

"The old Hegelian Dialectic," Mark retorted after hearing Ruth Ann's information.

"Oh, when you dig into this like our team has, Mark, it's beyond horrific that human beings can be this evil," Ruth Ann said.

Randsburg was small and quaint, so it wasn't hard to find the bar on the main street where Ruth Ann thought it would be. It also wasn't hard to find a parking spot in a town with so few people. Mark parked right in front of the bar.

"Hey! Welcome," Tom called out, as Mark and Ruth Ann

stepped into the tavern. Tom and his friend stood as Ruth Ann and Mark approached. They were seated at a corner table surrounded by a tufted black vinyl upholstered bench.

"This is good old Chip," Tom said, introducing his friend. "And these two characters are Ruth Ann and Mark."

No last names were exchanged, and everyone understood why.

"Nice to meet you, Chip," Ruth Ann said, making a point to repeat his name so she would remember.

"Chip, like in microchip. I know some people who actually use that as a memory jogger." He laughed at his own name and almost snorted when he did.

Mark ordered a bottle of wine and some glasses, and then turned to Chip. "Tom tells me you were an air traffic controller over at Edwards. That must have been quite an interesting career."

"Interesting, my friend, is one hell of an understatement," Chip responded, using both his hands for emphasis. "Hell, I had my very own CIA handler, how's that for interesting?" This time he added a smile and raised an eyebrow. "Most people think that spy agencies spy on each other—you know, like the old spy vs. spy, James Bond and all that. At least that's what I thought, but my handler, who'd been in 'the company' for over thirty years, told me one night over beers that all those spy agencies are in bed together. They meet once or twice a year in Katmandu and make those 'I'll scratch your back if you scratch mine' deals. They share their plans for nation building, government overthrowing and false flags. Doesn't matter if it's the MI6, the CIA, Pakistan's ISI, the Russian FSB the German BND, Australia's ASIS, the Chinese MSS or the Israeli Mossad, or freelancing black operators. Once those plans are agreed upon, they help each other feed their chosen outcome to the media, which they also control. You know, once I learned that one tidbit of information, it changed the way I watched the news. I even saw one news channel admit that their commentator was a retired CIA agent." Chip let out a burst of laughter that echoed in the nearly empty bar. "Everyone knows you never 'retire' from the CIA—once CIA, you're always CIA. If you step out of bounds, meaning you try to expose any of the spy agencies and their ruses, well, you can guarantee one of those agencies will hunt you down and silence you, and it won't necessarily be the agency you're working for or going to expose. Let's say you work for the CIA out of Langley and you're stationed around here somewhere and you know about one of their stunts, maybe you were even involved in that stunt. If they begin to think, for whatever reason, you're going to expose it, well, they'll call out a hit on you, your family and maybe even your dog. Some of the people working for those agencies are ruthless psychopaths; they don't ask questions, they do what they're told. Someone higher up the chain calls for a hit and it's done, no questions asked. Yep, my handler was quite the guy— he never said much unless we were up all night and finished off our shift with a few beers at a local hideaway. That's when he would get to telling me stories. The tales I could tell about my time working at that base could fill a book," Chip finished, and then ordered a beer for just himself.

"So, what's the strangest thing that ever happened to you while you were at Edwards?" Ruth Ann asked, slowly sipping her wine and hoping for a good answer.

"Well, I never tried to put my experiences into any sort of order of interest. I always knew that book would never be allowed to be written," Chip replied. He thought for a few moments and then said, "Several years back, oh, maybe fifteen or sixteen I'd say, we had a Russian Antonov plane fly right through our highly restricted airspace. I was told by my handler that the plane would be coming in through air space nobody receives permission to fly over, and landing at Mojave. It came in several Saturday nights for months. I never could figure out what that was all about, and most things that went on at Edwards, well, let me just say, if you weren't given the details, you didn't ask for them."

Ruth Ann and Mark looked at each other without saying a word. They were thinking the same thing, and it ended with them both ignoring the Denny's cashier's advice.

"Another night, not long before all hell broke loose with those terror attacks back east, I heard a Continental pilot screaming about a US Airways 757 that was flying VRF, just outside our restricted airspace down by Barstow. The Continental pilot had to use evasive action to avoid a collision. Needless to say, he was angry, confused and he wanted to scream at anyone that would listen," Chip began.

"Wait a minute; did you say a US Airways 757 was flying VFR?" Mark asked, making certain he heard both correctly.

"What's VFR?" Ruth Ann interjected, hoping someone would answer her question before the story continued.

"VFR stands for visual flight rules, but it's not something you would expect a commercial carrier like US Airways to ever be flying under," Chip answered. "You see, commercial carriers must file a flight plan. This US Airways 757 didn't file a plan until it reached Las Vegas. Then it filed a flight plan to Washington D.C.'s Dulles International Airport while it was in air. Well, once the dust settled and the Continental pilot had vented his frustrations, I went to the computer to see what was going on with that 757. I thought it was—well, let me use the word 'suspicious'—so I kept my eye out for it showing up the following week. You can imagine my surprise when the following Saturday it was flying VFR again just outside the restricted airspace surrounding Edwards. This time, I followed the bird and watched as a flight plan was filed once it was near Las Vegas. And wouldn't you know it—the flight plan was again to Dulles International."

"Did you ever figure out why a commercial carrier was flying VFR and filing a transcontinental flight plan once it reached

Vegas? Did you see where it departed from? How could a US Airways plane carrying passengers take off VFR with no flight plan?" Mark was firing questions faster than Chip could answer.

"All great questions, and all the same questions I had, once I started to see that it was happening every Saturday night around the same time. There was no US Airways plane scheduled into Dulles every weekend at the time that bird would have landed, if in fact it really did land at Dulles. But more importantly, there was no scheduled flight from anywhere I could see," Chip explained.

"What do you mean? Once a flight plan is filed, doesn't the plane have to go from point A to point B?" Ruth Ann asked, looking around to all three men as she spoke.

Chip answered, "After filing a flight plan in the air with Las Vegas controllers, he could certainly do the same once he was closer to Dulles. It's so out of the ordinary that it would catch someone's attention. A commercial jet flying VFR and requesting a flight plan while flying at seventeen thousand feet simply doesn't make sense. I had to start paying attention. But there's more than just a flight plan. If that 757 landed at Dulles, it would need a gate or spot to land so the people-movers could get the passengers to the terminal. Parking a bird like that costs the airline, and there was no nonstop flight on US Airways scheduled anywhere near where we found him each Saturday night outside of Barstow, California. I never could quite figure out where that plane came from. Flying so low, it had to originate from someplace close to Edwards."

Mark was wishing he had a map in front of him to confirm his suspicions.

Tom had been silent while Chip shared his stories. "You know, I'm not sure of any dates, but I remember hearing about that Continental pilot and that near miss. The controllers at the LA Center in Palmdale talked about it for weeks. I think the main reason was because nobody could get any information about that

US Air 757. Flying VFR, it had to stay below seventeen thousand feet, which was just weird. The controllers had no idea where it launched from and that's the sort of data vacuum that really bothers them. No wonder that Continental pilot was screaming."

Chip laughed. "Well, let me just say this. Around Edwards we had a little saying—our radar was so high-tech and so accurate, we could see up a sparrow's butt if it was flying over Salt Lake City. Needless to say, for any kind of flying object to escape our notice—especially a commercial 757—well, there was just no possibility of that." Chip thought for a moment. "I can think of only one scenario, but I can't imagine why the Central Intelligence Agency would be involved with a commercial flight, if indeed it was a commercial flight."

"You said you watched that US Air 757 fly along the outskirts of the restricted airspace outside of Barstow on several Saturday nights after that?" Mark asked, reconfirming Chip's story.

"That plane did the same thing for, oh, I would guess at least most of the summer and up until early fall. I don't recall it being seen after the terror attacks. Even though commercial flights were stopped for a few days, I never saw that US Air 757 fly along the Barstow corridor again, come to think of it." Chip's own words started his memory to kick into high gear concerning the terror attacks in New York and Washington D.C. "It was a Tuesday morning, early over here in California. I can't recall right now if that US Airways plane flew out the Saturday night before 9/11 or not. I might have to call around and see if any of the other controllers remember when that crazy plane stopped flying VFR through that corridor."

Tom piped up, "I might have to call some of the guys that worked LA Center too, and ask around. That bird's a mystery, but the near miss could have been a real big disaster. If you and Ruth Ann want us to ask around, shake up some controllers' cobwebs, just let us know."

For the next few hours Tom and Chip shared all kinds of stories with Mark and Ruth Ann about the planes that flew in and around that area over the years. Most of them had been classified at the time, but enough time had passed that they were free to talk about what they had seen. Finally, Chip looked at his watch. "I'd love to stay and talk with you all day and share stories, but I have to run—promised the Mrs. I would work on her honey-do list and I hadn't planned on a trip to The Joint. It's been a pleasure meeting you two, and Tom, always great to touch base with you. I expect you'll be up here to do some gold panning with me in the near future. No better way to leave the hustle-bustle behind, that panning. And you'll be surprised how much gold has been left behind."

Chip stood up and shook Mark's and Ruth Ann's hands, and said goodbye to the bartender as he headed out the door.

"So, Chip lives nearby then?" Mark asked, looking at Tom.

"When he retired, he settled up here in mining country. He claimed it would keep him busy and out of the house. That's why we met here today," Tom replied.

"Ruth Ann has something for you," Mark said as they left the bar and walked toward the car.

Chip waved as he found his car a few spaces away. "Great meeting you two. Let me know if I can answer your questions about my old life hanging around Edwards. I'm happy to respond to certain things, but I still have to be tight-lipped about the classified top secret stuff."

"Much obliged and great meeting you, Chip," Mark called out.

Ruth Ann handed the laptop to Tom and reminded him it was government property and would need to be returned at some point. "Use it as much as you'd like, wear it out, but don't lose it."

"Don't worry about me. I'll protect it, since it's just what I need. Thank you so much. I'll contact you via your Skype account later tonight to make sure it all works, once you've had enough time to get back to Vegas," Tom promised.

"Tom, this was a great meeting. Thanks for inviting Chip. He might be very helpful as we move this investigation along. This is quite the out of the way place to meet, that's for sure," Mark said as he shook Tom's hand.

Once inside the car, Ruth Ann looked over at Mark. "Well, I could almost hear the wheels in your head spinning. What did you think about those stories Chip shared?" she asked.

"We certainly couldn't ask for a better confirmation of Elmer's stories about the Russian cargo plane and the US Airways 757 flying out of the boneyard." Mark's voice carried a pitch of excitement as he spoke. "This information sure has my brain spinning. I kept asking myself, where did that US Air plane originate? How far away from that restricted airspace down by Barstow did it launch from? I think the answer is pretty clear, don't you?"

Ruth Ann was listening to Mark's thoughts as they rolled past his lips. "Let me pull up a map and take a look to see if any other airports might be within that area. I love Google Maps and Google Earth for looking at details like this."

Mark drove the rental car back down the hill toward the Mojave Desert, waiting for Ruth Ann's findings. He could see her typing and scrolling to zoom in and out on the map on her screen.

"Ontario International Airport is about seventy miles to the southwest. They couldn't have left Ontario under VFR and been flying at seventeen thousand feet all the way to Barstow," Ruth Ann surmised. "There's only one possibility, and that's Mojave Air and Space Port," she declared.

"We might have to visit that place again in the future. Elmer shared with us information we couldn't and wouldn't have found any other way. The chances of us getting those details about the

US Airways 757 parked in that boneyard were slim to nothing. But to meet with two air traffic controllers who confirmed everything Elmer had to say, well, I almost feel divinely led at this point." Mark chuckled and smiled at Ruth Ann.

"Do you think that the US Airways 757 could have somehow been involved in the 9/11 event?" Ruth Ann asked, her mind churning out possibilities.

Mark was at a loss for an answer. "I think we'll need to run all the details we have past Tom and see if his expertise can see anything in all those government radar files. I know it's easy to be blinded when you're told to look the other way. For a long time, pilots, investigators and even researchers into 9/11 have been looking at those faked flight paths the FAA put out. We have also been blinded by the lie that nineteen radical Muslims were flying those jets and that those planes were flown into the designated targets they showed us on television. With this new information, Tom can look for things that might have involved that US Air 757, and determine if it could have had a role in 9/11."

"Boneyard?" Ruth Ann was again typing into her laptop. "I remember a 9/11 researcher that had been crawling around the Pinal boneyard. He was planning to write a book about 9/11. He, according to the media, killed his two teenaged kids and the family dog, then shot himself at their home in California." She paused while trying to read the webpage on her screen. "He was a retired United Airlines pilot, trained in both the 757 and the 767, the two planes used on 9/11. But the real mind-blower is here. He was at one time a pilot for the Central Intelligence Agency," Ruth Ann exclaimed. "Oh, Mark, you don't suppose we have stumbled on what he was looking for, do you? Could the CIA have moved their operation from Marana to Mojave? Might this retired pilot, turned author, have been digging around the wrong boneyard?"

"It's hard to say. Wasn't he the guy that still believed that nineteen radicalized Muslims were flying those planes? I seem to recall his story when it hit the news, and when I looked at his book it made no sense to me that he would be murdered. If you're promoting the official story line that the planes were piloted by hijackers from the Middle East, there's no reason for you to be murdered. But the story of his death never sat right with me. The whole thing stank of a professional hit. From what I could tell, he was a retired pilot who had separated himself from the CIA years earlier. He claimed he had found something new he was intending to put into his next book, and nobody else knew what he had found."

Ruth Ann had been busy reading several websites about the retired pilot and his demise. "A retired NSA guy agrees with your suspicion. He writes there were far too many unanswered questions surrounding his death."

"Why wasn't his wife killed?" Mark wondered.

"She was in Turkey on a buying trip. She was starting up a new business," Ruth Ann read from the account.

"I wonder if she ever got that business up and running?" Mark mused.

"Well, now that would be interesting to follow up and see. I wonder why she was in Turkey, if she was from there or had some type of connection to the country," Ruth Ann added.

"Have you read anything about her that might indicate that she was also at one time involved with the Central Intelligence Agency?" Mark asked.

"No, not so far, but not many people believe this man would kill his kids and his dog and then take his own life. None of the neighbors heard any gunshots. Looks like your gut feeling might be right. I'll keep an eye and an ear open for more information on this guy and his wife. Next time I talk to Max and Gil I'll see if either of them knows anything."

The afternoon was slipping behind them, the sunset casting

hues of orange and pink in the desert sky as they pulled the car up to valet parking at the M. The drive seemed to have gone faster than the first time they'd driven it, but this time they had collected and confirmed valuable information which made the day a success.

"Don't be surprised if we hear from Tom soon. He's like a pit bull; once he sinks his teeth into something he's not about to let go," Mark warned as they walked through the lobby toward the elevators.

"I look forward to hearing from him. I'll email the crew back in D.C. with an update when I get into my room. That's about all I have energy for tonight. I hear my soaking tub calling me. I need to take some notes while it's still fresh in my memory. Let's meet for breakfast in the morning. Give me a call and a heads-up about twenty minutes before you want to meet. And I don't know about you, but after these long days of driving, we might have to rent a cabana and have a down day at the pool as well." Ruth Ann laughed, knowing that probably would never happen.

"Sounds like a great plan to me. Let's see what tomorrow brings, rest well, lady. We might be headed off to unknown places again."

fifteen

Jim Bowman was waiting at the security entrance when Dante's Corvette pulled up and was directed to park in the space provided. Farouk and Dante were quickly cleared by the Secret Service. Jim greeted them and introduced himself as another special assistant to the president, working with Max.

"So, you've had quite the morning already, it looks like," he said, looking at Farouk.

"I don't know what I would have done if Mr. Wilcox hadn't come out of nowhere to take control of the situation," replied Farouk.

Dante laughed. "Yeah, you'd still be back on the side of the road talking to those cops, who were probably never going to let you get away because they had no idea what they were investigating."

"What exactly were they investigating? What happened out there?" Farouk asked.

Dante looked at Jim as if to request permission to answer the question. Jim nodded.

"You were ambushed by one or two CIA snipers in an effort to keep you from arriving here on time, which means whatever you are about to tell these gentlemen must be pretty important. The CIA doesn't risk that kind of exposure on anything frivolous," Dante said softly, so as not to intensify Farouk's already obvious concern.

Jim led the way from the security clearing station into the West Wing of the White House. "Our meeting with Max is on the second floor, but I'd be more than happy to give you a quick Cook's tour of the executive offices on the way. I assume this is the first time in the White House for both of you."

Dante balked at the suggestion. "I thought I was kind of done here. I agreed to bring Farouk to you, but I don't really want to get involved in your discussions or investigations. I was under the impression that I'd told Max all I knew. I do have the slug I recovered from the tire, which I'd be happy to give you, but other than that, I can't see why you need me."

Jim was taken back by Dante's attitude. He had read his impeccable service record and just assumed he would be all in to help in any way he could. Leaving now, even before he had the opportunity to meet Max and be fully debriefed, was not anywhere close to military protocol, something Dante should have been expecting. "I'll tell you what, why don't we run upstairs. You can at least meet Max and give him the bullet, and then I suppose you can be on your way."

"I think I can do that. I don't mean to be rude. It's just that this type of involvement is a part of my life I've left behind. It makes me uncomfortable to relive my former experiences, and I'd just as soon stop before I get dragged any farther along that path," Dante said, but inside he was thinking how ironic it was that he was standing in the White House just days after unloading on Jamal and setting things straight with his mother.

Jim led the way, and seemed to forget about the short tour he had mentioned to Farouk. They entered the upstairs conference room and Max stood to greet them. After a few pleasantries, Max asked them to be seated at the table. Jim pulled Max aside and asked to speak with him privately. They stepped into Max's office off the conference room and Max asked, "So, what is it?"

"It's Dante; I don't think he wants to cooperate with us. He's not hostile—he's just not interested in being helpful, and I know we were kind of counting on him to help us with the investigation at Belvoir," Jim answered.

"What's his problem?" Max asked.

"My suspicion is that he is suffering from PTSD. I have no doubt he acted instinctively when he pulled over to save Farouk, but once he had time to think about it all, the disorder kicked in and now he wants to be dismissed. I think Vera might be able to help here."

"Vera? Why Vera?" Max asked, looking puzzled.

"His record indicates the possibility that he might have served with someone Vera met on a flight we took from Salt Lake to Minneapolis. If that's true, she can talk to him on common ground and maybe persuade him to help us," Jim explained. "Why don't you go get the bullet from Dante and rehash the roadside incident, and I'll call Vera and ask her if she can come and lend us a hand."

"Give it a shot, Jimbo," Max said, and he turned to head back into the conference room.

"Vera, Jim here. Remember that chief master sergeant you met on our flight from Salt Lake to meet Max last year?"

"I do; why do you ask?" Vera queried.

"I might have one of his Special Forces buddies down here in Max's conference room. He could be very helpful to our investigations, but he's anxious to get out of here. I think he suffers from PTSD and you might be able to ease some of his anxiety. Could you come down and meet him? And bring Kelli if you can. I think even she might help."

"I'd be glad to. We were just on our way to meet Joel, so it won't be a problem at all," Vera replied.

Jim proceeded to fill Vera in on all the details surrounding Dante and then said, "Thank you, my friend. I know I can always count on you."

Vera laughed. "I'll never be able to repay you, so just keep counting on me."

Jim returned to the conference room and gave Max a nod indicating that Vera was on her way.

"Well, Dante, now that I have the bullet, you're free to go. I can have you escorted back to your car, but I promised Farouk here that he might get the chance to meet the First Lady. She happens to be on her way down, and if you don't mind, I'm sure she'd love to meet you too. So if you can stay just a few more minutes, it would be my pleasure to introduce you both to her," Max said.

"I can do that," replied Dante.

A few moments later, the First Lady and Kelli stood in the doorway to the conference room. Everyone stood up to welcome them. Kelli wandered over and sniffed Dante's pant leg. He patted her on the head and scratched behind one of her ears. Kelli sat down next to where he was standing as if to say, 'I'll take this one.' Everyone smiled, especially those who knew Kelli's knack for choosing men of good character.

"Vera, allow me to introduce you to Farouk and Dante. These two men had quite the harrowing experience this morning, trying to arrive here on time. And we especially appreciate Dante for stepping into a dangerous situation and making sure Farouk arrived safely," Jim said.

Vera stretched out her hand and shook Farouk's. "It is my privilege to make your acquaintance. Max has told me about you, and I want to express my appreciation on behalf of the president for your willingness to respond to his call and step forward with information about what you know."

Farouk mumbled something through the ear-to-ear smile on his face. He caught himself in time to recover and add, "I'm so honored to meet you, ma'am. No one back home will believe me when I tell them, so I think I'll just keep it to myself and remember this moment forever."

Vera smiled warmly. She took both his hands in hers and

said, "I will remember this moment as well. And I will remember you, Farouk, and how much courage you have inside. You are a credit to my country and to yours. Thank you."

Turning to Dante, who was still reaching down with one hand to attend to Kelli, she said, "And thank you, Dante, for your service to this country and for your timely action this morning. You, sir, are the kind of hero who never dies. I'm honored to shake your hand and make your acquaintance."

"The pleasure is mine, ma'am. Thank you for taking the time to come and meet us. It means a lot to us," Dante replied.

"Oh, by the way, Dante, Jim tells me you were Special Forces in Afghanistan. Would you happen to know a Gary Gill?" Vera asked.

Dante's eyes became wide. "Why yes, ma'am, Gary Gill was the best weatherman in the military. We executed many a mission together. I haven't heard from him since I retired, but if you have his contact information, I would love to get in touch with him again."

"I think that can be arranged, but if you know Gary Gill then I know some things about you. If you have the time I'd like to talk to you about them," Vera suggested.

"If it won't take too long, I'd be happy to talk with you," Dante agreed.

"Well then, Max, if Dante is through here, Kelli and I will see to it that he gets everything he needs," Vera said.

"Thank you, Vera, that'll be terrific. Dante, thank you once more, and I hope to see you again," Max responded.

Dante nodded at Max and Jim and shook Farouk's hand. Then he followed Vera out of the conference room, with Kelli close by his side.

As they made their way into the hallway, Vera stopped and turned to face Dante. "I was actually on my way to see my husband when Jim called me and asked me to stop by and meet you and Farouk. Do you mind accompanying me to his office?"

"The Oval Office, the President of the United States—you want me to come with you? I don't think that would be such a great idea, ma'am. I have no business seeing the president. No, I would prefer not to do that," Dante pleaded.

"Dante, I know what happened to you at Tora Bora. The president knows what occurred there, and earlier in Kabul. I have no doubt he would like to apologize to you," Vera explained.

"But he wasn't the president at the time, and I've tried to forget about that. He owes me nothing," Dante replied.

"Trust me on this; it will be good for you both to meet. He needs you and you need him," she said, not taking no for an answer and proceeding down the hall. Kelli nudged Dante forward, as if she knew what they had been talking about and was sure Dante needed her help. Reluctantly, he followed the First Lady, and Kelli followed behind him.

When they got to the executive offices, Vera told the secretary to inform the president that she was here and that she had a guest with her. The secretary did as she was asked, and within a few moments the president was standing before them. He leaned forward and kissed Vera on the cheek, and patted Kelli on the head. Then he asked, "And whom do I have the pleasure of meeting?"

Dante felt like he needed to salute, but before he could say or do anything, Vera said, "Joel, this is Dante Wilcox, a retired veteran of the military, today's special hero, and a comrade of Gary Gill in Tora Bora, among other places."

"Mr. Wilcox, I don't know how you managed to find your way to my office this morning. As you know, not just anyone can wander in here, but I have to believe there's a certain amount of divine providence that made it possible for you to be standing before me right now, and I'm truly honored that you are. Please come into the Oval Office and let's talk for a minute. I have some idea of the pain you are going through, and I want to listen to what you have to say." With his open hand he pointed in the direction of his office, and placed the other around Dante's shoulders, hoping to reassure him that all would be well. Vera led the way and seated herself on one of the couches in the center of the room. The president sat beside her and motioned for Dante to be seated across from them. Kelli chose to climb up on Dante's couch and rest her head in his lap, hoping he would continue to scratch her.

"That dog is a perfect judge of character. The fact that she's sitting there near you and acting as if you've been her friend forever tells us all we need to know about you. You're honest, your heart is pure, you would do anything for a stranger, and you have exceptional intelligence. Is there anything I've left out?" the president asked.

Dante smiled and patted the dog again. "It must drive her crazy when congressmen visit your office."

Vera burst out laughing. "She's never invited to the State of the Union addresses. That might give her a doggy heart attack."

When the smiling subsided, the president said, "Dante, I know what happened to you, Gil and the others in Tora Bora. That decision could only have come from this office, or someone acting out of this office. I can't imagine what you've been going through all these years, knowing you went to serve your country, and your country was busy serving itself and its own private agenda at the hands of evil."

"Mr. President, I did my duty. I obeyed my orders and the chain of command. I was loyal to my country and I stood by her even when I had no idea what she was doing. I never openly questioned and I never refused to take part or to help, but I'm afraid that burden was too heavy to carry and it's destroying me from the inside out," Dante tried to explain.

"This country and its Commander in Chief have no right

to ask you to bear that burden alone. And yet, I'm afraid that's what's happened to thousands of terrific men and women who, like yourself, gave everything. And when you had nothing left to give, you were given the shaft and pushed through its opening. Now you're in free fall with no hope in sight. Am I correct?" the president asked.

"I've been searching for a metaphor to describe how I feel, and what you just illustrated is as accurate a picture as could ever be painted. Yes, sir, you are correct," Dante replied.

"You've suffered long enough, my friend. It's time you found the peace you so well deserve," Vera added.

"But how does that happen? I don't see a way out. The torment and guilt is unbearable at times, and you must know I've taken it out on the government, on the military and even on you, Mr. President. You represent the beast that has wrapped its tentacles around everything I hold dear. When I can't breathe, it's because you are sucking the life out of me," Dante said.

The president got up from where he was sitting and moved to the other couch, sitting down next to Kelli. He stroked the dog's back a time or two and then said, "I don't take that personally, Dante—I'm sure if I were where you are I would feel the same way. But you need to know I'm fighting your battle. I'm fighting against a nation's apathy, and against fifteen years of the public being brainwashed with a concocted story. I'm fighting against a Congress that is so entrenched in serving themselves that they no longer have any regard for the truth. Lies, cover-ups, and shifted responsibility are all my enemies. They try and thwart me at every turn. They place roadblocks in front of me to slow me down, and they craft their secret works so as to obscure the truth from all light. And yet, I'm not deterred because I have right on my side and honest men and women, like yourself, who buoy me up when it becomes more than I can bear. I lost my first wife in this battle, but I've been blessed with a second wife who is now the love of my life, and whose vision of truth and determination to expose it knows no equal. Together we are committed to get to the bottom of 9/11 and to prosecute those responsible for its execution and its cover-up. Forgive yourself and move forward with us. Let a flicker of our hope begin to once again shine in your soul, and with its light be able to see clearly. Don't let them win. Help me, help us, and help yourself to freedom from guilt, darkness and the gall of bitterness."

Dante sat in silence, stroking Kelli's head and thinking about what the president had just said. The words had pierced the barriers he had been building for years, to protect himself from the lies and evil in which he had participated. He knew what President Sherman had said was correct, but he wasn't certain he had the strength to overcome the shackles that bound him to indifference.

Vera could sense the agony that the battle inside was creating for Dante. She called the dog over to her so that she could have Dante's undivided attention. When his eyes finally met hers she said, "This morning when shots rang out and you knew it was sniper fire, you automatically reacted to save Farouk because that's who you are. There was no fight in you to resist or to hold back. You drew from your experience and risked your own life because you knew your importance to the greater good. In a sense, that's exactly what you're facing now. You've heard Joel's call to help. You're aware of the sniper fire that surrounds this country. Be the Dante that saved Farouk."

Vera's words more than pierced the barriers; they pierced his soul. Tears began to well up in the hardened soldier's eyes. He quickly wiped them away and stood at attention, facing the president. With a salute and a voice full of resolve he said, "Dante Wilcox, reporting for duty, sir."

sixteen

Max looked up from his desk and was pleasantly surprised to see Dante standing in the doorway. No words were exchanged as he motioned to an empty chair and Dante followed the invitation with his eyes. He stood quietly for a moment, staring, before he allowed his body to saunter over to the vacant seat and slump down into the comfortable cushions. He composed himself and looked Max directly in the eyes. "They'll try to make me pay for this, you know," Dante said, in a soft but all-too-knowing voice.

Max nodded and said, "And yet here you are. Was it the dog?" The slight smile on Dante's face told him all he needed to know. "Once Kelli exposed your soul to those two, there was no place left for you to hide, was there?"

"Well, something like that," Dante confessed.

"I think we both know you've paid the price already. There's nothing more they can extract from you," Max responded to the original claim.

"They'll go after my mother in an attempt to stop or silence me, and if that doesn't work, then and only then will they come after me. It's not what I know; it's what they think I know and who I might expose to the truth. In reality, they're cowards, but they're vicious cowards capable of anything in an attempt to preserve their lies. It's the lies they think shield them from exposing their constant desire to control and acquire their advantages, profits and rewards. In other words, the lies obscure the hiding place of their god."

Max listened to Dante with an uncommon intensity. It was

as if he was hearing himself speak words he would never utter out loud. Max kept his thoughts to himself, hoping others might pick up on their message through his actions. It was refreshing to hear Dante express the truth so simply, in a way that left no room for confusion. Max leaned forward and spoke slowly. "You don't need to explain anything to me. I've been where you are, and I know what it's like to be targeted and what it feels like when they think they've taken you out. And we're not going to let them do that to you or your mother."

The words Dante heard Max speak did little to assuage his concern for his mother's safety, but the way Max delivered the message galvanized his confidence that he had made the correct decision to help the president. It caused him to realize Max was definitely his ally, and they were in this fight together. That was a feeling Dante had not experienced for a long time, but one he knew he could trust.

"So how can I help?" Dante asked.

"I don't know how much Farouk told you about why he was coming to see me. It had to do with Fort Belvoir and his daily travel route to work, which was abruptly blocked on the morning of September 10th. That, combined with some other information we have received, has led me to believe that if a missile hit the Pentagon on the morning of September 11th, there's a good possibility it was launched from someplace on that base. So, my question is, what do you know about portable tomahawk cruise missiles, and where on that base might be a good launch site for such a weapon?"

Dante rolled his eyes, finding it hard to believe Max was asking him, a sniper, about that kind of military ordinance. The only problem was that he had some limited experience with that very kind of scenario, but the mission was so top secret that there was no way Max could have known he had been involved. He had been chosen with one other sniper group to protect an operation led by the CIA to launch a missile from Syria into Iraq, and to make it appear as if the Russians had become involved in the conflict. They managed to secure a warhead stolen from the Ukraine to an American tomahawk, smuggled it into Syria, and launched it in the dead of night. Two minutes into the flight the order came down to self-destruct. The agent in charge did as he was commanded, and immediately the trucks were on the road back across the border towards Mosul with perfect plausible deniability. A recon team was assigned to pick up what was left of the warhead, and as far as Dante knew the mission was never again mentioned.

Without trying to sound as if his one experience made him an expert, he calmly said, "I can probably show you the kind of location that would be necessary to launch such an attack. No guarantees, but you just don't pull into a parking lot, point and shoot. You're going to have to recover the boot, which means you have to have a pretty good idea where you want it to land."

Max rubbed his hands together and almost came out of his chair. "Good. Let's go on a little field trip with Jim and Farouk and see what's out there. I'll have the chairman of the joint chiefs arrange for us to be invited onto the base and then summarily ignored, so we can roam around at our pleasure without an escort. They won't like that much, knowing the military, but it pays to have friends in authority when you need them."

Dante smiled.

Jim and Farouk joined Max and Dante in Max's office to go over the route they planned to take entering Fort Belvoir. The initial purpose of the trip was to get a good visual of what someone might have seen while traversing the fort on Highway 1. Farouk explained to them the exact route he took every morning, and the men wanted to see for themselves what that road might reveal. The secondary purpose was to spend more time exploring the base, and to ascertain the location from which a tomahawk missile might have been launched. That part of the expedition needed to exclude Farouk.

"When we get through the fort, I've arranged for a driver to take you back home," Max said, looking at Farouk. "Your car was impounded by the State Police, but I've taken care of that and had it towed to a repair shop. Hopefully, by the time you and the driver arrive at the shop, your car will be ready to go. If not, he'll take you to Fredricksburg and I'll arrange to have your car delivered to you tomorrow. Are you okay with all that?"

Farouk smiled and replied, "Well, I was kind of wondering how I was going to get home and where my car was, not to mention how I was going to get it back in drivable condition, so that all sounds terrific and I thank you for being so helpful and considerate."

"That's the least we could do for someone like you, who's been so willing to sacrifice your time to help us," Jim said. "And in your case, you almost sacrificed much more than just your time," he added.

"With that all taken care of, I believe our car is waiting for us, and time's a-wasting," Max said, pointing to the door.

Jim drove, with Farouk in the front seat. Dante and Max hopped in the back, where they were pleased to be able to continue their conversation. It was clear the two of them were establishing a friendship based on a mutual respect that drew from their similar life experiences. They left D.C. along the beltway, and headed down I-95. Once they had passed the intersection with Highway 1, they turned the car around and headed north as Farouk directed. The entrance to Fort Belvoir was just a few miles off the freeway. The MP's at the gate were obviously expecting them. Once they checked Jim's retired military ID, they saluted him and counted to see if there were three other people in the car, then waved them through.

"I never liked generals much, but I guess they do come in

handy every now and again," Max piped up from the back seat once Jim rolled up the window. Dante and Jim laughed, knowing exactly what Max meant by that comment. Farouk looked slightly bewildered, but tried to laugh anyway, which caused the rest of them to laugh even harder. They drove through the base on Highway 1, looking in all directions for what a civilian might see while driving that route. For the most part the road led through the base, but there wasn't much to see. Most of the buildings were off to the left, and far enough back from the road that it was difficult to tell what they were for or what, if anything, they housed. They all seemed to have ample parking lots, but few cars in them. There were large areas of property on both sides of the highway, filled with deciduous trees or expansive fields of grass. Before long, they were at another guard booth on the opposite end of the base.

"There doesn't seem to be anything out of the ordinary here. It looks very much like it did fifteen years ago," said Farouk. "Can you tell me why they closed it down to us daily commuters?"

"I don't rightly know, Farouk, but Jim, why don't you turn this baby around and we'll drive through a few more times before we meet up with Farouk's driver. Maybe there's something we didn't see that's important," Max said.

They drove in silence back across the base, and then turned around once more to return to the far gate to let Farouk out. As they approached the north gate, Jim immediately spotted the car and driver that had been sent to collect Farouk. He pulled up close and signaled to the driver that this was the vehicle he was sent to meet.

Max got out of the car and opened the door for Farouk. Jim and Dante followed, and each of them shook Farouk's hand. "I can't thank you enough for coming today, Farouk. I know we didn't see anything earth-shattering, but your contribution to this investigation has been important. I hope your car's ready, and I'm really sorry to have put you through so much trouble, but we got to meet Dante here as a result, so it wasn't all bad," Max said.

"I thank you for your kindness and help, and especially want to thank you again, Dante, for saving my life. I hope you find what you're looking for out here. Remember, if you need me for anything I'm at your service, but send a limo next time," Farouk said, jokingly.

Jim opened the door to the back seat of the car and Farouk slid inside. Max signaled to the driver as Dante waved a final goodbye. The three of them stood in silence for a moment until Dante said, "You didn't think they were going to launch a missile from the highway, did you?"

"Not hardly, but after having had a brief look at this place, it's secluded enough that they could have done almost anything they wanted and no one would have been the wiser. I'm more convinced than ever that this base has a secret to share, and we're going to snoop around until we find out what it is," Jim replied.

The three of them climbed back into the car and methodically began to traverse the base, driving on every side road that looked interesting. It didn't make sense to drive through the base looking at the buildings, which were concentrated in a central corridor bisected by Highway 1. There was nothing out of the ordinary in that confined space; it was mostly the type of structures found on any military base: hospital, commissary, BX, military housing and general maintenance. The specific structures, like the Missile Defense Agency, were located in a more separated area, but still near the central corridor.

"I'm looking for a secluded area that is isolated from the rest of the base. All of these trees here would have been in full foliage in September. A launch team would have had all the privacy they required," Dante explained to Max and Jim.

Max concurred, "He makes a good point, Jim. Take the roads

that lead away from the main highway into more secluded areas. Anything that looks interesting, we'll explore in greater detail."

"Got it, gentlemen," Jim responded.

Jim took Warren Road out of the central area of the base, which led to Fort Belvoir's outdoor recreation area. Almost immediately the landscape changed to dense trees and underbrush. They drove up a side road that opened up into a large lot that looked like a construction yard. There were stacks of building materials piled up throughout the yard, and several vehicles in various states of disrepair. Jim had no choice but to drive around the lot, as the road in was the only way out. Dante looked at Max and shook his head no. Max pointed back to Warren Road and Jim turned right out of the construction yard. They passed a few roads on the left that they could see didn't lead anywhere, but about fifteen hundred feet farther ahead they saw a turnoff to the right marked Thayer Road.

"Turn here, Jim. This looks interesting," Dante said, looking straight ahead through the trees to what appeared to be a slight clearing.

Jim had barely made the turn and headed up the road when an MP truck with flashing lights pulled in behind them and grazed their back bumper, compelling them to pull over. Two MP's climbed out of the truck and approached the car from both sides. Jim rolled down both the front windows to see what they wanted.

The officers arrived at the windows at the same time. The officer on the passenger side placed his hand on his side arm, while the officer at the driver's side window bent down to inform Jim, in no uncertain terms, "This road is off limits to all vehicles and to all personnel."

Max smiled and indicated he would handle this. In fact, it was the exact kind of situation into which he loved to insert his whole personality. Looking past Jim and making sure the officer on the driver's side could see his face, he asked, "Under whose authority is this road closed, and who says we're prohibited from driving on it to the end?"

It was obvious the officer wasn't pleased with the question, and he took a step back so he could get a better look at Max. He too placed his right hand on his side arm and in his most authoritative voice replied, "Under the authority of the commanding officer of this base. I'm ordering you to back off this road or I'll place you all under arrest."

"Is that right?" questioned Max, not allowing the officer to respond. "We happen to be here under the authority and direction of the Commander in Chief—you've heard of him, President Joel Sherman—and the last I checked he sort of trumps anything your commanding officer has to say, now doesn't he?"

"That would be correct, sir," replied the officer.

"Now here's what I suggest you do. You call in to your superiors and report the make and model of this vehicle, along with who you can see inside. And then you wait for them to tell you to get the hell out of our way and allow us to go where we wish to go. If you can do that, I'll forget what a pain in the ass you both have been and all will be forgiven. If not, then I'm going to have to call the chairman of the joint chiefs, who arranged for us to be here, and report you both. Any questions?"

The officer on the passenger side remained, while the lead officer returned to the truck and could be seen making a phone call. A few minutes later he motioned to his partner to come back to the truck and they slowly backed off of Thayer Road and onto Warren Road, headed towards the interior of the base. Jim turned to Max and asked, "So what do you think that was all about?"

Before he could answer Dante piped up and said, "I think you've found your secret, and those boys weren't reporting back to their superiors—they were reporting to their CIA handler.

That means they know we're on to something, but aren't sure what, and I can promise you they won't forget. Now let's go see what's up this road that's so all-important that they want to keep the president from knowing."

Jim put the car in drive and proceeded the short distance up the road. They came to a paved clearing about an acre in size, completely surrounded by trees. Around the perimeter of the site were a few storage huts, some flatbed trailers and their accompanying tractors. Several vehicles used for loading and moving pallets could be seen tucked away in corners, but for the most part the paved space was wide open. Max directed Jim to pull the car into the center of the lot and turn the engine off. They climbed out of the car and stood looking around at the secluded nature of the location, and the collection of mostly junk that was stored there. "Unless there are some deep dark secrets in those storage sheds, there's not much here that would warrant such tight security," Jim commented.

Max looked at Dante, who was deep in thought, and who then began to pace off a few distances in the middle of the lot. "Have you ever seen a tomahawk cruise missile?" Dante asked.

"Not exactly," responded Max.

"They're transported covered by encasements, on flatbed trucks with special trailers that allow them to be raised above the horizon. The trailers are longer than your typical commercial carrier trailer, which has a regulated length for US interstates, so you're rarely going to see them on a highway without escort vehicles, and then only if they can't be transported by an Army train. This lot is the perfect location for launching such a missile. Look, it's elevated, surrounded by trees, and access to it can be closed off very easily."

"Do you think this is the location from which they launched the missile that hit the Pentagon?" Jim inquired.

"If it is, it would make sense they would close the base to

civilians on the 10th. That missile would have been stored at Langley and would have needed to be transported here a day early to be set up and properly programmed. If they brought that thing through the base it would have caused traffic problems, and it would have been remembered and questioned. Of course military personnel rarely question anything," Max interjected with a laugh.

"That's right. Now look how perfect this spot is," added Dante. "If they had launched the missile towards the river, the boot could have been dropped in either Accotink Bay or Gunston Cove, and may not even have had to be recovered. Send some divers down there, and you might even find it after all these years. Remember you can program these missiles to do anything. It could have taken off to the south and then flipped around so fast no one would have even noticed, and if you had wanted to put the 270-degree corkscrew turn in as ascribed to Flight 77, you could have done that easily. How far is the Pentagon from this spot, in a direct line?"

"I would guess about fifteen miles," Jim responded.

"At nearly seven hundred miles per hour, that's about a minute and a half flight time. Give it two minutes tops to run through its flight program. If they had closed the recreation area, or even just closed Warren Road that day, so that no one was in the recreation area, I doubt anyone would have seen a thing. And coming out of a dense forest like this, by the time it had acquired its target and was heading at full speed towards D.C., it wouldn't have formed a hint of a memory in anyone's mind," Dante explained.

"So you're sure this is the spot?" asked Jim.

"If this was all I'd seen, I'd be very confident this was the spot, but the fact we were stopped trying to enter this location when in reality there's nothing here—it's been fifteen years and they're still protecting it from prying eyes—tells me all I need to know.

You've found what you were looking for, boys. Now, what do you plan to do with this information?" Dante asked.

Max smiled. "You just leave that to me, my friend. When the time is right, this little field trip will prove to be a cornerstone in our investigation, and we couldn't have done it without you. You have my deepest gratitude—for what you know, what you've done, and particularly, who you are."

Dante could still feel a hint of hesitation in his resolve to be helpful, but this new and glaring revelation of truth accompanied by fearless and stalwart men such as Jim and Max focused the light that was returning to his soul directly upon the road ahead, and he was determined to follow wherever it led.

seventeen

Ruth Ann woke up to see a message from Tom on her Skype feed. He wanted to chat with her. She quickly grabbed her robe and changed her Skype status to 'online,' hoping he was still available. She messaged him back with an invitation to call anytime.

Tom was anxious to share what he had found. "There's something odd in the facility logs from the air traffic control centers. I wanted to run this past the two of you and get your opinion."

Ruth Ann got out her notepad and began taking notes.

"When an air traffic controller begins their shift," Tom began, "they do certain tasks and log details about their facility; these are details that affect that facility only. If, for example, certain runway lights are out of service or a radar array is giving them a problem or a radio frequency is full of static, that type of information is recorded in the log. Generally, these logs are written by hand and then fed into a machine that actually prints them. I have the computer printouts, but have been unable to locate the original handwritten logs." Tom paused, making sure Ruth Ann was following him.

He continued, "When I gathered all these pages of logs together and started reading through them, I discovered that around nine that morning, until after eleven, nearly every air traffic control tower or center was evacuated. What struck me as even more strange was that these logs all state that they were evacuated—our term would be 'ATC Zero'—but they don't say who ordered the evacuation or why. That detail should have been noted."

"Can you elaborate on that?" Ruth Ann asked.

"Sure," Tom said. "Let's say I receive a bomb threat out at the LA Center in Palmdale. My phone rings and someone on the other end says they've placed a bomb at our facility. I would note in the log, 'received a bomb threat via phone call, bomb squad called, evacuated center for thirty minutes.' Most of these logs from the northeast sector state 'ATC Zero,' meaning that there is nobody at the radar screens watching air traffic, but not one of them lists a reason. Then there is a time logged that they have returned to normal staffing. So, during a time when FAA headquarters and even NORAD thought there could be a dozen or more hijacked planes in the skies, nearly every air traffic control center around the northeast sector was evacuated at some point. I'll be digging deeper and organizing all the multiple copies I find, but it's beginning to look like something very strange was going on with our air traffic controllers that morning. Also, I found hundreds of copies of timelines or chronologies from that day, and they are all telling a very different story from what we were told by the government and the media. There appear to be more than two hundred versions of the chronology for the events of 9/11."

Ruth Ann had continued to take notes as Tom talked. She had no way of knowing, nor did anyone else on the team, what a facility log 'should' look like. She was trying to follow along with what Tom was saying and take notes in order to share the information with Max back in D.C. "Tom, it's amazing that you're able to see anomalies so quickly. What do you make of it?"

"I have to be honest with you, Ruth Ann; I'm not sure what to make of this. It's highly unusual," Tom admitted. "I'll continue to go through these files—there are a lot of redundancies and it's not an easy project. I'm beginning to feel like I'm looking for a needle in a haystack, and I happen to know from personal experience that nobody can build a haystack bigger or better than the government. Call it intuition, but I'm getting a sick feeling in my stomach that that might be exactly what's going on. Someone is hiding something. I'll compile a list of things that strike me as abnormal in these facility logs and the chronologies, and see if anything jumps out at me. All I can say at this time is, my spidey-senses are on high alert."

"You're saying there are almost two hundred timelines for that one day?" Ruth Ann asked, not certain she had heard Tom correctly or understood what he was referring to.

"That's correct; these are all timelines for September 11, 2001, the day that changed our world forever," Tom answered.

"I'll call back to the team members. I don't know what Bob had shared with them, if anything, but I'll soon find out and let you know. Tom, your help is greatly appreciated, and I know I'm speaking for the rest of the research team as well as the president and first lady."

"My pleasure. Ruth Ann, this gives me something fun to do. Retirement is sometimes lacking in excitement. It's either too hot or too windy to do much in my yard, and after I got that water feature built, I kind of hit the wall. This project of yours is right up my alley," Tom said, looking forward to the challenge.

Ruth Ann assured Tom she'd be available throughout the day in case he discovered anything else unusual. As soon as they hung up, she quickly dialed up Max and told him about the peculiar details Tom had shared. She was right; this was new information to them. If Bob had ever been aware of these anomalies, he hadn't shared it with anyone.

Max reminded her once more of the purpose of her 'vacation,' but thanked her nevertheless for her dogged determination to get to the bottom of these files and uncover anything that was hidden from the public.

"Max, I'm relaxing as much as I can, but the opportunity to

get the help that has popped up here—well, it's just too good to pass up. When things line up like this, it makes me think about my grandparents up in heaven, and I wonder if they might be directing the action down here. I feel like we're about to discover something our eyes might not have ever seen without the help we're receiving. Tom looks at these files and immediately sees things are amiss. His gut is leading him and you know that feeling, Max. The universe might be ready for a shift in consciousness, as they say. The truth about 9/11 will be uncovered and every piece of the puzzle will be put into place."

"I love your positive attitude, Ruth Ann. I hope you head back to Washington soon," Max said. As much as Max wanted her to relax and enjoy herself in Las Vegas, he knew she was right. The team was on the verge of discovery and they worked best when they were together in one place.

eighteen

"Dante, I thought the world had come to an end last night when you asked to stay over," Dora said, "and now here you are again, well past supper time, so I can only assume you've become homeless. What's up with you, boy?"

"I thought I'd stop by to see if your mother's intuition was alive and well, or if I'm going to need to prime its pump," he replied.

"Now, what are you talking about? I know you're not getting married, and I can't imagine you accepted a job from anyone, since you hate being told what to do. And please tell me you aren't moving to Baltimore with Jamal," she said, almost laughing.

"Nope, none of that stuff, but guess who I ran into today just by chance?" Dante shot back.

"Oh hell, I don't know. The President of the United States," Dora flippantly replied.

Dante's eyes grew big and he stared at his mother. "Have you been spying on me?"

"I gots better things to do with my time than spy on you. I've never known from one minute to the next where you were for most of your life, so what makes you think I'm going to try and keep tabs on you now? So tell me, who did you run into? Not your father, I hope," she said, smiling.

Dante stood stunned and quiet, not knowing how to answer her. He should have known better than to challenge her, because she was always right, even when she wasn't serious. Instead of responding, he walked past her, found his favorite chair, and positioned himself in a comfortable way that told his mother he was there to talk. Dora followed behind and sat quietly on the couch, waiting for some kind of an answer, or at least an explanation for his abnormal behavior. When enough time had passed that she felt she might not get an answer, she stood up and started to walk into the kitchen.

"No, wait, sit back down, mama. I'll tell you. I'll tell you what I did today," Dante instructed. "I actually did meet with the president and first lady in the Oval Office."

"Oh shut my mouth, you hate those two," Dora responded.

"I thought I did, but I was deeply mistaken. I'm now working with the president's team to get to the bottom of 9/11, and that potentially puts both you and me in danger," Dante explained with a sigh.

He then proceeded to tell her all of the events of the day—from rescuing Farouk, to meeting President Sherman and his wife, and finally the tour of Fort Belvoir. He took the time to explain how he felt and how those feelings began to transform as they drew strength from the principles she had taught him in his youth. Dante recognized those same core beliefs in the president, which had begun to melt away his hostility towards him and his policies. He also told her about Max and how they had formed an instant friendship, which allowed him to open up about things he knew concerning 9/11. Most importantly, he expressed to her his thanks for continuing to have faith in him even when it seemed all his hope had been spent. As mothers do, she continued to love him even when he was not particularly lovable. Dora began to weep. Dante rose from his chair and sat next to her. He put his arms around her and held her tight. It was something they both needed, and communicated all the emotions that had been buried for many years.

"I can't begin to tell you how proud I am of you, son," Dora began.

"No need, mama, I just needed your strength to remind me who I was. When I saw many of your qualities in the president and the first lady, I knew what I had to do in spite of the risks and dangers."

Dora wiped the tears from her eyes and sat up straight so she could look Dante in the eye. "Now, that's the second time you've said something about danger. What are you trying to say?"

"Mama, I know these people we're fighting against. I've worked with them. I know their tactics. Mostly I know they'll do anything to keep from being exposed. If they think for a moment I might be working with the president to uncover their involvement in 9/11, they'll stop at nothing to silence me. That means they'll even come after you if they think it'll prevent me from helping or from revealing what I know."

Dora shook her finger in front of Dante's face. "Now that's just plain ridiculous. Who would want to harm an old woman who's not the least bit afraid of them, and who would gladly exit this wicked, cruel world if it meant helping to uncover the truth about their dastardly deeds?"

"I don't think you understand. Do you remember hearing about that pilot that wrote a book about 9/11 few years back? He was one of them, worked with them even longer than I did. Apparently he got too close to uncovering something they wanted to remain hidden and they were afraid he was about to expose what he knew. They showed up at his house and shot his two kids and his dog before they put a bullet into him. Oh, they tried to make it look like he was the culprit in a murder/suicide, but anyone with a little common sense and some knowledge of how these bastards operated knew it was a hit. I don't want that to happen to you," Dante explained.

Dora smiled and shook her head. "Nothing's going to happen to me. I have no doubt you can protect me and even if you can't, I'll die a happy woman, knowing I've lived a good life, raised great children and fought the battle to the very end. There's comfort in that, son, a lot of comfort."

"Of course I'll do everything in my power to protect you, but I'll need your help. These guys don't just waltz into your house, guns a-blazing. They do a lot of surveillance work and planning so they don't get caught. That means if you see anything unusual outside when you are working in the garden, you let me know."

"What do you mean, unusual?" she asked.

"If you see a car or a van that you don't recognize parked nearby, or if anyone comes to the door and asks you questions that don't quite feel right to you, chances are they're scoping you out and charting your daily patterns. Look, Mama, your intuition is flawless—you proved that again tonight. If it doesn't pass the scratch and smell test, you contact me immediately. I'll worry about what to do next, but I need your eyes and ears on full-time alert. I don't mean to scare you, but please be vigilant," Dante instructed.

"I ain't scared. You've just pushed my busybody tendencies into action and given me something to do besides tend to my flowers and trim plants. And you tell that President Sherman I'm now on the job, working around the clock for him and his quest for information," she said with a laugh in her voice.

"Oh, I'll be sure to let him know, count on that," Dante replied.

nineteen

Ruth Ann felt restless. She tossed and turned most of the night, finding sleep to be impossible. She finally gave in, arose, put on her robe, and headed downstairs to the living room area of her suite. She sat looking out through the wall of windows to the Strip side of the room. The jungle of megalithic casinos with their high-tech flashing signs off in the distance filled her view. For some reason, her mind reflected upon the potential terror attack that targeted Vegas, detailed on the recorder pen that Vera had brought back from Grace's room in Paris. Had she and Jim not listened to that recording in time, President Sherman could never have prevented the thousands of deaths that would have resulted from that attack. Had all six of the planned attacks occurred, it could have led to total chaos in the streets of America, possibly martial law and the total abandonment of the Constitution.

A peculiar anxiousness began to surround her. In moments such as these she wished her grandparents were still alive and just a phone call away. She had grown up listening to their incredible tales of survival before they immigrated to the United States. Their stories always filled her with inspiration and hope. A large part of her needed that now. Somehow she had to replace her anxiety with something solid she could grab hold of and trust. She reflected back on the meeting in Randsburg and could sense that Tom knew the exact people to help him find what he called the needle in the haystack. Finding that missing piece would transform her anxiety into excitement. She could feel good news was coming soon.

That thought was just the spark she needed to open her laptop and click open a folder that contained hundreds of documents on 9/11. She clicked on the DEA report, sixty pages of the most incredible, yet overlooked story of the year preceding that fateful day. How could anyone inside the government not think these foreign art students were, at minimum, a security threat? She wondered. As she read through the report she recognized some of the names; being Jewish herself, she was familiar with many of the uniquely Jewish surnames. These young Israelis, claiming to be art students, had been discovered all across the country on various federal properties. They were found on military bases, and at the homes and offices of several federal agents including DEA agents, US Marshals, and even agents for the Internal Revenue Service. One astute government employee thought the students were worth looking into after he was asked about his building's security. That wasn't a question he expected from a foreign art student selling prints door to door. He began to gather data from other federal agencies about similar visits from these young students. The information that came to light was more than disturbing, and his report continued to grow. It stated that the art students' suspicious behavior had started in the spring of 2000. Many of the phone numbers associated with the students were linked to a massive Israeli drug ring that was under investigation in Florida, California, Texas and New York.

Some of the students had also been arrested carrying counterfeit Social Security cards, while others had been charged with marijuana possession or passport irregularities. One female student showed up at the front door of an EPA special agent's home to sell art, returning later to photograph his house. Another student was reportedly seen diagramming the layout of a federal facility. Many were found to be in possession of airline tickets for various dates into and throughout the year 2001. Of particular interest was one student whose father was a retired two-star general in the Israeli Army. Apparently, this general was so important that Israel named a spy satellite after him. This young man certainly did not need to be selling art in America to support himself, Ruth Ann thought as she continued reading. Just as that thought crossed her mind, she noticed another student of interest. This one claimed to have been a personal bodyguard for the highest-ranking general in the Israeli army, and a demolition expert. Her mind immediately replayed how Building 7 had collapsed late in the afternoon of 9/11, and she remembered seeing with her own eyes what very much appeared to be a controlled demolition.

Ruth Ann clicked open her email and began to write. Max, I've been up all night reviewing that sixty-page DEA report. I know you have this file. The troubling part is that some of the names are very similar to my kidnappers. A number of these 'art students' served in the Israeli Intelligence (Mossad) and many of them were demolition experts, bomb experts, explosive experts and even Patriot missile defense system experts. This is very troubling. Most of these students were arrested for overstaying their tourist visas. Maybe you can have Jerry Reitz look into the immigration status and data on these guys. There are about one hundred twenty-five of them that were supposed to leave the US by July, 2001. That is dangerously or, should I say, suspiciously close to 9/11. Demolition experts would have been very handy, and many of these guys questioned by federal agents said they were going to travel to other cities including New York. Also, run their names against that group of artists from Austria that were living on the ninety-first floor of one of the towers. I seem to recall the name Rubinstein as a member, or perhaps it was on the title page of that book they produced, The B Thing. Call it women's intuition, but I would like to check on when each of these Israelis left the country. Oh, by the way, another thing I found interesting was the language used by some of the US Marshals and others to describe these traveling artists. The same exact description that some of the passengers and crew members used to describe the hijackers: 'middle eastern,' one reported that they were either Israeli or Arabs. And one more detail while it's still fresh in my mind—most of these men were about five foot six or five foot eight, just like the supposed hijackers. Oh shoot, one more detail, they also carried driver's licenses from Florida and California, again, just like the accused Arab hijackers. There are probably more coincidences than that, but it's four in the morning and I'm tired. Let me know what you find out. ~ Ruth Ann

As she clicked on the 'send' button, she felt her exhausted body and mind begin to relax. She took one long last look at the view out her window, then climbed the stairs and crawled back under the covers.

twenty

Max opened the email from Ruth Ann, hoping for some new information. After reading her words and knowing that she had been awake all night consumed with this DEA report, he sent the PDF she had attached over to the printer. He tucked the report into his leather satchel and walked to his favorite coffee shop down the street. It had been some time since he had read the report; he recalled how troubling it had been that no one in the Bush administration thought having over a hundred Israeli military and intelligence operatives posing as art students and snooping around the country was worth a closer look. He remembered seeing the towers collapse and how they looked so similar to movies he had seen of nuclear explosions in the fifties and sixties out at Mercury, Nevada. Max was aware of the DEA report when it was released years after 9/11, and still to this day could not believe that no government agency had connected the traveling art students to the explosions of the towers and Building 7.

"I'll have the usual, little lady." Max smiled at the young waitress as she approached his table.

"I always have to check; you never know when a customer might go off the rails and try something new. I'm sure if I had just brought you the usual, that today would have been your day to try goose dumplings with pecan gravy or something." She laughed at the absurdity. "Your boring usual is coming right up, sir."

Max chuckled at her comment. He wasn't the kind of guy

that deviated much from anything that was usual behavior, but the goose dumplings did pique his interest. He opened the DEA report and started reading, occasionally jotting notes on his paper napkin. He read slowly, paying close attention to every detail that the federal agents managed to get from their interviews. Ruth Ann was right; he did need to get Jerry Reitz in on this to double-check these names against the INS data. Several of these Israeli men and women had told federal agents they intended to leave the country in July of 2001. Jerry could easily run their names to see if they had left, or were still around in August and September. Max quickly wrote down 'New York,' followed by a question mark. He knew Ruth Ann had a psychic sense about her at times; she'd laugh and claim it was the presence of her grandparents, but Max had personally witnessed her ability to draw out information by following her gut feelings or intuition. He knew if Ruth Ann was awake most of the night reading this DEA report again, there more than likely was some connection worth further examination.

The coffee shop was unusually quiet and Max was appreciative of that. Suddenly, he heard a familiar voice shout, "Maxwell?" Max looked up from his papers and saw Gil standing in the entryway.

"Gil, buddy, come on over and join me," Max invited.

Gil sat down in the chair across the table just as the waitress approached to fill Max's mug. "Just coffee for me, hon." He smiled and gave a quick nod in her direction. "What do you have there, Max?" he asked.

"Good old Ruth Ann was up all night last night in Vegas, and she emailed me to review this DEA report about the Israeli art students that were roaming all over the country trying to get on military bases and selling cheap artwork to federal employees," Max explained.

Gil nodded knowingly. "Oh yeah, I read that report a while

back. They were Israeli Defense Forces guys, and a few women, too. Several of them were explosive experts, if I recall. Their story about being art students never rang true to me, and I never could understand why they were here. It's more than unusual to go from being a demolition expert with an intelligence agency—in this case the Israeli Mossad—to selling cheap Chinese art prints door to door in a foreign country."

"That visual never quite worked for me either," Max replied. "I figure, if this information is what called out to Ruth Ann and kept her up all night, I'd better take a good hard look at it again. Now that we have easier access to some government agencies, maybe we can find out more information about these characters. As you know, Ruth Ann does have an uncanny way of gravitating to the right pieces of the puzzle."

Gil's coffee arrived and he took a sip. "I do know that about Ruth Ann—too bad her super-senses weren't working when those guys kidnapped her. She was probably preoccupied with that car of hers and let her defenses down. Considering what was supposed to happen to all of us in Chicago, you'd have thought she'd have been on high alert."

"She had a lot on her mind, and I think she felt she was far enough away from Chicago that she was safer than she really was," Max said. "Now, she's connected with some people over in Vegas that are going to be a real big help to our team. She's linked up with some people that only she could have found. I suspect she'll most likely be headed back here soon."

"Well now, that's the kind of information I love to hear," Gil shot back.

Max signaled to the waitress that he was good for one more cup. "Ruth Ann has met some experienced aviation types, including an air traffic controller that can read those radar files none of us could. I hope I'm not too excited about that, but I sense there's something very valuable there that's been hiding in plain sight."

"Max, I have to run, I have a few errands to take care of this morning. I look forward to what Ruth Ann has to share when she gets back. Can't wait for the meeting." Gil wiped his mouth with his napkin, stood, and saluted Max.

"Hey, next time you're here you should try the goose dumplings," Max responded with laugh.

twenty-one

Dante was in a meeting with Max when his cell phone began to vibrate, indicating a call was coming through. Not many people had his number, so when his phone did ring it was usually important. He glanced down at his screen and saw that it was his mother calling. "Max, I need to take this, if you'll excuse me for a moment," he said.

Max did not say anything, but pushed his chair slightly away from his desk and leaned back, indicating that the interruption was acceptable if not entirely welcome.

"Mama, what's up?" Dante asked.

"Your CIA friends paid me a visit this morning, and like you told me, I'm calling to tell you," Dora answered.

"Do you mind if I put your call on speaker? If you're correct, I want Max's input on how we should proceed."

"Fine with me," she said.

Dante looked over at Max and said, "She thinks the CIA paid her a visit this morning, and I want you to hear what she has to say."

Max raised his eyebrows slightly and nodded.

"Okay, mama, tell us what happened."

"A gas company truck pulled up in front of the house this morning as I was doing some weeding in the flowers, and two nice young gentlemen dressed in company uniforms approached me. They introduced themselves and showed me their company ID's. Then they proceeded to tell me that they needed to replace my gas meter with a new improved model that could send my monthly usage directly to the company. They gave me some song and dance about how it would save money in the long run and keep price increases down. But what they wanted to know was when they could make an appointment with me when I would be home for two to three hours. I was immediately suspicious. Why did they come directly to my house and not to any of my neighbors? Anyway, son, I made an appointment with them at nine o'clock in the morning the day after tomorrow. I hope that was okay."

"What makes you think they weren't really from the gas company? I know that's the sort of updating that utility companies are doing these days," Dante asked.

"Your mama wasn't born yesterday. I called the gas company and asked if those two men worked for them. I made a point to remember their names. They had no record of them. Then I asked if they were putting in new meters in my area and they laughed and said it would be five to ten more years before they planned to do that. However, I didn't stop there. I called Marla, whose husband works for the gas company, and she had him call me. I asked him what he thought and his opinion was that I was being set up for a robbery. So what do you think?" she asked.

"I think you probably nailed this one, mama. Let me talk this over with Max and we'll get back to you on what we plan to do. In the meantime, why don't you stay at one of my sisters' houses just to be on the safe side? Can you do that for me?"

"I'll think about that last part. I'm sure you'll figure out what's best to do, and remember I ain't scared, not today, not tomorrow or even the day after. We're going to outsmart these freaks, aren't we?"

Dante looked at Max, covered the phone, and said, "She's a tough old bird."

Max laughed. "Yeah, I had a mother like that too, and your mom just used my favorite word—'freaks.'"

"Okay, mama, we'll get back to you shortly. Keep your eyes open," Dante said.

Dante put his phone back into his pocket and said to Max, "I was right, wasn't I? They either identified me at the fort the other day, or when I was helping Farouk, and decided to act quickly."

"Yup, I'm sure they've scheduled a hit day after tomorrow. My guess is they wanted enough time to take her out, then stage it to look like you killed her. They would then immediately get a warrant for your arrest and you would be snared in a legal battle that would destroy you."

"That's exactly the way they do things. Got any ideas?" Dante asked.

Max stood up and walked towards the door. "Come with me. I have someone I want you to meet that can help us."

Dante followed Max to the lower level of the Executive Offices, then out through the portico that led to the White House. They entered through a side door that was positioned right in front of the Secret Service office on the main floor. Max scanned the area until he found Gordon. Gordon's face lit up when he saw Max, and he stopped what he was doing to greet him.

"Max, to what do I owe the pleasure?" Gordon inquired.

"Gordon, I want you to meet Dante Wilcox, maybe the best sniper the service has ever enlisted, and now working on my team with the president. Dante, this is Gordon Garcia, in my opinion, the finest agent the Secret Service has ever hired, and trust me—he is also Joel and Vera's favorite agent."

Gordon extended his hand to Dante as they greeted one another. "What brings you down to my office, Max? You look a little troubled," Gordon said.

Max pointed to a private office. "Let's move into that office where we can talk undisturbed."

Gordon led the way. Once everyone was seated Gordon asked, "How can I help you, Max?"

Max proceeded to bring Gordon up to date. He explained how Dante had come on board with his rescue of Farouk, and how he had helped explain how a Tomahawk missile might have been launched from inside Fort Belvoir. His update ended with the phone call Dante had just received from his mother.

Gordon listened intently and scribbled a few notes on the paper in front of him. "Where does your mother live, Dante?" he asked.

"In Richmond."

"You obviously explained to her what to be on the lookout for, so she knows her life is in danger. Is she someone we can work with to help solve this dilemma, or do we just need to protect her?" Gordon asked.

Dante smiled and looked at Max, then turned to answer Gordon. "Perhaps you can picture an old woman in her seventies with a Glock in each hand, firing at will as these two clowns come up her walk. That would describe how willing my mother is to do whatever is necessary to stop these guys. Of course, I know that's not a good solution, even though it would make Mama happy. But that's why we're here. Max tells me this kind of thing is right up your alley."

"Were you a sniper with Special Forces?"

"I was," replied Dante.

"Then I have a pretty good idea what your skill level and experience has been. Do you have a rifle with an appropriate scope and silencer for taking these guys out?" Gordon asked.

"From what kind of distance? I don't have the kind of equipment I had back in the day, but if you're talking fifty to a hundred yards, I'm well equipped," Dante replied.

"I don't know. It all depends on what her house and yard are like. Is there anywhere that would give you a good view of the front porch, but allow you not to be seen?"

"Oh yeah, there's a large tree off to the side of the house where a blind and platform could be set up in no time. You're talking a hundred feet at the most," Dante said.

"Does she have patio furniture on her front porch?" Gordon asked.

"She has kind of a bench swing and a few chairs. She likes to sit out on the swing in good weather and feed the birds," Dante explained.

Max shook his head. "Gordon, I don't see what you're driving at here. If you put Dante in a tree and his mom on the porch, you put her at risk if his job is to take them out."

Gordon smiled at Max. "You should know me better than that. My job is to mitigate risk and still succeed. We proved that once before, didn't we?"

"Okay, so what are you thinking?" Max queried.

"Dante can probably understand the concept behind this scenario. When assassins are assigned a hit and they approach the subject only to find them already dead, it throws their plans into chaos. None of their contingencies ever account for such an encounter, and at that point they're vulnerable."

The light came on inside Max's head, and he slammed both palms down on the table in front of him. "Didn't I tell you this guy was good?" he said, looking at Dante.

Dante smiled and said, "You said he was good; you didn't say he was a genius. No wonder the president likes him. I'll leave and go home to prep mama, and acquire the necessary things for the platform and blind in the tree. Then, I think I'll head over to the range for a little target practice. I'll call you tomorrow and let you know we're ready."

Dora was not at all surprised when her son showed up on her door step. She invited him in and he began to explain to her what was about to go down.

Dora listened quietly to the plan as her son explained it to her. She could sense the excitement in his voice, even though she would be putting herself in harm's way. If Dante felt it was the right way to handle the situation, then any fear she might have had dissipated and she was committed to doing her part. Dante spent the rest of the day and part of the following morning in the tree he used to build forts in as a kid. The setup for a platform on which he could lay prone and still have his rifle trained on the front porch was perfect. The tree had more than enough foliage to obscure the blind from both the hit men and the neighbors. His experiences in the service had taught him how to make his position almost invisible. Later that day, Gordon and Max drove down to Richmond and inspected the setup. It couldn't have been more perfect. Again they went over the details of the plan, and told Dora and Dante that they would arrive at eight the next morning to make final preparations. Gordon gave Dante the medication he would need and instructed him on the application and dosage. "Seven-thirty tomorrow morning, give this to her. By the time we arrive, she should be resting comfortably," Gordon explained.

twenty-two

The doorbell rang in Ruth Ann's suite. She was still in bed; her late night reading had left her exhausted. She quickly put on her robe, tying it around her waist, and hurried toward the door.

Through the peephole she could see Mark standing in the hallway with a silly grin on his face, holding two large paper cups of coffee. She wasn't sure what he was up to, but now that she was awake, the thought of coffee seemed very welcome. She opened the door and said, "Good morning. To what do I owe this kind of room service?"

Mark didn't answer; he simply reached out and handed Ruth Ann one of the cups. She gladly took it with both hands and stepped back into the room, indicating for Mark to follow. "Oh, man, how did you know I needed this? Let's sit over here where we can get comfortable and enjoy the view as the sun begins to splash across the mountains." She led the way toward the living room area and curled up in the large leather chair, still clutching her coffee with both hands. After taking several sips she said, "You must be psychic. Did you somehow know that I was up most of the night reading?"

Mark set his cup on the coffee table, lowered his computer bag onto the floor and replied, "And the psychic genie also told me to bring along some pastries, but I had to put them in my bag for the ride up the elevator." He laughed as he fumbled through the pouches of his bag to find the two sacks of pastries, and placed them on the table.

"Oh, this is just wonderful. I can't thank you enough. I suffered from a bit of an anxiety attack last night, and I couldn't quiet my mind. I got up and read through files on my computer. I had this crazy feeling that Bob had uncovered something, but it was so buried in his filing system it might never have been found. I have this feeling your friend Tom is on the verge of finding it, and it's very important. This really could be the break we have been praying for." Ruth Ann sat quietly for a moment, then reached for the pastry bags. "Which one do you want?"

"You choose. I haven't found one thing in that bakery that wasn't my favorite," Mark said with a grin on his face. "I was thinking the same thing last night about Tom. I read more of the documents you gave me, and I guess hindsight really is crystal clear. Looking at the details in those reports makes me feel foolish that I ever believed the official story. The hardest part for me was swallowing the story the media put out about how those 757's were flown. I should have immediately realized that there was no way an inexperienced pilot could pull G's in that bird. That's just not a plane that could have been flown that hard and fast. I wanted to believe the official story to the point that I convinced myself to not look at it with eyes that could see the truth. Who was I to question what we were all being told? So, I just did what I imagine many people, including professional pilots, did: we closed our minds and swallowed the story hook, line, sinker, tackle, and boat. That mentality has about downed this nation."

"I understand exactly what you're saying. The entire nation was brainwashed for at least three years. Then people started to look carefully at those towers exploding and they began to question. The towers did explode; they did not experience a pancake collapse. The story that woke me up came from the janitor that was on one of the basement levels. He heard explosions coming from the lower basement floors. As the elevator doors from the basement opened, one of his coworkers stepped out, his skin just hanging from his arms and face. I knew that the airplanes didn't cause explosions in the basement levels that could have caused that type of injury. This janitor, Rodriguez I think was his name, spoke of multiple explosions throughout the towers that morning. He even mentioned the foreign art students that had been living on the ninety-first floor the year prior to the attacks. When I found that DEA report of the Israeli artists traveling the country, I started to think in a whole new direction. I didn't want to think that our biggest and most trusted ally could have had any part in this. As a Jew myself, it was nearly impossible for me to entertain that thought." She sipped her coffee and broke off a piece of her pastry, then continued, "I had to let go of my own personal preferences, my Jewishness, and my own prejudices to research without emotion. It was very difficult for me, since I feel some strange obligation to the state of Israel. I can't even explain it; I don't know how or why I have it. I didn't enjoy my trip to Israel when I went. I found the people to be unhappy and harsh in their interactions. I don't know, maybe it was instilled in me by my grandparents and the stories of their experiences. Those stories had a profound effect on me."

Mark sat quietly, listening to Ruth Ann's self-diagnosis and observations. He could sense her inner conflict as she spoke, and was amazed that she had overcome it to the point that she could do outstanding research.

Ruth Ann's computer chimed three soft tones, indicating an incoming message on Skype. "It's Tom," she exclaimed. "Here, let me read his message to you. He says: 'I'm finding some interesting discrepancies in these files. I would like to hit it hard for another day, and then I think it would be best for us to meet in person. I realize this is an encrypted computer, but I'm dealing with a touch of paranoia. I'm convinced that none of these details were meant to be uncovered.'"

"Sounds like he might have hit pay dirt," Mark exclaimed,

with more emotion in his voice than Ruth Ann had ever heard from him.

She nodded in agreement as her heartbeat quickened. She typed back to Tom: Sounds great. How does your time look this next week or so?

Tom's message came back instantly. Remember, I'm retired. I'm free as a bird for the next several months. As long as my neighbor will water my yard, I'm up for anything.

Ruth Ann quickly typed: Let's connect tomorrow.

Tom's reply: Yes, I can do that.

Ruth Ann closed the chat box with: Good, tomorrow it is then.

She turned to look at Mark. "I'm going to need to talk to the team in Washington D.C. I can feel in my gut that Tom has found some of the information we've been searching for and never found. The team in D.C., including the president, will want to meet with him and hear this firsthand. It'll take some doing, but I think we're going to head to Washington in the near future. If Tom has found details that have him feeling paranoid, that tells me a lot. He's smart to keep our communication on the down-low. I have firsthand experience that these guys are killers, and they have eyes and ears everywhere."

"Chip has no doubt shared a lot of horrific stories and details about these spooks from his time at Edwards. It's no wonder Tom's feeling nervous. If he thinks he has found information that could be damning, then he knows that it can also be deadly to anyone who has it in their possession," Mark calmly added.

Ruth Ann quietly walked to the other side of the room and stared out the window as the morning sunlight illuminated the Las Vegas Strip in the distance. "I know you were intending to be on a vacation here for a while longer, but I'm going to need you in D.C. to help deliver what Tom has found. Are you game? I'm going to run this latest update by Max later today. I know him well enough to know that if I tell him I want both you and Tom to be at our meeting, he'll make the necessary arrangements."

Mark wanted to hear what Tom had to say the next day, but he was of the opinion that Tom most likely had uncovered something that needed to be shared with the research group and the president. He had not been back to D.C. since his retirement, and he couldn't remember the last time he had stepped foot in the White House. Mostly, he was pleased to think that Ruth Ann needed him and wanted to include him in the meeting. He finished the last sip of his coffee and said, "I'm at your disposal, ma'am. If Washington is where we need to be, then count me in and ready."

Both of them could feel that their vacation was rapidly coming to an end. Even to this point, it hadn't been anything like what either of them had planned, but it was Mark who voiced it all. "We're going to miss this place when we head out. I think I'll make an appointment for a massage later this afternoon."

"Oh, yes, an afternoon massage—I think I'd better do that myself. In fact, I think I'll spring for the works: massage, facial and pedicure. Meet me here in an hour and we can go have some breakfast, then stop by the spa and make our appointments. After that, I'll give Max a call."

"Sounds like a perfect plan. See you in an hour," Mark agreed, as he headed toward the door.

"Max?" Ruth Ann asked as the phone was picked up on the other end.

"Ruth Ann, how are you doing? What's up? Has your guy found anything yet?" Max fired his questions off so fast that Ruth Ann didn't have time to answer.

"Max, I believe Tom has indeed found something significant. I'll know more when we meet in person tomorrow. Our communication to this point has been limited, but his last contact this morning indicated that whatever he had uncovered had him feeling slightly paranoid." Ruth Ann spoke as fast as she could, before Max could launch more questions at her.

She could hear him take in a deep breath. "I already have obtained security clearance for both Mark and Tom. Now, when can you get here? When do you want to leave? How long will it take for Tom to get to you? I'll arrange for a jet to come pick you up. There's a small executive airport almost next door to your hotel. That'll make it easy for you if we fly in there."

Ruth Ann said, "We were planning to meet with Tom tomorrow. It's about a five-hour flight back to D.C., so that should give us time to talk. It will take Tom about four hours to get to us, though."

"So, should I have the jet show up around two o'clock?" Max asked.

"I think that'll work. I'll check with Tom and let you know," she replied.

"Now, I know that both Jim and I would love to accompany the pilots to collect you, but tomorrow morning I'm scheduled to help stifle a hit, so that won't be possible. You'll get in late to Andrews, but I'll arrange for all of you to stay at Blair House and have a car waiting for you on the tarmac."

"You're scheduled to do what?" she shrieked.

"It's a long story. I'll tell you all about it when you get here, but Gordon and I need to prevent something from occurring," Max sort of explained.

"Well, if Gordon is involved then I won't worry, but you be safe, you hear me?" Ruth Ann demanded.

"Great! I'll text your Skype when I've made the final arrangements," Max said, sounding excited. "As much as I know you needed a nice long break after that last ordeal, I have to admit, I'm very excited that your little getaway turned out to be a working vacation."

"Oh, Max, you know I'm committed to getting this truth out,

no matter where it leads. I've had a very enjoyable time here. As a matter of fact, as soon as we get off this phone call, I'm on my way to relax at the most incredible pool you have ever seen. After a few hours of sun and swimming, I plan to have a nice long massage," Ruth Ann informed him.

As soon as her call with Max had ended, Ruth Ann phoned Tom on Skype. "Tom, I would like to invite you to Las Vegas and then on to Washington D.C."

"I can probably arrange that, when do you have in mind?" Tom asked.

"We'll leave for D.C. on a government jet tomorrow afternoon. You can drive over in the morning, or if you can get here to the M tonight, I'll make the arrangements for your room and you can have dinner with Mark and me."

"Oh, that sounds most inviting. I can gather up my computers and externals and leave within the hour. It's not Friday, so traffic should be light. I should be able to be there sometime later this afternoon."

"Just check in at the front desk when you arrive. I'll have your room reserved and paid for. Mark and I will probably be at the spa, but text me when you get here and we'll meet up with you for dinner. Oh and Tom—Max, my boss, is very excited to meet you and to learn about what you've discovered. And once you're on that jet there is no more reason to fear."

twenty-three

At exactly eight o'clock, Max and Gordon arrived at Dora's house. Dante had given her the medication as instructed, which slowed her heart rate to minimum life-sustainable levels, but gave no indication of a pulse. The medication had also suppressed her breathing to a rate that was undetectable without the aid of a stethoscope. She was positioned on the porch swing to make it look as if she was sleeping in a sitting position. Dante climbed the tree and securely locked himself into his sniper location. Max went inside the house, while Gordon parked the car down the block, made his way back to Dora's property and hid himself in the bushes by the side of the house. Now they waited.

Shortly before nine o'clock, a gas company van pulled up in front of Dora's house and parked. Two men got out, one slightly taller than the other. The taller man was carrying a briefcase. They walked briskly towards the front door, making sure not to exhibit any suspicious-looking behavior in case the neighbors were watching. When they stepped onto the porch, they could see Dora asleep on the swing.

"Wake her," one of them said. "She's not going to do us any good out here."

The taller man went over to her and shook her, but received no response. He shook her again with more vigor, but still nothing. He reached for her wrist to feel for a pulse, but could not feel anything. He held his hand over her chest to see if she was breathing. He looked back at his companion and slowly shook his head. "I think she's dead," he whispered.

At that moment, Max appeared in the front doorway. "Can I help you gentlemen?" he asked. Before they could utter any kind of a response, Max continued, "Now, you put that briefcase on the ground. If either of you so much as twitches, Dante, the expert marksman who's in that tree, he'll put a bullet through your right ear." He pointed at the taller man. Pointing to the other agent, he said, "And it will come out your left ear."

Just then, Dante fired a shot that sailed inches over their heads and struck the post holding up the porch. Both men were very familiar with the sound of a silencer, and the briefcase was immediately on the ground as Max had instructed. Gordon stepped out from behind them with his gun firmly placed in the ribs of the taller man, while Max pointed his gun directly at the other. Gordon made sure both men were unarmed, and then instructed them to remove all their clothing, so that they were standing naked on the porch. Max brought the briefcase and their clothes inside, then went out to the gas company van to inspect it for other weapons. When he was convinced that it was safe, he signaled to Gordon, who had handcuffed the culprits together back to back. Gordon marched the two agents across the front yard to the van. Max opened the back and Gordon helped them climb inside. He then handcuffed their ankles and secured them to the sides of the van with rope, so they could not move.

Dante had climbed down from the tree and came to the back of the van to get a good look at the two would-be assassins. According to plan, he photographed the men so that their faces were clearly visible. "Excellent work, gentlemen," he said to Gordon and Max. "What do you plan to do with these jokers now?"

Gordon smiled. "Oh, I think we'll take them back where they came from. We'll dump them off at Langley, right in front of the CIA headquarters. I think their days as government employees are just about over. Nothing is more disruptive to a hit man's career than having the boss discover you naked in the back of your getaway vehicle with no good explanation how you got there."

Dante and Max chuckled and patted each other on the back. "I'll stay here with Mama and give her the medicine to bring her back around. Thanks again for all your help. And let's hope we've sent a message loud and clear that they don't want to mess around here anymore," Dante said.

Gordon drove the van and Max followed behind in the car for the ride to Langley. Max called the president, who had been briefed earlier concerning the operation, and told him that it had been successful. The president had the final role to play, and instructed Max to call him when it was time.

Dante attended to this mother, and quickly got her breathing and her pulse back to normal. He helped her into the house where she could be more comfortable. "I'm still alive, so it must have gone well, but what are all these clothes here in the middle of the floor?" she asked.

"After we disarmed them, Gordon made them strip and strolled them out to their van," Dante replied.

"And I missed all that? If I would have known he was going to do that, I would have demanded a different assignment," she said, laughing.

"Oh, Mama, you were the star of the show. You should have seen the look on their faces when they thought you were dead. We couldn't have done it without you. I'll stay with you until you're feeling completely back to normal, and then I have a lot of work to do with Max. We're on to something that will change how the world sees 9/11. Their attempt to stop me is proof we're on the right track."

Those words would have made Dora happy to hear them, but she had fallen sound asleep in Dante's favorite chair.

About a half-mile from the main gate at CIA headquarters,

Gordon turned off on a side road, then parked the van in a small clearing. Max pulled in behind him and Gordon jumped into the front seat for the drive back to the White House. Gordon called the president and told him it was time.

President Sherman instructed his secretary to get the CIA director on the phone. When he was told the director was waiting, he picked up the phone and said, "Paul, it's good to talk with you again. I've got something I need you to do for me. There's a Richmond City Gas van parked in a clearing about a half-mile from your main gate. Inside, you'll find two of your agents. I'd like you and a security team to personally go and arrest them. They won't give you much trouble; they're naked and shackled. We intercepted them attempting to carry out a hit on the mother of a member of one of my teams. Now, I know you didn't order this, nor did anyone else that reports to you, but it came from someone inside your agency. We've known for a long time there's a rogue element to the CIA, and they act according to their own agenda. I want you to interrogate these men and use every method at your disposal. If it means flying them to Guantanamo, I'm okay with that, but I want you to find out whom they are working for and who is giving them orders. Then we need to find a way to eradicate that element. Am I clear?"

twenty-four

The flight to Andrews AFB left Henderson Executive Airport on time as planned. The comfort of the government Gulfstream made the flight time seem much quicker than it actually was. Ruth Ann spent most of the flight talking with Mark and Tom about the team and their findings and experiences. She did her very best to describe Max, but made it clear to them both that Max needed to be experienced in person to obtain the full flavor of his personality. She elaborated on the fact that his dedication, experience, knowledge and research abilities far outweighed any quirky personality characteristics that most people found endearing. In spite of everything, Max was the perfect person to be the leader of the team.

When Mark questioned her further about Max, she felt it was time to share her kidnapping incident with him. She elaborated on the frightening experience and the role Max had played in securing her release. That, in turn, led to how she had met the First Lady and how they had become close friends. The entire kidnapping and escape had been kept from the media; no one knew that the president's fiancée, at the time, had been held against her will and rescued. Ruth Ann's revelation opened a complete dialogue on who Vera Hanson was and how she came to meet and marry Joel Sherman. Those details made it clear to both Mark and Tom that the First Lady's commitment to exposing the truth was due to her unearthing new details about the hijackings. Of course, with her duties now as First Lady, her participation in the group was not on a day-to-day basis, but nevertheless she was included in meetings and informed of all the new findings that passed through the team. Ruth Ann went on to explain the role Jim Bowman had played in recruiting Vera, and how his longtime friendship with the president was the catalyst for the two of them to meet and to marry. She assured Mark that he and Jim had a lot in common, and that they would likely become fast friends and confidants. She also explained Gil's role in the group, and described the loss they'd suffered when Bob was murdered in Las Vegas. In spite of his idiosyncrasies, his research abilities had been second to none, and the informational leads he provided to the team were already sorely missed.

"Max informed me about a new member of the team that he brought on board in the last couple of days. His name is Dante Wilcox. I don't know much about him, other than Max is very impressed with his abilities, so I'm looking forward to meeting him and discovering how he can be of help," Ruth Ann said.

"Dante Wilcox...I seem to recall that name from somewhere," Mark said. "I think he was assigned to a Special Forces unit, and I had the privilege of flying his team to Panama about the time Noriega fell. If it's the same man, I know why Max would be impressed," he added.

"We'll find out soon enough," she said. "Max has a meeting scheduled first thing in the morning. That will give everyone a chance to catch up and to meet the two of you, along with Dante."

Both Max and Jim were waiting for the jet's arrival on the tarmac, with a limousine to take Ruth Ann and her two new companions to Blair House. Ruth Ann gave Max and Jim a big hug, then proudly introduced them to Mark and Tom.

"It's our pleasure to meet you both. Ruth Ann has told us about you two, and about some of your findings. On behalf of the president, I thank you for taking the time to come here to meet with us. We're sure your skill sets will be a welcome addition to our group. This team of ours has been through a lot together, and it's time we smash through the barriers that have prevented us from reaching our goals," Max said.

Mark and Tom graciously accepted the challenge that Max indirectly presented to them, and expressed their desire to be of help in any way they could. Jim was pleased to inform them all that dinner was waiting for them at Blair House. Even though it was late in D.C., he knew they would be hungry and had arranged for them to share a meal before they retired for the evening.

"Well, in that case, time is of the essence and we need to get moving," Ruth Ann jokingly replied, trying hard not to let on she was famished.

Max announced that he had scheduled tomorrow's meeting for ten o'clock in the conference room outside his office, and he encouraged anyone who wanted to arrive early to take the opportunity to get to know the other members of the team. He informed them that Vera had been invited, but was not sure if she would attend due to her already busy schedule. The drive to Blair House was filled with light conversation about their experiences in the Washington area.

Everyone seemed to have taken Max's suggestion, and began congregating near the conference room the next morning around 9:30. Dante arrived shortly thereafter and was delighted to meet Ruth Ann, whom he had heard so much about. Mark and Tom met Gil, and immediately began to share information about their research. Jerry Reitz soon joined in, and Jim made a point to introduce him to all the new members. To everyone's delight, the First Lady arrived with notebook in hand, ready to participate and to represent the president. Mark and Tom were honored to meet her, and Max saw to it that they were seated on either side of her once they moved into the conference room to begin.

Max called the meeting to order. "Welcome, and we're happy to include our new members in this meeting—Dante, Mark and Tom. I can see that we've all had an opportunity to make your acquaintance, and we look forward to working with you in various capacities in the coming days. Several of the assignments that will come from this meeting today will have you working together, so I'm certain in no time we'll come to understand one another very well. Before we get to those assignments, I would like Ruth Ann to give us a brief overview of what she found on Bob's flash drives, and how that led to Mark and Tom coming on board."

"Well, as you know I went to Las Vegas for some much-needed rest, but things never quite work out the way you plan, especially with this outfit. Once I retrieved the last of Bob's possessions from the coroner, I couldn't help myself and began to look into what he had discovered that was so important. I started by looking at radar information, which was impossible for me to read. I had just met Mark at the hotel, and once I discovered his background as a military pilot, I asked him to assist me. He gladly obliged and helped to open my eyes to what I was actually looking at, but even he was having difficulty with some of the data in the FOIA documents. That's where Tom entered the picture. As a former air traffic controller at LA center in Palmdale, he was able to read most of the information that baffled us. His friend Chip, who was ATC at Edwards, also was helpful in explaining some of the data. My guess is that moving forward, we'll need to call on Chip again to give us the military perspective on some of the revelations that come to the surface. Bottom line here is that we have more leads, which need to be followed up on and distilled into the larger picture of what happened on 9/11. It's going to be a lot of work, but I feel confident we have the help we need to make it all come together."

Max thanked her and said, "For the time being, I would like Mark and Tom to continue to dig into those FOIA files of Bob's and report to Ruth Ann any findings you feel need immediate attention on our part or that prove to be a game changer."

Mark and Tom looked at Ruth Ann and nodded their acceptance and willingness to assist.

Max continued, "In the meantime, there are several emails which have come to my attention that need further follow-up. The first one comes from an anonymous source, but it has all the markings of originating from someone in the intelligence community. He could be referred to as our very own 'deep throat.' This message outlines some of the back channels relating to the art students that were residing in the towers prior to 9/11. I realize we have already gone down that path with some rather significant conclusions, but this email expressed foreknowledge on the part of the government, as well as details concerning these students planning more chaos. It also sheds some light on the fact that elements of the military, particularly those in Central Command were involved. They knew that planes could be used as weapons to create the illusion and deceive the public into believing that a terror attack had occurred. I would like you, Gil, to take a closer look at what we have, based on this email, and see what you can find out using the DEA report as well as any other sources to confirm or deny the claims of this intelligence officer."

"I'm all over that, Max," Gil replied.

"Now this other email might be of particular interest to you, Vera and Jim. It comes from a maker of maps who creates terrain maps for the flight simulators. He claims he has mapped nearly every airport, both civilian and military, and is very familiar with the terrain around them, using Google Earth. He says that near the end of the northeast runway at Westover there appears to be some kind of a bunker, hangar or something, buried with twelve to fifteen years of plant growth covering it. I know it's a long shot, but I think we should at least check it out. Will the two of you take on that responsibility?" he asked.

"You know, Jim, ever since we pinpointed Westover, I've wanted to visit that base. I'm certain my office can arrange for some kind of a ceremony or presentation that requires the First Lady's presence. Maybe a presidential award to officers' wives who have rendered service to the base or something. I'm sure we could get the commanding officer to give us a tour," Vera said with a huge smile on her face.

Max pulled another email from his file. "Dante, this one has your name all over it, and I'm going to join you," Max said. "This letter is from the son of a flight attendant; his father was a crew member on one of those fateful flights. I have to admit his message is rather disturbing. He claims that his father visited him the week prior to 9/11 and told him he was considering taking a job with the CIA, but it would mean that they would never see each other again if he did. I can feel there's something more here, and you and I will make arrangements to spend some time with this kid and see what we can learn about his father."

Vera, who had been quietly taking notes, blurted out, "What? Max, did you say a crew member on one of those flights told his son he was considering working for the CIA?"

Max nodded. "That's affirmative. And like I said, he told his son, should he decide to take this position, it meant he would never see him again."

Ruth Ann joined the conversation. "That doesn't sound good. There are intelligence agents that have wives and children they come home to. Why would he suggest he could never see his family again if he joined the CIA?"

Vera jumped to her feet. "You would say that to your kids if you were about to take part in a huge fake terror attack where the official story tells of your death. There were a few crew members on those transcontinental flights that didn't have enough years of seniority to hold those trips as a schedule. I had assumed they were reserves that picked up the flights last-minute. If the CIA had a working crew member onboard, then they pulled some real magic to get that person on the flight. Everything we do is based on seniority, or luck of the draw if you're on reserve." Vera found herself thinking out loud, while the entire room was trying to follow her train of thought. "Max, did his son mention how many years his father had flown?"

Max admitted, "I didn't notice that detail, but will get every bit of information I can from his son when we meet him."

"Find out when he started flying. By the sound of things, he knew he was seeing his son for the last time, and that means he knew he would be on one of those flights. The only male flight attendant I recall reading about had been a police officer prior to joining the airline, and he sure didn't have enough seniority to get on that flight as a schedule holder." Vera's heart sank as the reality of what she was learning seeped into her logical mind. She had never dreamed that a crew member could have been involved in this charade, but this man's visit with his son was indicating that the term 'inside job' carried an entirely different meaning. Her mind began to silently review every word from each of the crew members that made phone calls, and the personal details of every crew member on the four flights. Then it hit her—those that were not making phone calls were not following FAA hijack protocols either. Her mind raced to try to figure out how the Central Intelligence Agency could have convinced crew members to go along with this horrific travesty. Were any of the pilots involved? How many other crew members were working with the perpetrators? How could this be?

Max's voice interrupted her questions. "With the details this guy's son shared, at least this one crew member knew what was about to happen, and he knew he was playing a role that would mean he was about to be dead to his family, and dead to the entire world."

"How many more emails do you have, Max?" Jerry asked.

"There are hundreds, but only a few more appear to offer any relevant information worth a follow-up. Several of them seem to have a connection to aspects of the investigation we have already uncovered, so we're in a unique position to ask the right questions. But don't worry, I have lots of leads I plan to give to you and your NSA team," Max answered.

"Ah, Miss Lowy," Max said, looking at Ruth Ann, "I still feel badly your vacation was cut short and interrupted by research, but this little assignment you might actually enjoy. You remember how Bush's solicitor general kept changing his story about his wife's phone calls from Flight 77, which they tried to convince us flew through the thick walls of the Pentagon? Well, I have received an email from a woman in Kentucky who has done some digging into the solicitor general's new wife. It seems she claims to be an attorney, like his wife, Barbara Olson. Only this person emailing us works in a position where city, county and state documents are stored, and lo and behold, it seems Ted's new wife, whose name is Lady Booth, has no records. There is no history of a Lady Booth in Kentucky—no driver's license, no law license, no nothing. Now the writer claims she is from the area and has done extensive research trying to find this woman. I'd like you to find out what you can and report back to us."

Ruth Ann rubbed her hands together to express her excitement with the job. "Now you're talking, Max. This should prove to be fun. Jerry, I might need your help with a few of the details. I recall Barbara was an attorney for the same law firm that represented the passenger on American 11, that Israeli special operations Sayeret Matkal agent, Lewin. That same law firm was also associated with the company that employed the Israeli woman that was on United Flight 175, Applied Materials. Those connections go too far beyond coincidence to be ignored. Her husband, the solicitor general, was also the attorney for that Israeli spy Jonathan Pollard—now there is a serious connection between all of these people. I know most people found Ted's stories and his behavior to be disingenuous at best. If there is any history on Lady Booth anywhere in this country, I will find it."

"Just let me know what assistance you need and you'll have it," Jerry replied.

Max searched though his stack of files. He found a blue file and opened it. "I don't know why this email raises the hair on my arms, but it does. It comes from a woman who claims to have seen a pretty large four-engine jet flying low up the Hudson River prior to all the havoc in Manhattan. Now, we know that at the time, the only commercial jet with four engines was a 747. I have actually questioned her in email, and she is positive it was not a 747, but is fairly certain she saw four engines. Her certainty leads me to believe it could have been some type of military jet. Mark, I think you and Jim should follow through with this and see if you can interview her. Use your military backgrounds to find out what that plane could have been. I know it's not normal procedure to fly up the Hudson at a low altitude, so if it was military, they're going to need a good reason for that kind of behavior, especially on that morning."

Jim looked at Mark and pointed to him with a wink, indicating he was excited to work with him. "Good choice, Max. I think with Mark's experience and the little bit I know, we will figure out what she saw."

Max turned to Tom and said, "Now that you're aware of where these team members will be focusing their attention, I want you to look through all the data you have, and if anything aligns with the information they are following up on, make that avenue a priority."

"This meeting has been very helpful, and I'll keep their assignments in my mind," Tom assured everyone. "From what I have seen in these files so far, it is mostly FAA and NORAD radar and protocol files. They probably won't match up with everyone else's focus, but if anyone can find something out of place or not quite right or even faked in this radar data, I'm your man."

"I would like for everyone to follow up with your assignments as quickly as possible. I will schedule another meeting as soon as I hear you are on your way back or you have completed your task. Does anyone have any questions?" Max concluded.

Just as Max was about to adjourn the meeting, the president appeared in the doorway and said, "I hope I'm not interrupting."

Everyone stood as Max assured him that he was welcome. Joel could tell the meeting was adjourning, and wanted to meet the new members as well as encourage the seasoned ones. He took the time to speak personally with Mark and Tom. He pulled Dante aside, asked how his mother was, and thanked him for his courage. The president concluded by asking Max if his ponytail collection had collected any dust since he'd been in Washington.

"Who told you about them?" Max asked.

The president indicated his lips were sealed with his finger, but then pointed to Vera. Everyone laughed but Jim; he was in on the setup and pulled one of the ponytails from his pocket to give to Max to model for everyone. Max obliged and wore the partial disguise for the rest of the day.

twenty-five

Tom arrived early each morning to the White House, where he not only had access to the FOIA data, but also had all the other documents the team had been working with at his fingertips. The security surrounding the computers he worked on and the data he pored through provided him a level of comfort that eased his mind and allowed him to focus on the interpretation of the reports. He found Gil to be an immense help. Together, drawing from their distinct areas of expertise, they were able to find inconsistencies and anomalies that warranted further investigation.

As an air traffic controller for many years, Tom was familiar with the procedures established by the FAA that were mandatory in all control centers and towers. The problem for Tom was the FAA chronologies included abnormal details which caused him to wonder if many of these accounts had been added at a later date. Armed with his personal experience and knowledge, Tom began to scan through the many records that the FAA had included in the Freedom of Information Act requests. One discovery he made in the New York center's log was a notation that the ELT (electronic location transmitter) went off at least two minutes before American Airlines Flight 11 supposedly crashed into the North Tower. The only explanation for such an event was that the ELT for that flight was either manually or electronically activated, by someone on the ground or in the air that had knowledge of the frequency the ELT would transmit through. That was odd, since the ELT is a locator meant to assist in finding wreckage after a crash. It did not go off without a crash, nor did it go off minutes before a crash, since it activates on impact. Tom found himself mentally reviewing what he knew about the ELT, and questioned who could have possibly activated it at least two full minutes prior to the supposed impact. He searched through the other reports and noticed no mention of any ELT for the other three aircraft. Odd, he questioned, how three aircraft supposedly crashed without their ELT being activated, and here on the first flight to supposedly hit, the ELT goes off minutes before impact.

The FOIA data also contained the complete accident packages for the four flights. Gil and Tom made note that the NTSB (National Transportation Safety Board) did not provide their typical investigation, and this in and of itself seemed highly irregular.

Tom took note to share with the team: One chronology reported that the FBI was immediately headed to Dulles to pull the tape recordings between the flights and the air traffic controllers; they seemed to be fighting the FAA for the tapes. That appeared very peculiar to Tom, knowing that all air traffic control and aircraft incidents always ran though the Federal Aviation Administration first, then that information would be distributed to the NTSB, FBI and on down the line. But, here we have the FBI trying to get their hands on the tapes before the threat of terrorism was calmed. Tom took note again: WHY is the FBI pulling tapes before the FAA?

Tom began to explain to Gil the details of the facility logs, when he noticed that there were several mentions of long range radar and other radar being out of service that morning. Included on the list of radar out of service was the Doppler radar around Washington D.C. He jotted a note as he continued shuffling through the printed facility logs.

Tom had access to what appeared to be the voice recordings between air traffic controllers and every aircraft in the air that morning. He observed that the Boston center had noted a voice they assumed came from the hijackers onboard American Flight 11, but there was no proof of where it came from, and there was no notation of the frequency that voice was transmitted over. This seemed incomprehensible as it was standard practice to note the frequency of any transmission received, especially during a hijacking. With no frequency notation, the transmission could have come from anywhere.

Gil suggested they look at the typed transcripts, and compare those to the official story that had been circulating for years. They noticed that Boston center reported that American Airlines Flight 11 was several miles southwest of Albany at 8:28 that morning. Gil said aloud, "This says American 11 was almost forty miles southwest of Albany in twenty-eight minutes."

Tom recalled reading the official report that both the American and United planes that reportedly hit the towers were seen on radar near each other just south of Albany at 8:42, but United 175 couldn't have gotten that far in fourteen minutes. Tom was making notations on a form in front of him. "Gil, there are some huge discrepancies here. United 175 would have only been as far west as Westover Air Force base at that time." The discrepancy in the timeline made its way to his notes to be shared with the team. "No way did American 11 stay in the Albany area for fourteen minutes. That's impossible," he continued.

For years, the government had claimed that an official nationwide ground stop was ordered at about 9:40 that morning, and all planes in the air were directed to land at the nearest airport. Though there was ample evidence that planes did land in locations other than their intended destinations, Tom and Gil could not find any supporting evidence suggesting the FAA had ordered such a ground stop or that planes were instructed to land immediately. They read through typed transcripts and listened to tape recordings from that time period, and could not find any air traffic controllers instructing planes to land. Tom assumed the claimed ground stop time was included in the reports that were written long after September 11, 2001, to make the FAA look good.

There were transcripts that claimed Flight 11 was slowing to 250 knots and descending near New York, but that information was only confirmed on primary radar. The air traffic controllers were only able to see a blip on a radar screen that showed a location and some indication of speed, and since there was no transponder, that blip could have been anything. According to the official story, Flight 175 would have flown almost directly in front of Newark International Airport on its path to strike the South Tower. No one in the Newark tower noticed a plane flying that low and that slow, and the tower had a perfect view of where the FAA later claimed United 175 would have been. As Tom continued reading through the transcripts, he noticed one that appeared to be a conversation between the Newark tower controllers and those at the New York center. The controllers remarked that the object that hit the tower could not have been the missing 767; there were too many people that would have seen it, and the hole in the building appeared to be too small and circular, more like a missile strike. As the transcript continued, the controllers seemed convinced that they or one of the millions of people in the vicinity would have seen a large 767 flying low enough to hit the tower. Later, they remarked that it now finally appeared that wingtips were cut into the building and the outline of the hole more closely resembled that of a plane, but they still could not believe it was the United plane that flew into the tower. Tom had been in the Newark tower and remembered the remarkable view of the twin towers just a short eight miles or so across the Hudson River. The controllers and nearly everyone at the airport would have had a perfect view of planes flying at ten thousand feet and lower.

Gil and Tom discussed how NORAD used the same radar facilities that the FAA used. This was a product of MIT (Massachusetts Institute of Technology)—the SAGE system built in the 1950's, but updated with new technology as it became available. As Tom dug deeper into the reports, it became apparent that NORAD was unable to find any of the planes in question that morning on their radar. There was no plausible explanation why NORAD could not see the target planes on 9/11. The longer Tom thought about that, the more confusing it became. How could they not see these huge commercial aircraft? Was something blinding their radar?

Tom said, "When I was in California with Ruth Ann and Mark, I understood that these files were not meant to be seen by the general public. After what we've found and all the inconsistencies that don't match the official story, it's becoming clear these documents should never have been released. Are you sure Bob wasn't murdered over these documents?" he asked Gil.

"I was in Vegas with Gordon and Jim when we found his body. Agent Garcia was positive that it wasn't a professional hit, and the portable hard drive and his flash drives weren't taken. Based on that, we assumed that his research data was not what the killers were after," Gil replied.

"I was only beginning to get into this stuff when we were invited here, and I have to tell you, reading these irregularities made me pretty nervous. Now that I have a better idea what is contained in these files and how they conflict with each other, I understand why I had so much anxiety," Tom confided.

"Since we're working in the Executive Offices, we are the government, so to speak, and don't need to worry about retribution," Gil replied. "The problem I see is being able to explain this data to others in a way they can understand. Making it simple enough to the layman that they can comprehend the significance of what these findings mean. I'm thinking our job is going to be as hard on the communication end as it has been on the discovery and analysis end. Fortunately, Jim and Max are both really good at delivering this type of complicated information in easy-to-understand language."

"Do you think it's time to share these discoveries with Max? I know we've scratched the surface and a lot of what the other team members bring back from their investigations will augment what we've found, but should we start with Max?" Tom asked.

"Let me call and see if he's free to come see us. If we share this with him, it might help him to direct traffic with the others. Max is good at that, as you'll see." Gil smiled.

Gill phoned over to Max's office and invited him to hear what they had discovered. Max told them he would be there in forty-five minutes. Their meeting together lasted several hours. Max drilled down on several of the issues presented by Tom and Gil, and filled them in on information that he had. He agreed with them it would be necessary to formulate the message in a way both Congress and the public could understand. His direct comment was something about helping them understand much like you would assist a fourth-grader to read the Constitution. Tom, not being accustomed to Max's sense of humor, was silent.

"Look, it all comes down to what we have as a whole," Max said.

"What exactly does that mean?" Tom asked.

"You remember the assignments I handed out at our meeting?" Max asked Tom.

"Vaguely. Being new and not knowing anyone except for Mark, I did my best to comprehend what was being asked of the participants, but I must confess, it was a bit overwhelming to me."

Max laughed. "That was to be expected. I've been at this a long time, and none of what you have found comes as a total surprise. Some of what you've unearthed I've been anticipating and expecting. If the rest of the team is able to put together the outcomes I expect, we will be able to put this puzzle together completely. In a few days I'll call another meeting and we'll merge the team's results with your discoveries. And if all goes well, you'll begin to smell the cookies baking," Max said.

Tom let out a slight chuckle, which confirmed to Max and Gil all they needed to know about Tom's integration with the team and his acceptance of Max as the leader. Understanding Max's quirks was always a helpful hurdle to cross.

twenty-six

Before long, Max called a meeting of the team to discuss what the various members had discovered.

"I want to begin with you, Gil. Are there any more direct correlations between the traveling Israeli art students and the Gelitin art group that were living in the World Trade Tower, and the information provided by our anonymous intelligence source?" Max inquired.

Gil was prepared to respond to the first inquiry from Max, and had already opened his notes. "I do have some information to share about both groups of art students, but before I do I want to elaborate on a point made in the original email you gave me. This particular informant mentioned that the intelligence community, or at least the agency he was with, was aware of six targets on 9/11. Now, we know about the three planes that allegedly hit buildings that morning. I think it's safe to assume that Flight 93 was meant to look like it hit the Solomon Building—or what most people now know as Building 7 at the World Trade Center. That's about the only way you can explain why that building was wired for demolition, and how that BBC reporter—along with whoever fills her teleprompter—somehow knew it was going to collapse. So the question is, what were the other targets? In the chronologies we've been going through, we noticed some very mysterious posts. For example, the Secret Service called in to CNN and reported that a plane had crashed into Camp David around ten-thirty that morning. In retrospect, there was no plane into Camp David, but it clearly indicates the Secret Service thought there was going to be one, or quite possibly they knew there was going to be another plane remotely hijacked that was meant to look like it crashed into Camp David. One thing we do know for certain—Camp David is an extremely secure neighborhood, and it houses plenty of security agents who would have been onsite to report a crash."

Jim commented, "I remember hearing that report about a plane crash into Camp David from CNN, but then it was never mentioned again."

Gil went on, "There was a Delta flight from Boston—Flight 1989—that the FAA reported was hijacked, but in the transcripts, the pilot clearly states they have no problems onboard and that the flight attendants are serving breakfast. Regardless of the captain's report, the FAA headquarters insisted they had a hijacker and a bomb onboard and ordered them to land in Cleveland, which they did."

"Yes, it is rather strange that the FAA headquarters would insist to a captain that they were involved in a hijacking when they weren't. The FAA is in an office in Washington; they have no idea what is going on inside an aircraft unless the flight attendants report to the pilots and the pilots report to air traffic control, not the other way around. In this situation, what happened is completely backwards," Vera said.

"There has to be more to that story. That doesn't make any sense. How could the FAA know about a hijacking when the crew didn't?" Max asked shrugging his shoulders.

Gil said, "The only explanation I can think of was that this Delta Flight 1989 was like the other planes, tagged for an electronic remote hijacking with some handlers onboard, and something went wrong so that the remote takeover failed. They aborted the mission, and then the handlers got off with the passengers in Cleveland."

Tom joined the conversation, explaining, "The remote control device, whether it was an installed Flight Termination System or some military drone technology, they both work on the plane's HF radio frequency. Each plane has a specific HF frequency, which is much like a phone number for that specific aircraft. If there was a last-minute equipment change—or ship change, as we call it— the HF signal the perpetrators had for the flight they intended to take over would not work for the replacement plane. When they tried to commandeer that aircraft to land it at Westover, it wouldn't respond. The flight continued on along its filed flight plan heading to LAX. It's possible this Delta flight was the one we would have been told crashed into Camp David. Since Camp David was a highly secure and well-guarded installation, we would have likely never seen the wreckage, plane parts or bodies even if they were real. Coverage of that supposed crash would have been even more obscure than Flight 93 into Shanksville."

"Well, that accounts for five targets—what about the sixth?" Max asked.

"That's still a mystery. It might have been the White House, the Capitol, a monument on the mall, or perhaps—as Peter Hansen said supposedly from United 175—'they're going to fly us into a building in Chicago.' My guess is it could have been the Sears tower. Faking a crash into a Washington landmark would have been more problematic than faking a crash into the Pentagon."

"You are probably right, and if you are, that's one more black mark on the FAA," Jerry Reitz said, simulating counting on his fingers.

Gil started to laugh. "Wait until we get to what Tom and I have been uncovering in the logs and transcripts. The FAA isn't just getting black marks; it's starting to look more like black ops."

Max didn't want to allow the meeting to seek its own direction, so he brought it back into focus. "The art students; tell us more about them."

"The art students in the towers claimed to produce artwork

using boxes," Gil continued. "The only problem, in this case, was the boxes they used were from the Littel fuse company and clearly marked BB18. To the general public those letters and numbers mean nothing, but we were contacted by several professionals in the demolition business. Those letters and numbers correspond with a power bar which could have easily been used to wire a remote demolition." Gil looked around the table, then back at his notes. "These artists were actually living in the north tower at the Trade Center and produced a book titled The B-Thing. That book contained artwork that looked like it was drawn by a kindergarten class. Their book included some very telling photographs taken from the inside of the towers, with the wall space between the windows marked in big red letters spelling out EXIT. Their childish drawings were filled with sick notes and comments about people jumping from the towers. All a foreshadowing of what occurred on 9/11. The other group of traveling Israeli art students was roaming the country selling cheap art while on tourist visas; in almost every case, their visas had expired. Several of them were arrested due to those expired visas, and interestingly they were bailed out of jail by a couple of Israeli companies—AMDOCS and NICE. Most of these traveling so-called art students were connected to Israeli Defense Force Intelligence or more commonly, the Mossad. Many of them had either military or intelligence experience with explosives. Some of them were considered demolition experts. It isn't clear yet when or even if they all left the country. We are still looking into that," Gil explained.

"Any thoughts on this?" Max asked, opening it up to the whole group.

Jerry was the first to weigh in. "Gil and I have talked about these students, and I've spent time trying to run down their entry and exit documents. For the most part, they're missing from our files. That adds a big load of suspicion to what I'm already thinking. If 9/11 ever gets to a criminal investigation, those students, in my book, become prime suspects."

"I think what bothers me the most is how this DEA agent and his report were treated once this information was brought to light," Vera added. "It was basically circular filed, and only now is it coming to the attention of the team, more than fifteen years later."

"That is troubling," Max agreed. "Let's move on to the bunker the cartographer pointed out at Westover. What, if anything, were you able to find?"

"Vera and I weren't able to make arrangements to travel to Chicopee like we'd hoped, but I did spend some time with Jerry's satellite people scanning the entire area and looking closely for anything that might look like a bunker or a concealed storage facility. The mapper was correct; there is something that needs a closer look. I'm not sure we are the ones to do it, however. I can tell you, it does look as if at least a decade's worth of growth has covered it, which means it's not an area that's used on a regular basis. It may be nothing, or it may be the most damning piece of evidence we'll ever have. I suggest we work with the chairman of the joint chiefs to gain access to it under a military directive carried out by a Special Forces team. There may not be anyone on that base now that even knows it's there, or why it was constructed. So I doubt it's being protected," Jim said.

"If we can get Congress to open an investigation, what kind of priority would you give this?" Vera asked.

Jim thought for a moment. "I think a five or a six," he said, looking at Max for corroboration. "We have plenty of evidence that'll move an investigation forward without this, but in the end, it could be the truth from which the guilty parties cannot escape. I'd be careful when and how you present this for further investigation. Let's keep it as an ace in the hole. Do you agree, Vera?"

"I think Jim's right. When the time comes and events are lining up in our favor, we can follow through and find out what's there. The one thing we do know is that most of the passengers didn't leave that base alive."

Max nodded in agreement. "I think that's the prudent approach, but if anyone hears anything concerning activity around that bunker, we'll move on it immediately."

Max turned his attention to Dante, who had been silent throughout the meeting. Max was so anxious to hear what Dante had discovered that he pulled out a piece of paper to take notes, which was so out of character for him that it surprised everyone in the room. "Okay, Dante, you're on. I'm sorry I could never free myself to assist you so what have you got?"

Dante made a point to speak so the entire group could hear him clearly. "I called this young man; in fact, I spoke with him many times just to make certain I understood what he was telling me and how he felt about what he was revealing. To the best of my knowledge, this information is unknown outside our group. He had only shared his thoughts and suspicions with his best friend. Throughout his growing-up years, he had a very close relationship with his father. His dad went to all his baseball games, coached him in martial arts and spent hours with him on road trips discovering places that piqued their interest. Around the time he graduated from high school, his father retired from the police force and took a new job as a flight attendant. A job he explained would allow him to be with the family, and offer an opportunity for them to travel. About a week before the terror attacks, his father told him he was considering taking an assignment with the CIA. The problem was, he explained, if he accepted the CIA position, it would mean he would never be able to see this young man or his brothers again. Now as many of you know, I've had extensive involvement with several CIA agents. I know all too well, they may be gone from their families for extended periods, but they always return home to their wives and kids. This young man tried to talk his father out of taking the intelligence job, but he said the conversation went nowhere. He knew his father had already accepted the job and this was his way of saying goodbye. A few days later, he learned that his father was working one of the flights that reportedly struck the towers in New York. He, his stepmother and his siblings assumed his dad perished in the terror attack. As time passed, he began to reflect on the conversation they'd shared, and what he later learned were suspicious irregularities surrounding the events of that day. He's in his early thirties now and has kids of his own. I got the feeling from talking with him that he has read enough about what happened that day, how the military dropped the ball and failed to scramble jets and well, you guys know all the anomalies. He openly spoke about a gut feeling he had that his father had taken the CIA up on the job offer and that it somehow involved what happened on 9/11. That's why he contacted us through email. Bottom line was, he asked me if I thought there was a chance his father was still alive."

Vera immediately interjected, "If his father had recently changed careers about the time this young man graduated from high school, then he had been a flight attendant for less than a year when 9/11 happened. Like I said before, there's no way he'd have had enough seniority to hold that trip on a schedule. Those transcontinental trips go pretty senior at every airline. It's great time, a decent layover and a long enough flight to be enjoyable. He would have needed at least eight to ten years' seniority. If he was still on reserve, there's no way he coincidentally was assigned a flight the CIA needed him to work for them." As the meaning of her words struck her, she quietly sat back in her chair and jotted herself a note to look into this crew member.

"Good point. I was told that he knew at least a week or two in advance that he was scheduled to work that flight. In fact, he invited his wife to spend the weekend back east right before 9/11. The son's understanding was that she went back to Boston to sign some type of paperwork, but he wasn't certain," Dante said.

Jim asked for the floor. "Let's look at this from another angle. Assume that the flight attendant job really was the CIA job, and he was on that plane as one of the handlers. We know from our previous investigation there were handlers on all the flights; we just don't know for a fact who they were. If that were the case, could the CIA have managed to get him scheduled on that flight even without the necessary seniority?"

Vera thought for a moment about how that might be possible, then said, "It would be highly unlikely. As you know, Jim, everything in the airlines is based on seniority, and they would almost need to have one of the crew schedulers be in on the scheme. In other words, one of the crew schedulers would also have to have been employed by the CIA. That being the case, he could have called up a reservist out of seniority order and put this guy on that flight. Nobody would ever find out."

Dante said, "I know how the CIA works. They're patient and they go to great lengths to set the stage for an operation. If this was a CIA job from the start, they could have managed to get him hired in the first place. They could have also gained access to some crew schedulers and made them a deal they couldn't refuse, even threatened them or their families. All the morning crew scheduler had to do was add this guy onto the crew, right, Vera and Jim?" Dante paused, waiting for an answer.

Jim was still standing. "Yes, that could have happened, I suppose. The flights are usually scheduled for a minimum number of flight attendants, and more are added to accommodate heavier loads or, on occasion, to crew a flight out of the destination city— what we called crew placement. It would probably be easiest for a crew scheduler to put a reserve on a flight for the CIA than it would be to break ranks in seniority. That was a pretty small base for both airlines, and everyone knows who is both above and below them in seniority, let there be no doubt. About the only way a CIA employee who was sitting on reserve could be on that flight would be the crew scheduler. He almost had to be on reserve, with less than a year under his belt."

Ruth Ann interjected, "So I assume there is the possibility that his father is still alive somewhere and was willing to write off his entire family."

"That's correct. I got the impression that the boy's feelings were twofold: his gut tells him 9/11 was an inside job, and he badly wants to think or know that his dad is still alive," Dante answered.

"Good work, Dante, but until we have more information, I'm afraid we're going to have to set this one aside, since nothing is conclusive. But my gut also tells me this detail is going to be a game changer at some point. I can already see Vera and Jim are thinking through all the angles, and trying to digest the possibility that crew members might have been involved or working for the CIA. That does answer the question as to why the crew did not fight back, and why a couple of dozen well-trained flight attendants didn't follow the hijack protocols. If a fellow flight attendant was informing them that they were involved in some type of drill or exercise, they wouldn't fight back. That also accounts for the strange comment Betty Ong made from American 11, when she said 'she didn't know but they might be being hijacked.'" Max found himself reviewing details from the crew and their phone calls as he spoke.

"Now, Ruth Ann, what were you able to discover about Lady Booth of Kentucky?" Max inquired with a smile.

"Lady Booth, come out, come out wherever you are," Ruth Ann replied, laughing. "The email was correct. There is no record of her anywhere. I spent hours combing through every possible database Jerry provided me from the state of Kentucky.

I mean, nobody is going to name a baby Lady, so I looked for every possible female Booth woman within a five-year age span, and then tracked them to see if any of them had corresponding similarities with this Lady Booth or her husband. Zilch, zip, nada. As far as I can tell, this woman never existed until she married Ted, and even now she exists in obscurity."

"So here's the big question. Is Lady Booth really Barbara Olson?" Max asked.

"Is that kind of like 'who's buried in Grant's tomb?' I think the only way to find out is to get a court order to exhume Barbara Olson's body from her grave. If you don't find anything in there, then it would be safe to assume that yes, she is Barbara. The other possibility is to court-order a DNA test on Lady Booth and then hopefully find a willing participant in Barbara's biological family that would generate sufficient markers to prove or disprove the identity," Ruth Ann suggested.

"At this point, that's not going to happen. I get the feeling that Dante's assignment and yours have an element of commonality that'll prove to be enlightening," Max said.

"There is one other revelation I'd like to bring up that we either did not talk about or it was simply not assigned to anyone," Ruth Ann added.

"And what is that?" Max asked.

"Remember the gold that was being stolen from the vaults underneath the Trade Center buildings?"

"Of course, you mean where Kurt wrote his name in the dust, proving that the gold had been long gone well before those towers came down. What about that gold?" Max inquired.

"We have reports, not fully substantiated, about gold being flown into Mojave on a Russian Antonov, flown by British pilots, probably MI6. The fact that they received permission to fly over the most restricted air space at Edwards Air Force base, and that they did it every weekend for several months, makes me think that gold might possibly have come from those vaults," Ruth Ann explained.

"I'm not sure how you'd follow up on that," Max commented.

"I'm not sure you can, but I might be able to provide you with photographs showing the gold being unloaded into some old ammo bunkers at the Mojave airport, and that may prove to be very valuable in any upcoming investigation," Ruth Ann offered.

"Make that connection and get me the pictures," Max requested. "You're right, photos like that may be very helpful down the road."

Mark, who had been sitting patiently through the meeting, was beginning to feel as if his coming back to Washington might not have been necessary. Finally, he asked, "Max, are you going to ask about the plane flying up the Hudson on 9/11?"

"You've been so quiet, Mark, I was beginning to think you forgot about that assignment. Yes, I was just getting to that question. What do you have?"

Mark opened his file and began, "Jim and I contacted the woman, who very distinctly remembered that morning before any of the tragedy began to unfold. She recalled a four-engine jet flying up the Hudson River at a relatively low altitude. Since she sees planes all the time in the area on their way in and out of JFK, it didn't seem completely unusual, but she said this plane seemed different, and she would have forgotten all about it had it not been for the events that occurred later that morning."

Jim added, "What struck us as odd was that she was adamant about the plane having four engines. She felt that was unusual, and quite frankly it was rather astute of her, since the only commercial plane flying in those days with four engines was the 747."

"We questioned her about that, and she was convinced it wasn't a 747. When we asked her how she was sure it wasn't, she said two things that made us realize she knew something about airplanes. She said that she couldn't see any bump on the top, and though it was a large aircraft, it was smaller than a 747," Mark said.

"Her answer made us wonder if she had seen a military aircraft. We asked her if she thought it was a military jet, but she didn't think so, since most military planes were gray and this plane was all white. I suggested that we visit her again with photographs of various military jets which had four engines and were painted white, if we could find any, and let her point out to us what type of aircraft it could have been," Jim continued.

"So, did you go visit her?" Max asked impatiently.

Jim looked at Max somewhat incredulously. "Show him the pictures we took to her, Mark."

Mark handed a stack of a dozen or so photographs to Max. They were all of military aircraft, many of which had been painted white. Max quickly glanced through the photos, then asked, "Did she see anything she liked?"

"Only this one," said Jim, pointing at a picture near the top of the stack.

"That looks like a KC-135, except it's white and has no refueling boom in the back. But isn't that really a Boeing 707?" Max wondered aloud.

"You are correct on all counts, except that particular plane is the Speckled Trout," Mark answered.

"Whoa, whoa, whoa, hold the phone," interjected Tom, coming out of his chair in disbelief at what Mark had just said. "Did you say the Speckled Trout?"

All eyes in the room turned to Tom, who was flipping through his notes as fast as he could, and becoming more and more excited as he did.

"What is a speckled trout? Isn't that something you fish for when you're on vacation in the mountains?" Ruth Ann wondered, rolling her eyes.

Mark laughed. "Yeah, but in this case it's a military jet, usually reserved for Air Force generals. I've seen it a few times, parked at Andrews. I've never flown it or even been inside, but I know it's full of highly secret and very sensitive electronics and communication equipment. It was an unspoken rule; that aircraft was off limits to anyone who wasn't directly assigned to it. In those days, 'don't ask don't tell' meant, if it's not your business, keep it that way—and that especially applied to the Trout."

"So, what do you have, Tom, that has you all excited?" Max asked.

"A few days ago, I was looking in the trash folder included in the FOIA files and saw a flight plan for a Trout99, which just happens to be the Speckled Trout. When I saw a file marked trash, I thought they must have put the flight plan in the trash by mistake. Trash is something you are deleting off a computer and to me that meant look and see what was deleted. As I began to understand we were dealing with a cover-up with possible military involvement, I started to look at every detail of this large file that had been put into the trash."

"Why is this airplane and its capabilities so important?" Vera asked.

"This jet was designed to perform magic tricks. I've heard my friend Chip talk about it. I can't remember all the fancy tricks this bird is capable of, but I know Chip has all the details. He was based at Edwards when they were putting it together. It was named after a woman who was involved in the project, whose last name was Trout. If you don't mind, Max, I think we should give Chip a call and have him explain more about this plane. The flight plan shows it took off from Andrews Air Force base at nine minutes after seven that morning."

Ruth Ann looked at Max and said, "I've met Chip. He can be trusted. I agree with Tom; I think we should call him."

Mark nodded in agreement.

"Is it too early in California to call him now?" Max asked.

"He'll be awake. Here's his number. Do you want to call him, Max, or do you want me to?" Tom asked.

"Go ahead and call him. Give him a brief rundown of why you're calling him, and then let me talk to him on speaker, if that's okay," Max replied.

Tom immediately took the phone and dialed Chip.

"Chip, Tom here. I hope I'm not calling you too early."

"There's no such thing as too early with me, but why the hell are you bothering me?" Chip asked, laughing.

"I'm in Washington D.C.. At the moment, I'm in a meeting with Ruth Ann, Mark and several other important members of the team she was telling you about when we met in Randsburg. The subject of the Speckled Trout came up, and I told them you knew more than anyone about that bird. So if it's not too much trouble, I would like to give the phone to Max Hager and let him explain why the hell we're keeping you from searching for gold."

"Put him on," Chip replied.

Max took the phone. "Chip, thanks for taking the time to chat with us. I understand you were at Edwards when the Trout was being outfitted. Could you share with us all you know about that plane? And do you mind if I put you on speaker?" he inquired.

"As I told Mark and Ruth Ann a while back, I'm happy to help you any way I can. Put me on speaker and I'll let her rip."

Max switched the phone over to speaker and gestured the others to begin the conversation.

"Chip, this is Mark. Give us an idea, if you would, about the plane's purpose and abilities, as well as the modifications that took place at Edwards. I'm aware the aircraft was in existence from the late fifties, but I understand that, from the time that jet spent at Edwards and the upgrades and modifications it has undergone, it now has some incredible abilities."

"You got that right. Originally the plane was used to fly VIP's around the world and run various flight tests with equipment they would install to evaluate performance, weather and efficiencies. But someone got the bright idea in the late eighties to turn the Trout into a command and control center. When they were finished applying all the bells and whistles, that old bird was better than new, filled with the latest technology. There was nothing that airplane could not do. It has a communication system onboard unlike anything the public is even aware exists, that plane can communicate with any phone in the world. For instance, it has radar and satellite technology most of us can't comprehend. That plane is a flying command center and from there, a war can be orchestrated by the bigwigs. Lots of what it can do is still top secret. The guys from DARPA were all over that bird at Edwards. DARPA had been perfecting their drone technology in Operation Homerun. Back in the mid-eighties, they were flying drones made from a hundred different types of aircraft. Mojave Airport was used to convert older F-4 Phantoms into drones that were flown and landed up near China Lake. One night when I was working as a controller there, I was frantically trying to guide this plane up by China Lake away from traffic; I had no idea there wasn't a pilot onboard. Later that night on my break, one of the intelligence guys took me down to an old hangar not far from the tower and introduced me to the pilot I'd been talking to. He was flying that plane I was so worried about by remote control, sitting right there inside that hangar."

"Hi, Chip, Ruth Ann here. What do you mean by 'nothing that Trout couldn't do?' Did it have the technology to take over those planes remotely, on 9/11? Is that Operation Homerun something they could have used on those four commercial jets? You said it had technology to make phone calls to anywhere on the planet, and more?"

"That baby could have taken over as many as eight aircraft remotely, and flown them to wherever they wanted," Chip said.

Jim looked across the table at Vera, who was having no trouble reading his mind and agreeing with everything he was thinking, her head nodding slightly as if she and Jim were on the same wavelength.

"This is Mark again, Chip. What about radar? What kind of capabilities did it have?"

"The Trout had direct satellite control. They could reposition any satellites, including the military's top secret ones. They had the ability to shut down radar and make airplanes appear and disappear, as well as control what other aircraft could or could not see. In addition, they had a direct tie-in to the FAA's control centers. Its communication package knew no equal. They even had a direct line into the White House. The modifications were meant to allow this aircraft to command a war from the air. These days a lot of that technology and capability has been superseded by the E4B's, which is why the Trout has now been retired, but the bottom line is there was nothing that baby couldn't do," Chip continued to explain.

"What about the crew who flew that plane? Were they assigned to it specifically?" Mark inquired again.

"I'm not sure about the pilots. They could have been associated with whoever was onboard, but as far as the crew who operated all of that sophisticated equipment, they almost had to be attached to the aircraft. They were highly trained and needed to be able to work in complete synchronicity for it to function at full capacity," Chip surmised.

"Max again here. Chip, I want to thank you for allowing us to bother you this morning. Your information has been invaluable. We may need to contact you again, but until then, keep your gold pan up and your pants dry."

"Will do, sir," Chip replied, laughing.

Once the phone call ended, the room buzzed with conversation about what they had just heard. Vera walked over and stood behind Jim and Max, so they could hear what she had to say. She leaned down and said, "Basically what Chip just said indicates that the Speckled Trout was possibly equipped with something similar to the software that Ptech company had—backdoor capability that could have entered into both the FAA and NORAD's computer systems, and created quite a lot of chaos in the skies for air traffic controllers who are depending on a blip from a transponder on a screen. From what Chip just told us, most of what happened that day could have been directed from that plane. This is worse than we thought. Our own military were the hijackers, and this really was a much different scenario than we were all led to believe."

Both Max and Jim stared at her silently. Their own thoughts had been spinning circles around her assertion, and their conclusions were daunting. Vera understood their silent message and was glad they were in agreement. She returned to her seat as Max raised both his hands in an effort to calm the chatter and call the meeting back to order. "Now that we have more understanding about the Speckled Trout and what it's capable of, why don't you tell us, Tom, more about what you have uncovered in that trash file, or in any of the other files you've searched through."

"According to its flight plan, the Trout left Andrews shortly after seven that morning, headed for Budapest, Hungary. Its flight path took it directly over New York City, then slightly eastward, and by 8:10 a.m. it was over Massachusetts, about 40 miles east of Westover. Its planned route was to take it just south of Greenland on a northerly route to Europe," Tom said.

"That would put the Trout awfully close to Westover, and right at the time communication with American 11 was lost," Jim interrupted.

Mark began to wiggle in his seat, shifting from side to side and appearing to be very uncomfortable. "I read the book that the Chairman of the Joint Chiefs of Staff wrote about that flight. I also read the stories his navigator and assistant wrote. All three tell a very different story; none of their timing is in sync. Knowing that his aircraft was equipped the way it was and its capabilities and possible involvement in the remote takeover of those commercial flights, well, it makes sense now why those three told very different accounts. They were all lying. I found it nearly impossible to believe the general's claim that air traffic controllers wouldn't let his plane return to US airspace. He was the most powerful man in the United States military."

Tom let out a loud laugh. "He said that? He actually claimed that air traffic controllers wouldn't let his plane, the ultimate flying command center carrying the top brass of the US military, return to Andrews?"

Jim spoke up. "By nine that morning, nobody seemed to know what was going on except the news media. I remember seeing banners across the screen on all channels, reading 'America at war' and 'America under attack.' I sure as heck thought we had just been attacked, and so did everyone else I know. But the general claims they refused to give them clearance to return?" Jim stopped for a moment, then continued, "The FAA hadn't closed the skies; there is no way they were refused."

Mark stood up and joined in. "No air traffic controller is going to tell the military, especially to top guy in the military, what he and his plane can and cannot do!" he blurted out. "The general has all the power to tell any air traffic controller what he intends to do, and the controller would make his way clear. The general's story is obviously not true, but what was really going on? I hesitate to bring this up because it touches close to home for me, being military for most of my life, but this insane story is impossible."

Max looked over at Dante, who he knew understood exactly what Mark was experiencing.

"Dante, do you have anything to add?" Max asked.

For some reason, Max's invitation did not catch Dante off guard; he knew exactly what to say. "The military, for all its esprit de corps, semper fi, integrity first, and service before self, is laced with lies. One thing I learned in the military is that war is all about profit. You know the saying—all wars are bankers' wars. As a kid I learned about something called the military-industrial complex. I wasn't certain what it was until I was well inside that monster, doing its bidding as a hired gun, a military hit man. The machine doesn't care about the human, and the military-industrial complex is the machine that continues to drive us into endless wars. There is nothing those at the top level of the Pentagon wouldn't do to promote an unwinnable war in some God-forsaken country. Nothing, including killing a few thousand innocent people in a couple of skyscrapers and a few airplanes. Everything the Speckled Trout was capable of doing that day was most likely done from that plane, not much doubt about that in my mind. The media in this country is just another tentacle of the evil Octopus that orchestrates the public's opinions and reactions through its illusion and deception. Most Americans are so busy trying to either one-up their neighbors or just simply survive, they don't take the time to research the truth. They were taught years ago to trust the television news. These days everything you are shown is on the screen for a psychological reason. The powers that be use the media to keep this country divided. You surely have seen that when you started to question what happened at the Pentagon and Shanksville, two places where you were clearly shown no sign of an airplane crash, yet were told those aluminum planes broke the laws of physics. Yep, this one day in history, the laws of physics no longer applied. The media cleverly manipulated our emotions, and through repetition, embedded the impossible into our minds. They also painted anyone like yourselves, who questioned any of the details, to be some insane lunatic or unpatriotic jerk that was siding with the terrorists."

Mark sat straight up in his chair and said, "According to the general, the Trout was clear up by Greenland when they heard the news about the plane crashes in New York. Now that isn't even possible, unless they deviated from the flight plan. From my own personal experience flying to Europe out of Andrews, I can say that by the time the first tower was hit, the Speckled Trout had just barely entered Canadian airspace; it's about an hour thirty to fly from Andrews to Bangor, Maine. As we learned from Chip, that plane had every high tech communication device imaginable on board. They would have heard the news immediately. There is no way in the world that aircraft took orders from the FAA. It was an excuse to have plausible deniability or to remain out over the Atlantic."

Ruth Ann had been pulling up information on her computer, then added, "The Speckled Trout claimed to have finally received permission to enter United States airspace from the FAA late in the afternoon. The general wrote in his memoir that they returned and flew over the trade center moments after the towers had both collapsed. If so, they would have been back on the ground at Andrews around noon."

Tom stood and interjected, "According to these flight strips in your FOIA data, his plane, Trout99, landed at Andrews at four-forty that afternoon. I would place my money on these flight strips being more accurate than anyone's recollection. These are computerized flight strips. They wouldn't be easy to manipulate, even for the military."

Gil asked, "What about all those radar sites that were out of service along the northeast corridor that morning? That included the long-range radar out of North Truro. Do you suppose that the Speckled Trout could have caused those radar installations to become inoperable?"

Dante quickly added, "That plane is equipped with the most

advanced electronic warfare capabilities; it could blind or render any radar site inoperable in a heartbeat. Heck, they could have been adding targets to air traffic controllers' screens, causing more confusion. Remember, during those supposed hijackings, the controllers were very confused and thought that nearly a dozen other planes had been hijacked."

Tom added, "And there were all those air traffic control towers and centers that were evacuated that morning, with no reasons listed in the logs. We had nearly four thousand commercial flights in our skies, and air traffic controllers were running away from their radar screens and evacuating their buildings. That is hard to believe, and until I read those facility logs, I had no idea that there had been so many evacuations. Now, since I have spent many years inside the FAA's air traffic control system, I have to add, the phone numbers and locations of those air traffic control centers are not readily available to the public. My best guess is that, although it is not reported on the logs, someone with inside knowledge phoned in to the centers and made some type of threat. Once I gathered all the logs and started noting the many evacuations, I realized that we were not only put in a very vulnerable position, but with the number of planes still in the air, this was a very dangerous situation. Since there was no reason listed for the evacuation, it appears that the order to leave the building may have come from the FAA headquarters back here in D.C."

Max chimed in, "I suppose it's possible for radar to go out from time to time. Equipment fails on occasion, but there's no way nearly every radar in the northeast could have gone on the fritz by chance. Something had to have neutralized them and from what Chip told us, the Speckled Trout could have done just that. Get him on the phone again and we'll ask him."

Tom dialed Chip's number once again. "Chip, have you found any gold yet?"

"It's a good thing I'm not fishing. I can pan for gold with your interruptions, but your calls would scare away the fish. What the hell do you want this time?" Chip asked jokingly.

"Max again, Chip. I have a quick question for you. Could the Speckled Trout have taken out radar sites along the northeastern corridor if it wanted to?"

"I suppose it could have, but if that was the objective I would think an E4B would have been equally as efficient at that kind of dirty work."

"Do you have any more questions for Chip?" Tom asked, looking at the entire group.

When the call to Chip ended Max asked, "Does anyone have any information about an E4B in that area about that time? If not, then I'm going to assume the Trout did the deed."

"What was on that paper I gave you last night, Ruth Ann?" Tom asked.

"To be honest, I haven't had a chance to look at it, but it's right here so let me see," she said, holding it up in her hand. Ruth Ann scanned over the document, then looked up from the paper and smiled. "Got 'em. One of the four E4B's, nicknamed Sword 31 was airborne that morning. It was in and out of Andrews a couple times, but it was definitely in the skies between Maryland and Massachusetts. I recall on the news that people reported seeing a large white aircraft circling in the skies over New York and Washington D.C. The media mentioned it in their reports and even showed a grainy camera shot of it, but the military denied any E4B's were flying."

Max pursed his lips together as he tried to make sense of what he was hearing. He looked around the room at each member before he spoke. "So are we at an impasse?"

Tom shook his head no, "I have a flight strip here from Andrews Air Force base that shows an E4B taking off on a 270 degree heading which is due west right over the Pentagon just minutes before it was hit and exploded. It's impossible that a hijacked 757 headed for DC would not have been intercepted by an E4B."

"So the bastards were lying again, imagine that," Max said.

"That's not all that's weird. There's something I found noted in several of these chronologies. It sure doesn't explain anything, but it makes no sense to me."

"What's that?" asked Max.

Tom collected his notes, reread them quickly and said, "Sometime around three o'clock that afternoon, it's noted that the White House contacted the FAA and informed them that a possibly hijacked US Air flight was returning to Madrid. Now, there are a few different versions of this account, one claiming it to be flight number 930, and another calling it Flight 937. There doesn't seem to be an exact time that matches on any of the timelines. What is wrong with this, is that it says the White House contacted the FAA about a possible hijacking outside of Madrid, Spain. I know the general public might not be privy to this information, but the flights from Europe are not monitored by the White House, or our FBI or even the FAA. Those flights are monitored by Europe's flow control, and they had stopped all departures or diverted all flights bound for the US at about nine-thirty that morning. When I saw that report claiming the White House told the FAA about a plane in a possible hijack situation near Spain, well, let's just say a huge red flag went up. There is just no way in the middle of this huge terror attack that the White House was monitoring flights out of Europe. So, this notation is one real mystery. Any of you have a clue?"

Vera immediately responded to what Tom had said. "International flights are usually one or two-digit flight numbers, not three. That alone says there's something odd about that message. I'm somewhat familiar with US Air because we stayed in the same hotel with them in Rome. Most all of the flights to the United States leave Europe between eleven in the morning and noon, which is about five or six in the morning here. By three in the afternoon, there were no flights bound for the US leaving anywhere from Europe. There definitely is something fishy about this story."

Jim leaned toward Mark and whispered something in his ear. They seemed almost animated as they conferred with each other. The rest of the room stopped and watched as their private discussion continued. Finally, Jim noticed that everyone was watching them, cut Mark off and said, "Mark and I have been talking about White House communications. They don't monitor flights, and if there was communication between them and the FAA about a flight, the call would have originated from the FAA to the White House. How in the hell would the White House know a plane, thought to be hijacked, was turning around?"

Mark rested his arm on Jim's shoulder and said, "Before you go there, Jim, we need to figure out what plane that even was. I've done a little quick research on my computer and found out US Air's one scheduled flight from Madrid to Philadelphia was Flight 11, and it was scheduled to leave Madrid at 11:45 local time. Now, that's 5:45 a.m. here on the east coast, so there's no way the plane the White House called about could have been that flight. That would have meant Flight 11 had been in the air for eight hours, and it wouldn't have had enough fuel to fly back to Madrid. From a pilot's perspective, this really doesn't make sense."

"It says in this typed transcript that Brussels air traffic control called the FAA headquarters upon learning about the first three planes, and stopped all air traffic at nine-forty. By that time, US Air Flight 11 would have been instructed to land at Shannon, Ireland or maybe Greenland. That mysterious call from the White House was nearly six hours later," Ruth Ann interjected.

"I'm not sure we're getting anywhere here. It makes no sense that we have a 757 flying over the Atlantic all day—I wouldn't think it had that kind of fuel capacity. And who on that plane would have contacted the White House concerning a possible hijacking? We have a report coming out of the White House to the FAA about something going on in European airspace, and we have a three-digit flight number that wasn't really the US Air flight from Madrid, and we have a 757 flying beyond its fuel capacity," Max reviewed. "We have stumbled upon a real mystery here."

Both Mark's and Ruth Ann's eyes widened as they looked at one another. The vibes charging back and forth between them were almost visible to the others. The room returned to silence as everyone watched the two of them silently communicate something important. Mark pointed to Ruth Ann and said, "Tell them."

Ruth Ann turned to Tom and said, "Remember that US Air flight flying VFR that almost hit the Continental jet near Barstow years ago?"

"Yeah, what of it?" Tom responded.

"Mark and I have it on pretty good authority that plane was equipped with a fuel bladder and could fly halfway around the world," she replied.

"What are you saying, Ruth Ann?" Max asked.

"Let me answer that, Max," Mark interjected.

"When Ruth Ann and I were poking around the Mojave airport, we met a couple of old guys that like to keep an eye on the planes in the boneyard there. They told us about a US Air 757 that was parked among the planes that had been equipped with a fuel bladder. That plane would take off out of Mojave every Saturday night, after a busload of people had boarded. When we met with Chip the first time, we discovered that there was a US Air 757 involved in a near-miss as it was flying VFR, which everyone knows a commercial jet cannot do legally. We have two mysterious Boeing 757's here right now. We have this plane flown VFR out of the boneyard every Saturday night headed to Washington's Dulles airport. And we have this supposed flight from Madrid to Philly with the wrong flight number, the wrong departure time and somehow the White House knows about it before the FAA. We also have the possibility of working crew members involved with the Central Intelligence Agency on the supposed hijacked planes, and now we discover that we have the highest ranking military general flying onboard the most advanced aircraft fitted with electronic warfare technology, and a couple of our E4B's in the air too. That right there is enough technology to stop any hijacking, yet nothing could be done to help those four commercial flights? What we were shown on television was completely impossible, so what really did happen? Could this US Air 757 be a getaway plane? I don't want to sound like a conspiracy nut, but we clearly have the possibility that some of the passengers and crew were not victims, but were working with the CIA. We know that Westover had been evacuated prior to 9/11. Was that 757 parked in one of the hangars all ready to go?"

There was an audible gasp from all the members of the team. Immediately they began talking to and over one another. Mark's speculation had fueled all kinds of possibilities, which flowed from the experience of each team member and the research they had done. Max could sense the information being discussed was most likely useful, so he remained silent.

Finally, Dante stood up, which drew everyone's attention and caused them to stop talking. As they waited for him to speak, Dante calmly pointed to Mark and said, "I believe Mark is correct. I saw that plane land in Madrid the night of 9/11. It was indeed a US Air 757. I questioned its fuel capacity then, because we knew that Brussels had stopped all internationals to the states by around three-thirty that afternoon European time. US

Airways didn't have inter-European flights, so it had to be coming from across the Atlantic. It just didn't fit with all the details we had been given. In fact, that plane has haunted me ever since. I watched through my scope as the passengers deplaned, and the flight attendant we talked about earlier certainly could have been one of them. It's even possible that Barbara Olson was on that plane. You've talked about various handlers who facilitated the hijacking and phone calls. They could have all been on that plane. I was still on the lookout for my target but this US Air 757 got my attention, so I looked at each of their faces through my scope as they carried their luggage down the air stairs. It never made sense to me. I'm your eyewitness. What Mark is telling you is correct."

Jerry Reitz, who had been silently listening to all the conversations, motioned to Max to be recognized. "I haven't been buried in this research like you folks have, so in many ways I'm an observer. In spite of that, I know the golden piece to the puzzle when I see it, and I believe that's what we have here. Maybe one of you military boys can answer better than I can, but if that plane was the getaway aircraft, it would have been very helpful for the radar all along the northeastern part of the United States to be shut down. Having the air traffic control centers and towers left unmanned would have also been key in a successful getaway. Nobody would have seen them on radar, that's for sure."

Jim nodded in agreement. "It also explains what the Speckled Trout could have been doing flying over the Atlantic for so long. If any one of those military jets that were finally patrolling the skies saw a US Air flight airborne, they would have been right on its tail attempting to force it down. The Trout could have easily hidden that plane from any pilot or air traffic controllers, with its radar capabilities onboard. Heck, they could have tagged it as a military aircraft and nobody would have asked a question. In fact, the Trout could have made that 757 completely invisible.

This escape plane was the grand illusion, the third act to every magic trick, the 'prestige.' Once the Trout had given the US Air plane the needed navigational assistance to get across the Atlantic, they contacted the White House. Remember what Chip said, that plane had telephone access to anywhere in the world, and it had direct access to the White House. That notation on the timelines was their code that the operation was complete and a success. The getaway plane was past the point of no return and in the clear. The Trout then returned to Andrews late in the afternoon."

"That also explains why they had to create some nonsensical excuse that gave them plausible deniability and covered up their involvement in this charade," Vera added.

"I suppose that also explains how the official story added the report that this mysterious US Air Flight 930 never existed and it was just one big mistake," Ruth Ann said. "I guess they discovered that someone at the FAA had included the report from the White House, so they cooked up a cover story."

Tom had been quietly reviewing a page of flight strips as each team member spoke. Suddenly, he blurted out, "Oh no, ladies and gentlemen, you are not going to believe what I just laid my eyes on. These flight strips from Andrews." He stopped talking and leaned closer to his computer screen. "This right here," he held up his screen toward his audience, "Do you see the E's in front of the numbers? These are three medevac planes, DC 9's." Again he paused, took a long slow breath and continued. "These medevac planes are used for..." he cleared his throat, "these are used to transport injured soldiers and dead bodies."

The room fell silent as everyone grasped what Tom was saying.

"I only have the arrival time into Andrews, but it looks like they all came in from the same area, and they are three and six minutes apart in their landing sequence. The only information in this flight strip is their last way point, which is just to the northwest of Andrews. These planes could have come in from Westover. They landed about nine-forty that night."

Jim was first to comment. "There were no soldiers injured or killed that would have been flown in. The only military personnel that were killed or injured were at the Pentagon, a short drive away."

Dante stood and spoke the moment Jim had stopped. "I'm familiar with those medevac planes; they can carry about ninety bodies or more."

"Why would they be transporting bodies to Andrews?" Ruth Ann asked.

"There's a crematorium at Bethesda. If they gassed those passengers and crew at Westover, they had to cremate them," Mark said.

Gil added, "If the bodies had been buried, they could have eventually been uncovered."

"Cremation would have destroyed all the evidence," Max finished.

Tom was obviously shaken by this discovery. "I would bet there is no record of where those three medevacs departed from. By now, we probably can't find their flight plans. I will continue to look for them, now that we know they came into Andrews. They had to have departed from somewhere."

Max was no stranger to diabolical acts and their accompanying cover-ups, so it was not hard for him to swallow all he was hearing. "I don't want to believe this, but I think Jerry's right. This revelation is another of the missing puzzle pieces, but the reason this one is golden is because it connects the military and several government agencies to that fateful event. I can't help but recall Thomas Kean's quote about the FAA and the Pentagon providing so many misstatements and confusion during the 9/11 Commission hearings, that he considered opening an investigation on both of them. For the country's sake, I wish he had opened inquiries into those organizations, but his committee had a pre-assigned and directed outcome, and all the investigation in the world wouldn't have changed that. We have been charged with finding the truth, and I believe we have done that. It hasn't been easy, and the task may never be completely over, but I think we have enough information and enough facts to lay out a case to the president. Once this information is heard and understood by the American people, we will get our hearings. Until then, I'd like you all to keep researching and asking questions. Months ago, I'd have never imagined we'd be where we are today. I feel it's been divine providence that has led you, persuaded you, in some cases, and protected you so that you could participate in pulling back the covers of the greatest illusion ever foisted upon the people of the world. You will never get the thanks you deserve, but you have my thanks, and you undoubtedly have the gratitude of those who lost their lives that day, along with their families, who will call your names blessed forever."

Max rose from his chair and in a demonstration that was foreign to him, went around the room, shaking the hand and embracing each member of the team. When he finished, he said, "Vera, Jim and I will take all of this information to the president in the coming days, but I have a feeling a little bird will spill most of the beans before we get there." He winked at Vera. Turning to the group he said, "I'll keep you all informed as we move forward. Your presence in meetings may be necessary from time to time, and I have no doubt you'll all be called to testify before Congress when that time comes. So take a deep breath, relax and prepare yourself for the next battle, which is sure to come. Thank you again. You're all dismissed."

twenty-seven

Max was in no hurry to schedule an appointment with President Sherman. He hoped some time would bring to the surface more details that might have been overlooked or had escaped the team's purview. He was encouraged to know that Vera would tell the president much of what had been discussed, which meant that when they did meet there would be no need to explain all of the details surrounding the evidence. In the ensuing discussions he had with Jim, they both concluded the attorney general should be included in the first meeting with the president, since there were criminal considerations that had arisen and they were certain criminal aspects would continue to come to the forefront.

Ruth Ann and Mark discussed the possibility of returning to Las Vegas to finish their vacation. As fantastic of an idea as they felt that was, they knew it would have to wait until they had an idea of how quickly the president could proceed. Their expertise needed to be part of the guiding light to help Congress plow their way through any investigation. Mark didn't seem to mind remaining in Washington D.C. for the foreseeable future. Ruth Ann had been correct in her prediction that he would strike up an abiding friendship with Jim, and the two of them often spent time together telling airplane and flight stories. Ruth Ann became acquainted with Jim's wife Mari, and the four of them would often dine out together at the many well-known restaurants around D.C.

Gil and Tom could not leave the FOIA data alone, and together they continued to devour every detail of the information. It wasn't long before Gil fancied himself as an air traffic controller, as he had become so well versed in reading the radar, flight strips, daily logs and chronologies. He shared with Tom how he had once wanted to become an air traffic controller, but life had taken him in another direction. Now, it seemed he had come full circle and was enjoying all that Tom had to teach him about a career he never had. They called Chip often, sometimes to bug him, but more so to field his input on military data they were unfamiliar with. Chip was more than willing to help and even offered to come to D.C. if he were needed. They held that offer in reserve, knowing the day would probably come when his presence was required.

When Dante was not working with Max, he would slip away and visit with Gordon to learn all the ins and outs of the Secret Service. He questioned him about the call the Service made to CNN about the fictitious plane crash at Camp David on 9/11. The only conclusion either one of them could arrive at was that the FBI or CIA had something to do with planting that information. Gordon knew it was highly out of character for anyone in the Service to act unilaterally without direction from another agency. Dante confirmed that no follow-up investigation into the reported Camp David plane crash had been conducted, so it essentially had been swept under the rug. With so much fear and tragedy occurring that day, the rug was deep, wide and offered no resistance to anyone trying to hide something. The agent who made the call to the media was no longer with the Service, and many of the agents assigned to Camp David at the time had retired.

After a few days, the president called Max. "My friend, it's time you came to see me. I'm prepared to hear all you have to say, and move forward with whatever decision we make. Would tomorrow morning at ten o'clock work for you? Bring Jim, and

I'll make certain Rudy is present. Vera and I will be waiting for you."

"That would be fine, Mr. President. We'll be there," Max replied.

Max relayed to Jim the meeting schedule, the anticipation of which prevented both of them from sleeping the night before. It was not meeting with the president that caused them anxiety, but rather the weight of sharing their findings and proof that the United States and allied governments were involved in the events of 9/11. Their commitment and friendship with the president prevented them from doing anything other than wishing they weren't the ones to reveal the ghastly and hideous facts.

"Gentlemen, welcome and thank you for coming," the president said to open the meeting. "I've cleared my calendar, so you can utilize as much time as we need to help Rudy and me understand the kind of evidence you have uncovered."

He went on, "Naturally Congress is reluctant to open a new investigation. They are so tightly attached to the status quo they cannot see past its horizon. After my State of the Union address, I received the expected 'dead on arrival' type comment from a lot of them. But I also know it began to stir many of their constituents into action, and since that address several members of Congress from both parties have offered their support should I decide to open a new 9/11 investigation. I've become aware of the flood of email your team has received. I also know that my announcement stimulated many people to contact their representatives. In addition, that speech sparked more enthusiasm on the part of Congress to be helpful, rather than the anchor they have been to this point. I'm not saying this will be easy sailing. The majority is still content to believe the 9/11 Commission hearing report, but we're moving in the right direction and I have great hope," the president finished.

The president had a way of reassuring Max and causing

him to relax in stressful situations. "Let me begin by telling you what we have, so you're prepared and armed to face Congress. There are a number of eyewitnesses who have come forward with new information. With the release of the First Lady's and Jim's theory about Westover, several people have contacted us with information about the base closure, the evacuation of all personnel, and the time frame before anyone was allowed back on the base. More importantly, we have had a few eyewitnesses who saw commercial airliners obviously on their way to land at Westover on the morning of 9/11."

"Will any of these people be willing to testify before Congress or in a court of law?" the president asked.

"Some gladly will; others may need some gentle persuasion from the First Lady or even yourself when the time comes. But I have every confidence they'll do what any good citizen would do when their country needs them," Jim replied.

The president smiled and motioned for Max to continue.

"With Dante's help, we think we discovered where the CIA launched the cruise missile that struck the Pentagon. We have it on primary radar, and if we can get access to any or all of the surrounding surveillance tapes the FBI confiscated, then we should have it on film. Dante did suggest we send a dive team into the Accotink Bay and Gunstone Cove to look for the boot that would have jettisoned from the missile when it launched. With that evidence, it would be almost impossible to refute the existence of the missile or its launch site. Another option might come from the interrogation of the two agents assigned to kill Dante's mother. If you can determine where their orders came from, you have a whole new avenue from which to mine information," Max said.

The president turned to Rudy and asked him what limitation there was on extracting information from these prisoners.

"I'll look into that, Mr. President, and get back to you with various possibilities. Obviously, we wouldn't want any kind of coerced confessions, but since there are two of them you may be able to offer one of them immunity and get him to testify," the attorney general explained.

Max continued, "The FAA might need to be investigated, to get to the bottom of their involvement. At the very least, a complete and thorough investigation will lead to criminal indictments, I'm certain."

The president turned to Rudy and said, "I want you to work directly with the FAA's inspector general and begin an internal investigation, regardless of what Congress decides to do. If what Max is saying is correct, the FOIA documents alone may very well have the evidence necessary to indict current and former employees of that organization."

Jim volunteered to continue. "The most glaring problem I see, Mr. President, is the Pentagon. If Dante's missile discovery was the only thing to worry about this might be easy, but based on what we have discovered with the Speckled Trout, the challenge will be to find out who at the Pentagon was in on this. Now, your current chairman of the joint chiefs of staff is on board, and I remember him clearly stating that he would be there for you if and when you needed him. Well, sir, you are going to need him, and it's not going to be easy. I think only if Congress decides to investigate will you ever understand how involved those in the Pentagon were. We can give you specific evidence and even an eyewitness to some things, but you will need to access all their records, and that is where the general can help."

"How would you suggest we pursue this, Rudy?" the president asked.

"I think Jim is correct. We're going to need the help of the chairman of the joint chiefs, but that won't be enough. If the team can provide us with the names of those directly responsible, we can approach their subordinates with immunity propositions, to help get them to testify against their bosses. That is really the only way," Rudy said.

"Oh, we have names all right. That won't be a problem. I'll have them in your hands in the coming days, with a list of violations perpetrated on this country and its people," Max offered.

"What about foreign government involvement? We have produced evidence that certain intelligence agencies were involved. Some were assigned to steal gold from the vaults of the Trade Center, and other foreign nationals participated in carrying out some of the most horrific aspects of 9/11—certainly the ones that killed the most people," Vera said.

"That is, if you don't count all the deaths associated with the wars 9/11 was designed to create," added Max.

"I'm sure that'll be a little trickier, since they're foreign nationals, but if their nations are confronted with the evidence it'll be easier to apply the appropriate thumbscrews to get them to cooperate. I'm not opposed to bringing the full force of this government to bear on any recalcitrant country who wants to stonewall our investigation or prosecutions," said the president. "Max, I'd like your team to put together a dossier with the salient points and facts that I can share with leaders of foreign countries, but more specifically with the Speaker of the House and Senate majority leader. I want them to be able to see with their own eyes the kinds of evidence you have."

"We're already working on that, and you should have it on your desk in a few days, perhaps even tomorrow," Max replied.

"Excellent," said the president. "Is there anything else anyone would like to add?"

Vera hesitated, wanting to say something, but not certain this was the right moment. Joel knew her well enough to encourage her to speak her mind. He put his arm around her, drew her into him and kissed her on the top of the head.

She said, "For many years I lived in horror, thinking it could have been me on any one of those planes that day. It made my job nearly impossible to perform, knowing what I knew. Every day I wondered what would come next, and I never again felt safe doing my job as I did prior to 9/11. Then when Jim and I began to discover what really happened and how insidious it all was, that horror magnified and was accompanied by anger. Ultimately it was that anger that encouraged me to retire. I knew others in the airlines who felt the same way. We didn't talk about it much, but when we did, it was clear to me 9/11 had affected every airline employee. After I began to learn more, I realized it was far more than just me and my circle of airline employees that 9/11 affected. Look how the military was involved and what it did to countless good people like Dante. Our entire country has suffered in countless silent ways since those attacks. You must be successful in persuading Congress to investigate these atrocities and hold the people responsible accountable, no matter who they are. The nation's survival depends on it and, more importantly, its people need to be freed from the lies they've endured all these years."

Joel whispered, "Amen."

Max and Jim nodded in agreement, and communicated with their eyes that they were in harmony with her. Rudy began to understand how special this woman was, and how she and the president worked as one. As the meeting concluded, the challenge in front of the president was clear. Success was the only victory, and victory was at hand.

twenty-eight

The president spent several days reviewing the dossier that Max had provided to him. He continued to ask questions in an effort to make certain he thoroughly understood every issue surrounding the arguments for a new investigation. He also met with advisors to discuss the potential pushback that leaders of Congress might present to stall the new hearings. When he felt fully confident he could present a persuasive argument to congressional leaders, he called a meeting in the Oval Office with the Speaker of the House and the Senate majority leader. As an extra incentive, he invited them for lunch with him and the First Lady.

Following the luncheon, Vera excused herself as the three men walked together along the portico leading from the White House to the Oval Office. President Sherman invited them both to be seated on the couch in the center of the office as he positioned his favorite chair in front of his desk so that he was seated just off to the side, but still maintained a position of authority.

"Gentlemen, I appreciate your willingness to meet with me this afternoon. I have often thought these types of meetings should occur more often. If they did, I believe more could be accomplished and if not, we would at least know the reasons why," the president began.

Both leaders smiled and nodded in agreement.

"I'm sure it comes as no surprise to you that I want you to put aside the orchestrated 9/11 Commission report and open a joint hearing and investigation on what really happened that day. I would like the hearings to be open to the public and televised, so that the American people can see and hear the people who will come before you and testify," the president continued.

"Mr. President, I don't think the American people have the stomach to scratch off the scab that has healed over the wound that was 9/11. I can assure you that we in Congress don't have the appetite to go down that road again, only to arrive at the same conclusions," the Speaker replied tersely.

The Senate majority leader added, "I'm positive the Senate has no interest in rehashing the details about how nineteen radical Muslims caused the devastation they wreaked on the public. It's a nonstarter, sir, and it's not going to happen."

The president leaned forward slightly in his chair and said, "I'm not surprised you feel that way. To be honest, that is the response I expected from you. The problem is, you don't know what I know. My team has been researching diligently for years, and more recently has been laser-focused on issues overlooked or neglected by the original commission. With the help of the American people, former members of the military and Freedom of Information Act documents, we have come to some sound and rather startling conclusions about what occurred and who was ultimately responsible for 9/11. Some of the more salient points of the investigation have been included in the dossiers I have had prepared for you. I think if you read through these findings, you'll begin to see things differently."

"I don't think you understand, sir. If your information said that little green men from Mars arrived on Earth on a Tuesday morning and destroyed the Twin Towers, wrecked the Pentagon and shot down a plane in Pennsylvania, we're still not interested in moving forward with your request. That was the past, and we have no intention of going back there to stir up what should remain dead and buried," retorted the Speaker.

The president rose from his chair, walked over to the couch

where the men were seated and glared down at them. He placed his hands on his hips and said, "Now I realize that you haven't had the benefit of reading what's contained in the dossiers yet, and for that I'll give you the benefit of the doubt and tolerate, for the moment, your unwillingness to do the right thing. But I need to explain to you what I'm prepared to do if your stubbornness persists, and you continue to thwart the will of the people. What is contained in our research is shocking, alarming, devastating, and provable beyond question. At the present, it's known only to a few. Soon I will begin making it known to the world. Remember, I don't answer to any party. I have no financial backers demanding I toe a specific line. And that means, gentlemen, I can use the full power of this office, unrestrained. I'm sure you've never seen that occur in your political lifetimes, but I can assure you when fully unleashed it can be devastating to the opposition. I will utilize the bully pulpit at every opportunity. As I make the facts known to the people, they will demand that you act because I will hold you both directly responsible if you fail to engage in new hearings. The people have been complacent about the government's answers about 9/11, but you know as well as I do they are not satisfied. They know the story shoveled up to them was full of holes. I have the facts before me, and with them I will fill every one of those holes. When I do, they will rise up and demand that you act. We were overwhelmed by the public's desire to provide information following my last speech to the nation. Imagine what will happen when I speak to them again and show them what happened and who was responsible. Do you think you will be able to stomach that kind of a response? Do you think your appetite might be stimulated sufficiently to share in the feast of truth that will rain down upon you? I certainly hope so, gentlemen. This country deserves that. Its people need to be liberated from the lies we told them and you need to rise to the occasion, in spite of your reservations, and act on behalf of the nation."

The president returned to his chair and continued to look through the souls of the men before him. "Now go. Take your time, educate yourselves with the facts, and then call those hearings to order."

When the president finished speaking, the door to the Oval Office opened and Gordon Garcia graciously ushered the Speaker of the House and the Senate majority leader into the hall.

Several days passed, and the president had not been in communication with either the Speaker or the Senate majority leader. It did not worry him, however; in his heart he knew they would respond to his request. They were good men who had been caught up in the influence-peddling that had become the Congress of the United States. He was certain it would dawn on them both that his influence trumped theirs, and as a result they would come to see eye to eye with him on moving the 9/11 hearings forward.

Early one evening, Joel and Vera were sitting in the great room watching a Gene Kelly movie together—something they rarely were able to arrange—when they heard a slight tapping at the door. It was Mike, the president's valet.

"Come in, Michael my man. I had no idea you were a Gene Kelly fan," the president said.

"Did he play for the Eagles, by any chance?" Mike asked.

The president looked at Vera and they both shrugged, indicating Mike was a hopeless cause. "So what brings you here tonight, Mike?"

"I knew you would be interested in this communiqué from the Speaker's office," he said, as he handed the printout to the president.

Vera stretched to be able to read it with her husband.

The Associated Press: The Office of Speaker of the House, in conjunction with the Senate, announces that joint hearings and a full investigation into the facts surrounding 9/11 will commence on Monday. The Attorney General is prepared to appoint a special prosecutor in the event that the hearings reveal criminal activities or treasonous events perpetrated upon the American people. The hearings will be televised to the public, and no closed-door executive sessions will be held unless approved by the president.

The president handed the paper back to Mike and looked over at Vera. He reached for both her hands as tears began to roll down her cheeks.

"Plunge into the depths until you reach the truth."
Imam Ali

Rebekah Roth

A FINAL WORD

With the completion of Methodical Conclusion the Methodical series has come to an end. The purpose of the three works is to expose the truth of 9/11 in a way that could be easily assimilated by those who believed the official government stories and open their minds to begin asking questions.

It was never my intention to write books. Like many of you, I too believed what I was told, but it never quite set well inside. As I begun to do some research into the events of 9/11 so many questions arose that were in direct conflict with my thirty years of training and experience as a flight attendant that I had to find the answers. That set my life in a new direction.

For months which turned into years I read and digested everything I could find concerning 9/11. I had to sift through a lot of garbage from conspiracy theorists, 9/11 truthers who were mostly interested in the attention rather than the truth, and crazy theories that wilted in the light of fact. Nevertheless, there were nuggets to be found which combined with my own personal experiences allowed me to discover where the four airplanes were taken so that the phone calls that convinced people of the government story could be made. That information constitutes the message in Methodical Illusion, which I was compelled to write so that other could understand what I had found and begin to see the truth. In my wildest dreams I never thought more than fifty people would read that book. To my surprise tens of thousands of people have read and become enlightened to the truth.

Though I knew my research wasn't over I thought my writing days were. At this point providence smiled upon me and brought to my attention elements of the events of 9/11 that I could never have found on my own. A researcher, who had been collecting FOIA, requests shared his data with me. It was a wealth of information, most of which I was unable to read or comprehend, but what I could understand compelled me to write the second novel Methodical Deception. That book began to point to the people involved in perpetrating this horrific event. I wasn't ashamed to expose what I had learned and point the finger in the direction of some of the culprits. That is when all hell broke loose and I began to be attacked by those who were unable to abide the truth and wanted to see me and my research put to an end. What they failed to realize was this was never about me. It was always about the truth and the truth stands up in the face of adversity no matter how much difficulty is created.

None of this was easy for me. My emotions were battered and bruised often as I learned how people, religions and countries were affected by the lies I was uncovering. In addition, the trolls, who were determined to silence me, attacked my family, friends and people I didn't even know on a regular basis in a coordinated effort that spawned from the depths of hell. But I was not deterred. Once more, divine providence smiled upon me and pointed the light of truth in the direction I needed to follow.

I knew that the huge volume of FOIA data contained secrets that would tie up many of the loose ends I had encountered in my research, but I was unable to decipher its language and solve its mysteries. That is when help arrived. Aviation experts, flight controllers and pilots both military and commercial found me and offered to help. Together we dove into the data and were able to analyze it and pull from it the truth which is now contained in the final book Methodical Conclusion.

Collectively these three books paint the picture of what

really happened on 9/11. It uncovers who was involved and how they pulled off the grand illusion. It isn't a pretty picture. I have spent sleepless nights and agonizing days coming to grips with the results of my research. And though my soul is pained by my discoveries my heart is bolstered by the truth I have found. It is the truth that I bring to my readers with the hope that they too will be encouraged to fight the good fight armed with light which will allow them to vanquish the evil which at the present, rules this world. Join me, share the truth, stand up against the lies and let's win this war.

Rebekah Roth